D1452681

ROGUE COMMUNITY COLLEGE

BOOKS BY DAVID R. SLAYTON

THE LIBERTY HOUSE SERIES
Rogue Community College

THE GODS OF NIGHT AND DAY SERIES
Dark Moon, Shallow Sea

THE ADAM BINDER NOVELS
White Trash Warlock
Trailer Park Trickster
Deadbeat Druid

DAVID R. SLAYTON

Published in 2024 by Blackstone Publishing
Cover and book design by Sarah Riedlinger

Printed in the United States of America

First edition: 2024
ISBN 979-8-200-96677-6
Fiction / Fantasy / Contemporary

Version 1

Blackstone Publishing
31 Mistletoe Rd.
Ashland, OR 97520

www.BlackstonePublishing.com

To Brian—

Have a great summer!

1
THE UNDERTAKER'S BOY

The house could give up the ghost at any moment.

Isaac scented blood, which was no surprise in a place like this. Old and new mixed with a sour flavor, chemicals and something wild, something strange he couldn't place.

Sad, scraggly trees ringed a red stone facade that might have been beautiful a century ago. Garbage piled around the foundation and plywood covered the windows on the first floor. Soot stains spoke of an old fire, but the grass was shaved to the ground, probably by the city since citations and tickets plastered the front door.

Isaac circled to the side to avoid detection and scaled the wall. His fingers found easy holds in the ruddy stone. Hefting himself atop a porch roof, he crouched to peer through an open window.

A trio of prayer candles, white wax in glass tubes, gave the room its only light. The scents grew stronger.

A twin bed took up most of the space. An elf lay stretched atop it, gagged, his ankles bound with rope. They'd handcuffed his wrists to the headboard.

A steel gurney waited against the wall.

Isaac climbed through the window.

"Haven't seen one of those in a while." He pointed to the antique embalmer waiting beside the gurney. It had seen recent use. He could smell it.

The bound elf's shock of black hair curled around his ears and forehead. His pale skin had a faint bluish cast, but he wore dark jeans and a T-shirt with some faded band name on it. His eyes were something darker than night, something more like ink. He narrowed them at Isaac.

"If I ungag you, will you keep quiet?" Isaac asked.

The elf nodded.

It was hard to tell, but Isaac would put him around his own age, maybe a few years younger. It would be hard to know without a taste, and he did have to wonder what sort of blood ran through those veins, what secrets it contained.

That wasn't the job though. Isaac was here to rescue the guy and get arrested in the process.

He drew a knife and began to saw at the ropes binding the elf's ankles. He considered nicking the elf and spilling just a drop . . . but no. He needed to keep his eye on the prize, the endgame—the future.

Isaac shook off the temptation and jerked the gag down.

"What are you doing?" the elf demanded. "You're ruining it."

"Ruining what?" Isaac eyed the handcuffs. "Where's the key?"

He might be strong enough to break the wooden headboard, but he'd lose any element of surprise. Then again, the elf might even the odds. If he was an elf. He had the ears, but something felt off.

"What's your name?"

"Huh?"

"Name," Isaac stressed. "I can't keep thinking of you as *the elf*."

He made air quotes with his empty hand.

"Vran." He sighed. "And you really should go."

"What?"

"Tie my feet back up and go please."

"Do you want them to drain your blood?" Isaac waved his knife at the embalmer. "Because that's probably the plan."

"Of course not." Vran jerked his head to the window. "But seriously, just leave."

Isaac blinked. "Talk about mixed signals. You don't want to be rescued?"

"I do. Very much, just not by you. I'm waiting for somebody else."

"That kind of hurts, dude. You don't even know me."

"Exactly."

"What in the hells?" a voice asked.

Three figures had filled the bedroom's doorway. Short, green-skinned, and broad, they had bulbous noses and long, pointed ears that flopped to the sides of their heads.

They smelled like body odor and noodles on a crowded summer bus.

"Now you've done it," Vran said.

"Me? I told you to be quiet."

"And I told you to leave. She's going to kill me."

"That's what I was trying to tell you," Isaac said, jerking his head toward the largest of the creatures.

"Not *her*," Vran said. "She's just a goblin."

"Is that what you are?" Isaac waved a finger at the handcuffs. "I don't suppose you have the keys for these?"

The goblins bared thick, yellow teeth.

"You can't have it," the largest said.

She wore a beaten leather biker jacket and combat boots. Isaac had no doubt she could kick his ass in a fair fight.

That was okay. He never fought fair.

"You're going to drain him?" He jerked his thumb at the vials and table. "You know that's seriously illegal, right?"

"What do you care?" the goblin demanded. "You a Guardian or something?"

"Hey. No need for insults." Isaac waved his knife. He liked this one. A British commando. Black, double-edged, with a decent throwing balance if it came to that. "Do I look like a Guardian?"

"They come in all shapes these days," the goblin said. "Even human."

"I was just passing by," Isaac lied. "And who said I was human?"

The goblin's sallow, bloodshot eyes fixed on the knife. She squinted.

"I've heard of you. You're the Undertaker's boy, aren't you?"

"Not anymore." Isaac made a gimme motion with his empty hand. "Keys, please."

The goblin squeezed into the room. The goblets moved to flank her. Isaac kept his focus on the big one, but they all posed a threat.

"His blood will go for plenty." The goblin nodded to Vran as she slammed her fist into her open palm. "But maybe you'll go for more. Maybe your old master wants you back."

"He doesn't." Isaac drew a second knife.

"How about in pieces?" one of the goblets asked in a high-pitched voice.

"You're a lot squeakier than I expected," Isaac said.

Two hands. Two blades. Three goblins. Not the best odds.

"If the Undertaker won't pay, we'll see what your blood will go for," the largest goblin said. "Whatever you are."

Vran sighed and pulled his wrists apart, snapping the handcuffs. He leaped to his feet. Something cold and clinging, like fog in the Graveyard, crept across the floor.

Greenish light filled the edges of the room. The shadows crept and coiled. They had hungry, shining eyes.

The air chilled until Isaac's breaths came out in little clouds.

"And I thought my magic was creepy."

The goblins charged.

Isaac whirled as the big one slammed into him. He dropped one of his knives as they tumbled to the floor.

Damn it. He'd gotten distracted by whatever Vran had conjured.

Isaac tried to roll her off him as she punched him hard enough to rattle his teeth. He tasted blood.

That was no good. His own was useless.

He slashed out with his remaining knife, not to kill, but to scratch.

The goblin reached for his skull and took it in both hands, intending to pound it against the floor as the shadows slithered closer.

Isaac licked the knife.

He'd never tasted goblin blood. He had to force aside any memories, any thoughts riding it. He didn't need those. He needed her strength.

The cut inside his cheek closed.

Healing. Nice, he thought.

Isaac grabbed her by the wrists and forced her off him.

Her eyes widened.

The goblets had backed against the wall. The shadows circled them, swimming through the air like eels.

No, the goblin thought. Isaac heard it through her blood. *My babies.*

They weren't minions or underlings. The goblets were her children.

"Don't kill them!" Isaac shouted to Vran. He faced the goblin. "Surrender. Just let us go. I'll call him off."

"We surrender!" she said, relaxing her grip. "Just don't hurt them."

Isaac wasn't certain Vran had gotten the message. His eyes had gone all black. Blue sparks swam in their depths and dark lines had crept up his neck and over parts of his face.

The elf looked strained. Isaac got the sense he was trying to hold back the swarming shadows.

Their thrashing shook the house, slashing holes into the walls. Dust and plaster rained from the ceiling.

"Run!" Isaac told the goblins.

They broke for the door as a chunk of roof crushed the bed.

Isaac did not know what to do. He could nick Vran, try to drain off some of his power, or maybe counter it, but he didn't know what the elf was, what his magic was, or how to use it.

He didn't know his limits either. With the goblin blood still pulsing in his veins, Vran's weird power might prove too much. Isaac could burn out like a spent match.

The decision was taken from him as the house imploded.

A flash like cold lightning swept away the shadows.

"What happened?" he asked.

He couldn't see, but he wasn't standing where he had been. Whatever was under his feet wasn't dusty, splintered hardwood but something soft, like spongey moss. The scent of the air had changed to green, heavy with rain and damp, growing things.

"You'll be able to see in a moment," a new voice said. She had a clipped accent, not British, but something like that—stuffy and formal.

"Are you all right, Vran?" she asked.

"I think so," the elf said. He was coming into focus, a slender shape dressed in shades of black and blue.

"Glad to hear it, because I'm going to kill you."

"Literally?" Vran sounded very young.

She sighed.

"Probably not."

Isaac could see her now.

Another elf, but not the same sort as the boy she glared at.

Her skin had an almost metallic sheen. Her eyes were the grayest gray, untouched by her ruby red dress. It sparkled with gems. The look clashed with the long sword in her hand.

"No," she decided. "Definitely not, though I am sorely tempted."

"Excuse me, but where are we?" Isaac asked, his eyes widening as he took in the landscape.

They still stood on a street, but the buildings were overgrown with vines and branches. Old, thick trees shot through the roofs and split the sidewalks.

The house was gone. A crater stood in its place.

Light from a bright green moon filtered through the leaves.

"This is the Spirit Realm, Isaac Frost," the woman said. "I brought you here to save you from what Vran unleashed."

"And you are?" He already suspected the answer and didn't like it.

"I'm the Guardian who's taking you in."

Isaac groaned.

Guardians were a pain. They lorded over races not privileged or powerful enough to sit on their council. They made all the big decisions from the top of the food chain, leaving the little folk to struggle.

The worst part was that they weren't very good at their jobs. All sorts of trouble fell between the cracks, escaping their notice, which was how the Undertaker made his unliving.

Granted, Isaac had never met a Guardian. He only had the Undertaker's word, but he didn't like anyone telling him what to do, not even the Old Man, which was why he had to do this job. Someday he'd be in charge, or at least be the right hand of who would be.

The Guardians had too much power. They ran the Watchtowers, the magical anchors that crossed the Spirit Realm. They were also the tool of the Council of Races, a collection of the powerful.

That was another reason to take this job. Isaac and his brothers were just the sort of people who fell through the cracks, beneath the Guardians' notice, unless they slipped up. The council saved their pity for their patrons and vassals, for the ones who kept the system going.

"It's his fault." Vran jerked a thumb at Isaac, bringing Isaac back to the moment and the elves.

"Isaac did not destroy the house, Vran. You lost control. *Again.*"

"I'm sorry, Argent," Vran said with a pained grimace.

"In his defense, it was a crappy house," Isaac offered. "And, uh, you know who I am?"

She cocked her head at him, looking every bit like an eagle or some other predatory bird on the verge of eating him.

"I do, and I know what you are. You're the boy who ran away from the Graveyard. Why are you here?"

Isaac held up a hand. "What I *was*. And I was passing by. He was in trouble, so I helped."

"Not the sort of altruism I'd expect from an Undertaker," Argent said.

"Like I said, I'm not one anymore."

"Why not?"

Isaac paused.

"It's just wrong, you know?"

"And you just happened to be passing by?"

"I smelled something." Isaac shrugged. "I got curious."

"Why do you look like that?" Vran asked.

Reaching out, he brushed Isaac's ear with a fingertip. He lingered there, just for a moment, before pulling his hand away.

Isaac peeked beneath the cuff of his jacket. His left arm remained green, the skin thick and leathery.

"It will wear off."

"He's a Phage," Argent explained. "A mimic. He sucked up some goblin blood in the fight. You know, the goblins he let escape."

"I barely nicked her. She was trying to bash my head in." Isaac jerked a thumb at Vran. "*He* was going to kill them."

"Not on purpose." Vran faced Isaac. "If you drank a turtle's blood, would you become a turtle?"

"It doesn't work like that. Wait, why a turtle?"

"I like turtles."

"How old is he?" Isaac asked Argent.

"Older than he acts."

Isaac could taste snow in her exaggerated sigh.

"Either way, we didn't get what we came for," she said. "We don't need the goblins. We need whoever holds their leash."

"So it was a setup?" Isaac asked. "That's why you wanted me to leave you there."

Vran's expression was full of *duh*.

The elf was cute, and he'd touched Isaac. That sparked a feeling in his chest that he'd almost call warm. He couldn't remember the last time someone had touched him outside a punch or a sparring session.

"Yes, it was a setup," Argent said. "And you ruined it."

Isaac cracked his jaw. His teeth weren't loose anymore. The goblin's blood had done its work.

Argent assessed him with cold, gunmetal eyes. He wondered what she'd taste like, but instantly realized that it would be like diving into liquid nitrogen. A drop of her blood would freeze him solid, and after that, he'd probably explode into snow.

Her involvement made his job trickier. He needed to get it done and get out. He wouldn't survive a fight with her.

"So now what?" Vran asked.

"Isaac is going to help us track them," Argent said.

"Wait, what?"

"You have a bit of their blood in you. You should be able to use that to help us find them."

"I don't know how to do that."

"That's all right." She crossed her arms over her chest. "We'll teach you."

"I don't work for you, and I don't want to."

"You're not going to *work* for us, Isaac Frost. You're out here on your own, without the Undertaker's protection. Those goblins were ready to drain you dry, and there are plenty of beings who wouldn't mind taking a shot at you just to see if your old master cares."

"So?"

"So we'll train you, teach you how to protect yourself, and how to best use your powers."

"She's kidding, right?" Isaac asked Vran.

"No," Vran said. "She means it. You're coming with us."

"Where?"

Vran smiled wistfully.

"Back to the school."

2
ROGUE COMMUNITY COLLEGE

The castle loomed over the plain. Many of its stones weren't held in place by mortar. Instead, they floated in formation, bound by emerald light. Inconsistent crenels lined the walls and roof like the crooked teeth of a giant in need of a dentist.

Other towers drifted around the main one, orbiting slowly on jagged rocks.

The campus's fantastic features couldn't hide its blockish architecture.

"I thought you said this place was a school?" Isaac whispered to Vran as they neared the grounds.

"It is."

"It looks like a *prison*."

"It's that too."

"Does that make you a student or an inmate?"

"Both. Neither." Vran ducked his head. "I'm on probation."

"Why?"

"Long story. Who's this Undertaker person?"

"My old master. He took me in. He takes a lot of boys in."

"Like *adopted* you?"

"Sort of." Isaac tried to sound nonchalant.

"Just boys?" Vran asked. "That's sexist."

"He's old."

"A lot of people use that as an excuse to be jerks."

"Even elves?"

"*Especially* elves," Vran said. "This Undertaker of yours, he's not a good person, is he?"

"No, no, he isn't."

It was the truth, but Isaac still tensed when he said it. It felt wrong to say it aloud.

He pointed at the birds that pecked about the lawn. Their eyes glowed with a green fire that he could only take as malicious.

"What's with the—" Isaac paused to squint. "Are those geese?"

"Dire geese. You want to avoid them."

One of the birds fluttered, showing long spines of bone along its back and wings.

"Why would you have those things here?" Isaac hurried to follow Vran up the steps toward the castle's heavy, medieval-looking gate.

"They promote dexterity among the student body," a woman said. "Though I'll admit they're a bit of a pest. Their leavings are hell on the lawn."

"Who are you?" Isaac asked, taking her in.

Middle-aged and broad-shouldered, she wore a dark pantsuit so stiff it made him think of armor. Her hair lay piled in a tight bun atop her head.

"She's the dean," Vran said.

"Isaac Frost." Her icy tone would have scared him if he hadn't been raised by a monster.

"That's me."

"The queen says you're to study with us." She started walking and gestured for Isaac and Vran to follow. "We'll get you a dorm room."

"Will it have bars?"

"Do you need them?" She cocked her head at him. "Show me your arms."

Isaac took off his jacket, revealing the tank top he wore beneath.

He held up his pale arms, twisting them for her to see.

"And your shoulders?"

He pulled the edge of the tank top back so she could see that they were bare.

"What are you looking for?" Vran asked.

"Feathers. Tattooed feathers." The dean's eyes scanned Isaac's arms and shoulders.

"Why?" Vran asked.

"The Undertaker trains assassins. Killers for hire. Each kill earns them a feather."

"I don't have any." Isaac tugged the neck of his shirt down to expose the heart drawn at the center of his chest and the two black birds flanking it. Their wings were short. "I ran away so I didn't have to earn any."

The dean scoffed as Vran took Isaac in.

"*Earn*, like it's some kind of a game." Her eyes narrowed. "Your master—"

"Former master," Isaac cut in.

"Your former master will want you back. He'll want to recoup the investment he made in your education."

"Well, he can't have me."

"You can put your jacket back on." She led them inside and the world changed, just a little.

They stood outside an institutional-looking door, the kind with a narrow window and wires crisscrossing the glass.

The dean nodded to the knives strapped to Isaac's belt.

"Are you any good with those, Frost?"

"You're not taking them."

"I don't intend to. You're going to need them." She opened the door. "Show us what you've got."

"What's in there?" Isaac nodded at the blackness. He couldn't see through it.

Vran sighed.

"It's the gym."

"That's right," the dean said. "Time for a pop quiz."

Vran stepped through, shoulders slumped, and vanished.

Isaac paused at the door.

"You may consider it an entrance exam, Mr. Frost."

Isaac knew what this would have meant back at the Graveyard, and he knew he could handle it. Whatever these would-be Guardians could cook up would pale in comparison to the Undertaker's training regimen.

Isaac followed Vran through the door. The light changed. The air tasted like old sweat and wood polish. Blood had been spilled here, often, but not recently and not in great amounts.

The large room had bleachers and a track for runners around the center. The lights above were yellow. They mimicked incandescent bulbs, but squinting, he could see they were tiny suns. None of those details helped him absorb the sight of the massive beast standing at the center, somehow without crushing the wooden floor.

The dinosaur was just the right height to gore Isaac with its central horn.

He drew his knives but didn't think they'd help. Even if he could get through its hide, he didn't scent any magic from it. A mundane beast had no power to steal and would likely stomp him for the effort.

A trio of other students had just been through that. They lay sprawled and winded, dressed in an assortment of clothes.

"At least there isn't a uniform," Isaac muttered as Vran stepped forward, his pale face determined.

Isaac froze, torn between stopping the elf and letting him have a go.

Whatever Vran had unleashed on the goblins would likely be enough to stop a triceratops.

Isaac could toss a knife. Maybe he could hit the lizard in the eye or some vital spot. Then again, he might hit Vran.

The elf stepped into goring range.

"What are you doing?" Isaac shouted. He started running, but Vran reached up with a slender hand and pressed it to the dinosaur's jaw.

The beast lowered its head as Vran scratched the leather hide around its horn.

"You're a good girl," he cooed.

Isaac froze, mid-dash. He felt more than a little stupid and sheathed his knives.

"Very good, Vran." The dean swept her gaze over Isaac and the rest of the students.

"Not everything calls for an attack, or even a counterattack."

"How did you know she wouldn't hurt you?" Isaac stammered.

"She's a triceratops," Vran said. "They're herbivores, not usually predators. She's just scared."

"You know a lot of dinosaurs?"

Vran nodded happily.

It settled in that the dinosaur was real. Something that had been extinct for millions of years was standing right there, alive and, now that the tension was defused, looking pretty cute. The smell was strong, like the time a nest of garter snakes had picked one of the crypts to mate in. Isaac and Samuel had shoveled them out as carefully as possible.

"Did I pass?"

"Oh no," the dean said. "You failed spectacularly."

He sank. The Old Man would not be happy.

"So I'm out?"

"Absolutely not, Frost. This only proves you need this school and the education we can provide you."

"I'm not a child."

"Obviously."

She didn't sound like she meant it.

Her eyes swept the room. He wondered how much she saw, and if she could see through him.

"All of you are here because there are gaps in your education."

"Like which dinosaurs are a threat?" Isaac asked.

"About what does and does not constitute a threat," she said sternly. "Being a Guardian means you will encounter species far different from yourselves. Appearances can be deceiving."

Isaac forced himself not to flinch at her implication.

They were training Guardians here. They wanted to train *him* to be a Guardian.

"You didn't know that triceratops don't eat people?" Vran asked.

Isaac shook his head.

"It wasn't in the curriculum at Murder School."

Vran considered Isaac's answer.

"That's really sad," he said.

The triceratops let out a disappointed grunt when Vran stopped scratching her.

"This way, Frost," the dean said. "I'll find you a dormitory."

Vran followed them back through the door.

"Go home, Vran," the dean told him.

"We don't have to stay here?" Isaac asked.

"*Vran* doesn't have to stay here," the dean said. "You are required to reside on campus."

"See you," Vran said with a half wave before sulking off.

Behind them, the gym had vanished. He wished he'd gotten a better look at the other students. He needed to size them up, figure out what they could do and if they'd be a problem.

At least he was in. That was step one. The Old Man would be pleased.

"That's not fair," Isaac said. "You can't just keep us here."

"We can, and if half the things I've heard about your former master are true, you'll be safer for it."

She might be the dean, but she was also the warden. He hoped the food didn't suck.

"I've seen Vran's magic," he said. "How come he gets let loose?"

"Vran lives with a member of the ruling court."

"You mean like the scary lady with the sword? The queen?"

"Exactly like that. You are welcome to petition them for the same."

"Yeah, no thanks."

"I thought not."

Somewhere in their walk the flooring had changed from vinyl to stone. It happened so subtly that Isaac hadn't noticed. That bothered him. He'd been trained to notice his surroundings.

There weren't windows here, just long slits that let in the emerald moonlight, nothing wide enough to climb through.

The dean paused at a medieval-looking door. Wooden, arched to a point, it wasn't unlike the crypts back at the Graveyard. At least something felt familiar.

It even had the same dampness, though the air here tasted of wood smoke instead of old rot and death.

"Sleep tight," the dean said, turning to leave.

"Wait, what if I get hungry? Where are the bathrooms?"

"You'll figure it out, Frost."

"Another test?" he asked, pushing at the door.

"Yes." She put her hands behind her back. "But not one I'm conducting."

Isaac flicked the light switch on and found himself in a simple room with a lean bed, a desk, and lamps.

It looked utterly mundane except for the walls. They rippled and undulated with the wind. He could probably kick his way through if he needed to escape. He tried poking one. It floated free but didn't drop. He backed away as it drifted back into position.

"Weird," he muttered.

Still, it was cleaner and far larger than his crypt back in the Graveyard.

Isaac didn't have a watch. He didn't even have a cell phone, but he did have a creeping sense of dread that told him he was late to check in.

He locked the door, sat cross-legged on the floor, and drew a knife to prick his fingertip. It healed instantly, using up the last of the goblin's blood, but he only needed a drop.

Putting it to his tongue, Isaac closed his eyes. His own blood tasted lifeless and dry, but also expectant, like a garden ready for watering.

He felt it before he saw it, a misty place that existed as much in his memory as in the world. The school felt similar, someplace not quite real, but he pushed that thought away. The connection wouldn't last long.

Isaac could taste the storm clouds. There was always a lot of rain as fall came on.

"About time, Dove," a voice said as Isaac rounded the corner, moving into a clearing among the crypts.

Flowers grew here in rows. They always surprised Isaac, that the Undertaker took the time to add bright colors and beauty to the hillside. He chose hearty plants like irises and lilacs, things that would survive the Graveyard's gloom and weather. It wasn't unlike how he chose his charges.

Isaac found him toiling in a plot, digging it with a shovel, as he made all his boys do. He never slacked on the work, never asked them to do what he wouldn't or couldn't do himself. Isaac respected that. He respected the Old Man too, even as he hoped and plotted for a change.

The Undertaker had shed his tattered trench coat and draped it across a nearby tombstone, leaving his lean frame exposed in a white, time-stained shirt and suspenders.

He added another shovelful to the pile of thick red clay and eyed Isaac from beneath his weathered top hat. He didn't need it for shade. He wore it to keep the drizzle out of his eyes. The sun shone long in the valley.

The fresh grave spoke of another successful job. They only buried certain targets in the Graveyard, the ones meant to disappear, to never be found. Plots like this, with their unlettered markers, littered the hills.

"I should have sent Kenji," the Undertaker groused.

"Kenji wouldn't be able to fool them. You need me for this job."

Isaac's brother had a full sleeve of feathers, each a name, each a life taken. In time, Isaac's arms and chest would match.

"Have you found your target yet?" the Old Man asked, his beard almost pure steel, with just a few threads of black woven in.

"I only just got picked up."

"I know that," the Old Man spat. "There's a clock on this kill, Dove."

The threat was clear. Plenty of boys didn't come back from their first job. They lost the nerve at the last moment, the target got the upper hand, or they ran, which was never a good idea. Isaac knew that firsthand.

"I can't go too quick or I'll give myself away."

Isaac had to find the school's heart, its beating, living heart. He didn't really understand it, but magic was like that, and it was always tied to life. The job, in theory, was simple: find the heart, destroy it, and get out before the Guardians caught him.

The main issue was that it wouldn't be easy to find his goal. It would be hidden, guarded, not just behind some labeled, unlocked door like a janitor's closet.

He'd doubted, when the Old Man had explained the job, that a knife would be enough; but the Undertaker had assured him it would do.

"Just get it done. Don't make me send Kenji in to finish it."

It wasn't like the Old Man to be so cagey about a job. Isaac wondered who the client was and why taking out this school was so important to them. He gave his curiosity a hard kick.

The first thing the Undertaker drilled into them, by rote and beating, was that it didn't matter. The client's reasons were unimportant, only that they paid.

The fee was usually magic. It had been a while since the last time the Undertaker had demanded an orphan, a new charge to join his collection of misfit boys.

Isaac didn't mind that. He'd spare anyone from this life if he could. That was the whole point of his and Kenji's plan. They'd change everything if they got the chance.

"I'll figure it out," Isaac said. "I'll get it done."

"See that you do."

3
THEY DON'T EAT THE DINOSAURS, DO THEY?

Isaac crept along the shifting halls and noted the architecture's change from medieval to modern and back again. The temperature never changed, but the smells went from antiseptic to something sweet with an occasional bout of mold.

He tried to memorize the layout but found himself somewhere new whenever he backtracked.

No one had said he *couldn't* explore the school. The dean had even kind of encouraged it, but he planned to tell anyone who challenged him that he was hungry, which was the truth.

He circled back to his room, finding it again and again, though he couldn't say how, and he couldn't map the way.

It felt like the school was taunting him.

I will figure you out, he thought. *And then I'll kill you.*

Because that was the job.

Every slit or window showed the emerald moon and twilight sky of the Other Side.

Undertakers often worked in the Spirit Realm. The older boys, like Kenji, even went beyond or below, but Isaac was a lot of feathers, a lot of tattoos and kills, away from that.

He passed a hall lined with classroom doors, took a left, and found three students waiting for him.

They stood in a triangle, facing him, a Black girl with dark purple lipstick at the point. Her outfit was heavy on the goth look, with raggedy skirts and a leather jacket in considerably better shape than his own.

The boy on the right towered over Isaac.

His skin was riven with deep crags, looking like tree bark, at least on the left side of his face. A line ran straight down it, separating him in two. His left hand matched. That eye glowed green like a firefly. The right half was fully mortal, including a dull brown eye.

The second boy was harder to describe. He was utterly normal, so much so that he faded into the background. Isaac had to squint to see him. He couldn't even remember what the guy was wearing.

The three didn't look threatening. Isaac had his knives. He didn't reach for them, though his palms itched to hold them.

"Is this some kind of hazing?" he asked.

"We just came to say hi." The girl extended a hand.

She wore gloves like his, the kind that left the fingers exposed. Her nail polish was purple and sparkly.

"Do you know Vran?" Isaac asked.

"Of course we know him," she said. The boys nodded.

"Do you exchange fashion tips?"

The girl cocked her head. He didn't think he'd offended her but couldn't quite tell.

"We thought we should meet the latest inmate," the half-wooden guy said.

He wore a varsity jacket, the kind jocks got in high school, not that Isaac had gone to high school, but he'd seen them on television.

He squinted again, trying to pinpoint the other student. A boy—definitely blond, but the details remained hazy.

Were his eyes blue or green? Even his age was up for debate.

A bit like Vran, Isaac thought.

The elf wasn't blurred out like this kid, but his age was hard to pin down. Vran looked mature, out of his teens, but came across as innocent.

Isaac hoped he wouldn't have to fight him.

He pushed thoughts of Vran aside.

Any of the students could be a threat. He needed to focus and learn what he could about them.

"I'm Hex," the girl said.

"Ford," the tree guy said. "Like in Norway."

He pronounced it like the truck, not the geography, but Isaac decided against correcting a guy who could smash him with one hand.

"That's Shy," Hex said, nodding in the general direction of the boy Isaac couldn't quite see. "He doesn't talk much."

"Getting that," Isaac said. "Is there anything to eat? I just got here and no one gave me a tour."

"The dean did her cryptic you'll-figure-it-out thing, didn't she?" Hex held up her hands to make air quotes.

"How'd you know?"

She shrugged.

"I could say that I'm psychic, but it's really just a good guess. She loves that kind of thing."

"We thought you might be getting hungry," Ford added, "and decided we'd help you figure it out."

Isaac liked that they weren't a bunch of rule followers. That might be useful.

"So there's a cafeteria?"

"Not exactly." Hex stepped to one of the classroom doors. "We're hungry. Can you take us somewhere to eat please?"

The door opened by itself. Like with the gym, swirling ink obscured what lay on the other side.

"The school listens to you?"

"If it's in the mood," Ford answered before slipping through the door.

He moved gracefully for a big guy. He had a lot of muscle but carried it well. He'd be trouble in a fight. Hex went through.

Shy followed her, a boy-shaped blur like a heat haze or a shadow.

Isaac didn't feel anything when he stepped through, just a slight change of air pressure and temperature. Then the smells hit him, a mix of people, mostly human, and many types of food. His stomach grumbled, reminding him that he was actually hungry.

The space was brightly lit, full of artificial cheer and neon signs. People milled about, carrying bags or leading children by the arm.

Bright signs announced brands, fast-food places he knew and a few he didn't. The ceilings soared above them. Some trailing vines lent the space a little green.

He took in the sprawling structure and the massive, tiered fountain better suited to outdoors.

"A mall?"

"Yeah," Hex said. "It always drops us somewhere with a lot of options."

The door to the school had vanished.

"Where'd Shy go?"

Nothing happened, no shimmer or scent of magic. The guy had been there, just a little. Now he was gone.

"He's harder to see the more people there are," Hex explained with a nod to the tables of shoppers and bored-looking teens.

"Ah."

That was good intel. Shy wouldn't be a problem if Isaac was alone with him. It might nullify the guy's invisibility.

Isaac hoped it didn't come to that.

He was only here for one kill, one feather.

"So where are we?"

"Hard to say," Ford said, sizing up a sandwich joint.

The wooden part of him was hidden now. He looked like any college-aged jock, broad-shouldered and kind of hulking, but nothing that would draw attention.

"Nice glamour," Isaac said.

"Thanks," Hex said.

"Last time it was the Mall of America," Ford said.

"We could be anywhere?"

"Yeah, but it tends to default to Denver," Hex said.

"Why Denver?"

"We think it's because the old Eastern Watchtower was destroyed there," she said.

"I think the school just likes Denver," Shy said from somewhere to Isaac's right.

Isaac definitely didn't jump. He would have described it more like a tactical flinch.

"Wait," he asked. "We can just walk out of there anytime?"

"Anytime we're hungry," Ford said. "We joke about being inmates, since the Guardians recruited us, but there aren't a lot of rules. The school's not a prison."

"At least not for us," Hex said.

"What do you mean?"

"We're training to be Guardians," Ford said. "They have to put the things we'll lock up somewhere."

"I thought the Guardians were all elves and dwarves," Isaac said.

Ford shrugged.

"Things change. They want diversity, not just the immortal races."

"Why?" Isaac said. "And what exactly are you supposed to lock up?"

"Don't know why," Ford said. "But a lot of nasty got set loose when the old tower exploded."

Isaac imagined that wasn't only it, that more than a few people who disagreed with how things were run would find a home in a cell.

"And that somewhere is the basement," Hex said. "It's a labyrinth."

That piqued Isaac's interest. A maze sounded like a good place to hide a heart.

"The whole school's a labyrinth," Isaac said.

"We don't really get lost though. The place takes care of us." Ford said with a smile. "But down there . . . Let's just say it's somewhere you don't want to wander around."

"Because of the prisoners?"

"And the guards," Hex said.

"What are they?"

"Don't know, and I'm not stupid enough to go find out."

"Even the professors are scared of them," Ford added.

He headed for the sandwich place and Isaac followed.

"I like this place," Ford announced after ordering two foot-long sandwiches.

"Me too," Isaac said. "I thought they'd all gone out of business."

He ordered and thought while he waited.

If he was going to hide the school's heart, putting it in a labyrinth full of monsters and mysterious guards would be the way to go. He had to get down there, but it was too soon to press for more details.

"Anyway, welcome to RCC," Hex said, waving her hand when they'd all sat at a table in the corner.

Ford put a plate down in front of an empty seat.

"RCC?"

"Rogue Community College," Shy whispered.

If Isaac tried, looking out of the corner of his eye, he could just make out a dip in the seat's cushion.

"They never should have let us name it," Ford said with a shake of his head.

"They let you decide what to call it?"

"Yep." Hex paused with her sandwich at her mouth. "We all got a vote."

"So why did you name it that?"

"It's a joke, sort of," she said. "There are other schools, elven schools mostly. But we're the misfits, the rejects."

"And the school doesn't seem to mind," Shy whispered.

Isaac assumed he ate. The fries on his plate slowly vanished.

"So it's alive?"

He already knew that from the intel the Old Man had gotten from the client, but confirmation was always good.

"We think so." Hex took a long sip from her drink. The straw and lid made that familiar squeaking sound. It reminded Isaac of his little brothers.

"Have you asked the teachers?"

"Professors," she corrected. "And yes, but they won't tell us much. They want us to find things out for ourselves."

"What's the good of a school if they won't teach you?"

"Oh, they teach us." Ford had already made it through one sandwich. "Like how to hide, or fight—just not each other."

"And topics like magical theory," Hex said gravely.

"Or math," Shy complained.

Isaac tried to scent Shy's blood and couldn't. He'd make a great Undertaker.

The Old Man should have scooped him up.

"Are we it?" Isaac flicked a finger over the table, making sure to include the empty chair. "All the students I mean?"

"Well, there's Vran," Hex said. "He's in our class along with a few others."

"And there are other classes," Ford said, eyebrows crinkling. "We think."

His expression didn't quite keep up with his words. Hex's spell wasn't perfect. There was a lag between his words and movement, like a video out of sync with its audio, so she wasn't that powerful, at least not yet.

"We see hints of them, stuff on chalkboards from other lessons, but no other students," she said. "I think they're on another plane."

Isaac wanted to ask about Vran, about where he ate and who with, but held back. The Old Man had told him time and again that curiosity was bad for business. Asking the wrong questions could be fatal.

If pressed, Isaac could argue that he worried more about a fight with the elf than he did these three. A drop of Ford's blood would give him enough strength to put Hex and Shy down. The bruiser wasn't likely going to be used to dealing with someone skilled with a blade, but Vran's power was strange. During that moment in the house, Isaac had been overcome with the sense that it could swallow them all. Maybe he was the key to this job, to taking down the school. Vran's power was unstable. If Isaac could set it loose, it might be like burning down a crime scene—he could use Vran to cover his tracks.

Or perhaps it would be like handling dynamite.

"So what are you?" Ford asked.

"Ford!" Hex said. "That's rude."

"Why?" he asked with a shrug. "He knows our powers. It's not like they're subtle. Or are you human?"

Ford's eyes went wide and the glamour slipped enough for Isaac to see the green sparks in his one eye.

Isaac was prepared for this. It went against his instincts. You weren't supposed to hand an enemy any advantage, and knowledge was power.

"I'm a Phage. I eat blood."

"Like a vampire?" Ford eyed Isaac's sandwich.

Isaac laughed.

"No, just a drop or two."

"Why?" Shy asked.

"I can pick up some of the host's power for a bit," he said. "That's why they want me at the school. They're hoping I can help them track down some goblins."

Hex nodded sagely.

"Cool," Shy said. "A real mission."

"We just go to class and train," Ford said. "We don't get to do anything important."

Hex raised a finger. "Not yet."

Isaac smiled, trying to fake sympathy.

They never would, not if the Undertaker's client got their way.

4

EVERY PART OF THAT PLANT IS POISONOUS

Isaac was up before the bell clanged outside.

He couldn't remember having ever slept so warmly. There was something, maybe, a time before the Graveyard, before the constant taste of earth and rot, before cold stone walls and a hard slab for a bed. He prodded the almost-memory, knowing it wouldn't help. It was no clearer now than any of the other times he'd tried to tease it to the surface, so he let it sink back into the darkness.

His first foray into infiltrating the school had gone well. He'd followed Hex and the others back to RCC and found his room without effort. It had changed a bit in his absence. A stack of books lay on the desk, along with a cup full of pens and a new notebook. He'd found the bathroom stocked with a toothbrush, toothpaste, and other essentials. There were even clean towels, but most importantly, the shower had hot water.

This was nothing like his crypt back at the Graveyard or the common showers in the mortuary.

It won't save you, he thought at the school.

Saying it aloud was too risky. He didn't know who or what might be listening.

He needed to appear a little lost, even a little innocent. He hated to admit it, but neither was much of an act.

Isaac ran his eyes over the books: bestiaries, histories, and—he stifled a yawn—literature. He could already tell that lessons here would be different than those in the chapel.

He'd laced his boots when someone hammered on his door.

"Good morning, Frost," the dean said when he opened it.

"How can you tell?" he asked, jerking his thumb toward the emerald light creeping through the nearest casement.

"The bells will orient you in time," she said. "Please follow me."

"Where? What will I need?"

He scanned the stack of books on his desk. He'd never been a fan of reading, but the bestiaries might have pictures and diagrams of veins and weak points.

"You're not going to class. Doctor Cavanaugh, our physician, will see you first."

"Why? I'm not sick."

"We need to make sure you've had all your shots."

Isaac flinched at the memory of needles, the tattoo gun grinding into his chest. Still, he chose not to argue. Everything he learned about the school, about its layout and staff, would help his mission. The sooner he got it done, the sooner he'd go home and see Kenji and the others again. It was only the first step in his and Kenji's plan.

The dean marched along.

Isaac wondered if she ever let her hair out of that bun or if she ever showed any emotion other than slight disapproval. Even the Old Man was more expressive, though he tended toward disappointment or anger.

Isaac didn't get a whiff of magic or power from the dean, just a bit of perfume and something tangy he assumed was her hairspray.

He noted the doors and hallways as they walked. There were no locks he could see, no keyholes. That didn't mean his job would be easy. He didn't see any stairwells or any way into the labyrinth below.

They passed vending machines, one stocked with snacks for the human students and one with packages of glowing fruit or writhing flower petals.

That meant there were people here, though Isaac couldn't assume they were students. They might be the mysterious guards the others had mentioned.

His stomach gurgled at the sight of the candy bars and chips, but he doubted the dean would let him pause to choose something. Besides, he'd been trained to go without, to get by on whatever he had to. He could wait a little while longer.

The physician's office was on the first floor. It felt sterile and kind of cold. A wordless tune, soft music, came from somewhere.

Isaac had seen places like this on TV, the few times he'd watched TV, but he'd never been in one.

There was no one behind the receptionist's desk.

Posters on the wall detailed cross sections of body parts. Those were familiar. Every assassin needed a good knowledge of anatomy.

Pamphlets were laid out in the waiting room. The ones he could read had titles like *Your Body and You.*

He shot the dean a look and read, "*So You've Been Impaled*?"

"Accidents happen," she said with a shrug and with what might be considered an expectant smile. "I'll leave you here."

Isaac was about to take a seat when the door to the back opened.

"Hello?" Isaac called.

"Come in, Mr. Frost."

He walked through to find a willowy woman in a lab coat holding a clipboard. She had straight red hair and a serious expression.

"Doctor Cavanaugh?" he asked, taking in the modern office.

"You look surprised."

"I was expecting a more medieval setting."

"Our students come from many backgrounds," she said. "We need to be prepared to support their needs."

He nodded.

Another human, she didn't wear perfume but had a faintly chemical scent: a mix of deodorant, unscented soap, and hand sanitizer.

"Take off your shirt and boots and have a seat." Cavanaugh nodded to the paper-lined bed.

"What is this exactly?" he asked.

"A physical."

He blinked at her.

"Have you ever had a physical?"

Isaac shook his head. This felt like a waste of time.

She scowled and wrote something down.

"How about a dentist?"

"Uh, no," Isaac said, pulling off his shirt.

She looked at him over the top of her glasses and scribbled another note.

"Mr. Frost, are you saying that you've had no medical care whatsoever?"

"Not like this," he said, waving a hand around them.

"Well, we're lucky your former guardian had the foresight to see that you got a tattoo."

He flushed a bit, remembering the needles, the long hours on the cold metal table, the same kind of table the goblins had meant to strap Vran to. The cold steel pressing against his bare back had been a comfort. He'd focused on that while the Undertaker had marked him with a thousand little jabs, deep and sharp, like the Old Man had been drawing on his bones.

"It was kind of required."

"Fetching," she said in a dry tone devoid of sincerity.

He sat to unlace his boots, focusing on the large squares of the tile floor as he removed them.

When he was done, she pressed the metal disk of a stethoscope to his heart, listened, and nodded. She wrote again.

"Any major illnesses?"

"No," he said. "Colds and flus sometimes."

Those had been the worst, lying feverish, shivering in his crypt despite the heat flooding his face. Kenji had brought him water and food. Kenji, who could be so gentle, despite all the kills he'd racked up.

That was what Isaac hoped to be, gentle. He hoped he could change the Graveyard, and the Undertakers, but he couldn't do that until he'd earned his feathers, until he was strong enough, respected enough, for Kenji's plan to work.

"What about broken bones?"

"My arm once. At the wrist."

He held up his right arm.

She felt along it with gloved hands.

"It was well set, but not perfectly. They didn't take you to a hospital?"

Isaac shook his head. The Undertaker had taken him to one of the embalming rooms, set the break, and put a cast on it. He'd given Isaac one of his potions, some foul concoction that tasted like mud and went down with a similar texture.

"Let's hope Phages are resistant to blood-borne pathogens. Stand on the scale please."

Isaac perked up. This might be worth his time after all.

"Do you know a lot about Phages?"

"No," she said with a shrug. "You're remarkably rare."

She slid the metal things around, captured his weight, and wrote it down.

"Does that make you want to dissect me?"

"Not at all, but it does mean I want some of your blood, quite a bit of it actually."

"Why?"

"We need to know that it's safe for you to interact with the other students and to train with them."

"I'm not going to eat them."

"I didn't think you were, but even if you're resistant, it doesn't mean they are. I need to know you're not carrying something deadly that could infect someone else."

Isaac thought back to the gym, to the smell of blood. Accidents happen, the dean had said. Maybe that was how he could pull it off, make it look like an accident.

"Oh. Well, okay then."

"You can get dressed now. After I draw blood you can go to class. You appear to be in good health."

"You sound surprised."

She tsked.

"We don't know much about the Undertaker or what he does with the children he takes."

Isaac tugged on his shirt.

"He trains us to kill, to fight, and survive. That's basically it."

"Well, he at least protects his investment. You're not malnourished, a little underweight, but that's nothing a few weeks of better eating won't cure."

"The dean said there might be shots?"

"Let me run tests on your blood first. I don't know how you'll react to anything."

Isaac couldn't understand why she wasn't pressing him to learn about the Undertaker. They had to want to interrogate him and learn as much as they could about the Graveyard. The Undertaker worked hard to keep himself, and his affairs, hidden from the Guardians.

"One more thing, Frost. How old are you?"

"I—I don't know."

It was her turn to blink.

"He never told me."

"I'm writing down early twenties with a question mark," she said. "What about your birth parents? Any history of illness? That could be important later in life."

"No idea."

"You don't sound concerned."

Isaac shrugged.

"Assassins don't usually live long enough to retire."

She cocked her head at him and he wondered if maybe there was a little sadness in her expression.

Was sympathy the right tactic here? Pity probably wasn't the dean's style. The other students, well, they might be around his own age, give or take a few years, but they were way more innocent than him.

Whatever this school was putting them through, it wasn't like his training.

It had been hard. It was meant to be hard.

They were taught to endure anything, and to never die unless they took their target with them.

Isaac was used to blood, but he felt weirdly dizzy as the doctor put the needle in his arm and took vial after vial of bubbly red fluid.

"Now I go to class?"

"Registration. But first, have a cookie."

She offered him a little package like the ones from the vending machine.

Isaac bit into the waxy cookie and felt a weird flutter in his stomach at her expression.

"Do you know where I go for that?" he asked between bites, hoping this wasn't another test.

Isaac had never been to school. He'd had lessons and tutoring at the Graveyard, but not actual *school*. While he wasn't looking forward to it, he could go for a training session, the sort of one-on-one sparring they'd done almost daily.

He didn't like this feeling of being lost, of needing help. Punching something would help. Stabbing would be even better.

"No, but your buddy should be waiting for you."

The door to the waiting room opened.

"Buddy?"

"They assign every new student a buddy to help with orientation."

Her attention was back on her clipboard and the vials of his blood.

He wandered out to the waiting room to find a pretty girl sitting in one of the chairs.

She was dressed in nice jeans and a fuzzy pink sweater. Blond and delicate, she smelled a bit grassy, rougher than whatever perfume the dean wore. She sprang out of her seat and waved a gloved hand. Blue silk, the gloves reached all the way to her elbows.

"I'm Daffodil," she said perkily. "You must be Isaac."

"Daffodil?"

"Like the flower. Or you can call me Daff. Most people do."

"Doesn't anyone around here have a regular name?"

"Sure they do." She led him into the hall with a little wave. "We just don't use them."

"Why not?"

"It's more like we're superheroes or something like that. I think it helps with the whole freak-show school thing."

"So what's your power?" he asked.

She wiggled her fingers at him and grinned.

"One touch and you die."

"Really?"

Isaac took a step back.

She laughed.

"Maybe . . . poisoned at least."

She started walking and he followed, though with a little more space between them.

"You weren't at dinner last night," Isaac said.

"I was studying with my boyfriend."

Isaac didn't ask how she could have a boyfriend if they couldn't touch. It was too bad the Old Man only recruited boys. She'd make a killing at killing.

"Besides . . ." Daff shrugged. "Putting me in a room where a little kid could stumble into me or something like that isn't a good idea."

"It's happened before?"

"It started in the middle of my senior prom." Her bubbly light dimmed a bit. "During the first dance, when my date kissed me."

"I'm so sorry."

Isaac couldn't imagine what that would be like. He hadn't had a prom of course, but most teens would want one, right? To get dressed up, dance with a guy you like, only to kill him when he kissed you—Isaac shuddered.

"It's all right. It feels like a long time ago, and they let me keep the crown, probably because they were too scared to take it away."

She smiled at her own joke, but her eyes crinkled with sadness.

Daffodil stopped at an office door.

"Let's get you registered," she said, the cheer back in her voice.

"How does this work?"

"Registration?"

"That too, but I mean, well, all of it."

"Don't worry," she said. "I'm with you all day today."

"Thanks."

He couldn't imagine a better watchdog. He probably wouldn't be able to cut her or get too close without her putting him down. Why else would she share something so personal or give away what she could do so freely? She wanted him to know she was a threat.

They stepped into the office. The dean waited behind a large wooden desk with a plaque that read *Dean Ryan*.

"Now what?" Isaac asked.

"More tests," the dean said. She gestured toward a smaller desk in the corner of the room. Several sheets of paper and a pen waited for him.

"Why?" he groaned.

"We have no idea what you do or don't know," the dean said. She had a large metal mug of coffee in her hand. "We can't register you for any classes until we do."

Isaac thumbed through the pages.

"How long do I have?"

"This is a knowledge assessment. It's not about performance. Take as long as you need."

Isaac sat with a sigh and began.

The first questions were more personal, things like his preferred pronouns and plane of origin. Then they got harder, moving into questions of math and history, neither of which were his strong suits.

"Can't I just stab someone?"

"We know you know how to do that. What we need to know is if you know *when* not to stab someone. Do your best, Frost."

He wanted to joke that it was all about how much he was paid, but he swallowed it down. The dean didn't look like she'd find it funny, and he was supposed to make this work, at least long enough to complete the job.

Isaac ground through the rest of the pages and handed them to her.

He stood waiting as she went through them with a red pen, slashing and circling. Not knowing what to do with his hands, he took his seat again.

It took her nearly as long to assess them as it had him to complete them.

Setting them aside, she started typing on her computer.

"There." She nodded to the printer in the corner as it awoke and started whirring. "That's your class schedule until we need to adjust it."

She whipped the page across the desk and he took it cautiously.

"Do you usually handle this yourself?"

"We're a small institution. You get the personal touch here. Go on."

Isaac scanned the list of topics.

"Transplanar Literature? What does that even mean?" He waved the sheet at her. "Do I really need to learn all of this?"

"The point of that particular class, Frost, is to expose you to ideas other than your own. I think a better question might be, can you learn it?"

She took a long sip of her coffee.

Isaac was sensing a theme, and while he wasn't certain, he thought she might be insulting him.

The dean continued, "Our curriculum might be largely remedial, but we're here to offer our students an education, a foundation to be able to thrive in a larger universe than most of them hail from or have comprehended."

"But I already know what's out there."

"Your test scores say otherwise."

"You can't just read about stuff or hear it in lectures."

"I think you'll find that we incorporate plenty of practical exercise into the curriculum."

"What does that mean?"

"That you'll have plenty of opportunity to stab something . . . once Doctor Cavanaugh clears you."

Isaac smiled until he read the class sheet again.

"And literature will somehow help me understand the planes?"

"Yes, but that's just for starters, your first semester. Like I said, we'll evaluate and adjust as you go."

"How long am I in for?" he asked.

"This is higher education, Mr. Frost, not a prison sentence."

"That's not how the queen put it."

"The queen does not have the final say here. I do. You'd do well to remember that."

He intended to.

The school had one thing right. Knowledge was power. Maybe they'd teach him something he could use to help Kenji overthrow the Old Man.

"How did it know?"

"Excuse me?"

"The books in my room. They're all for these classes, right?"

"I would assume so."

"How did the school know those were the ones I'd need?"

"I guess that's one more thing you'll have to learn."

5

BUT LEARNING ISN'T VERY FUN

"Excuse me, Professor Lin?" Isaac asked, raising his hand.

"Yes, Mr. Frost?"

"What does any of this have to do with being a Guardian?"

He knew he shouldn't push it. He needed to fit in here, act grateful that they'd taken him in, but the endless lectures on the politics of the races and realms had him grinding his teeth. He'd only been here a few days, and he wasn't certain he was going to make it.

He'd been hard-pressed not to stare out the window and hope for an attack of some kind.

Professor Lin even managed to make the assassinations and duels, like the recent death of the King of Swords, sound boring.

Xenobiology was going better. Literature was almost as bad as this, Social History of the Planes, but that was mostly reading and he could do it on his bed.

Professor Lin was a slight woman with long, curling brown hair and severe features. She always smelled like lemons and toothpaste. She scowled at Isaac's interruption.

"Etiquette and interspecies customs are crucial to building bridges and understanding, Mr. Frost. That's why we teach you the history of the realms and their interactions."

"But you're training Guardians," he countered. "How does any of that help us with taking someone or something down?"

Lin took a breath and Isaac got the sense she was holding in a sigh.

"Because violence isn't the answer to most situations. Not everything can be solved with a knife."

Isaac leaned back in his seat.

"Are you sure about that? Have you tried?"

Lin sighed.

"Why do you think you're here, at this school, Mr. Frost?"

He waved to indicate the other students.

"Because we're dangerous."

Daffodil shook her head. Ford shrugged. Isaac couldn't read Shy's response. The invisible kid was a blur in his seat.

"Speak for yourself," Hex said. "Some of us *want* to be here."

Lin moved behind the lectern and gripped it with her hands as if she could use it to steer the conversation back on track.

"We're not training an army. This isn't a barracks or a boot camp. Despite your special circumstances, it's not a prison or a punishment either."

"Then what are you doing?" Isaac asked. "Why are we here?"

"Because, yes, violence has been tried as the answer to all of our problems, and it didn't work out so well. You're here—all of you—because you need our help and we need yours. In the past the Guardians were an army, or have been used as one. RCC is meant to change that."

"But what if we don't want to be Guardians?" Isaac asked.

"Then don't. It's as simple as that. We'll train you to use your gifts, but we won't compel you. When you're ready, you can leave, if that is your choice."

Isaac didn't believe her. There was no way the school, the royals, would invest the time to train them if they could just walk out the door when they wanted to.

The others were naive to believe it. He should be grateful. That same blindness meant they believed that he could have gotten away from the Undertakers, that the Old Man would let anyone go.

"Now, can anyone tell me what occurred in the Christmas War of 1984?" Lin asked. "Vran? You haven't said anything all hour."

"I don't want to talk about it," the elf said, tilting his head up from where he'd almost slumped against his desk. "Not if I don't have to."

"You do not," she said but sounded disappointed. "Anyone else? Mr. Frost?"

"I didn't raise my hand."

"No, but I'm still asking you."

"Is that the one where people were beating each other up over dolls?"

"Not exactly, though you have the correct time period."

Daffodil raised a gloved hand.

"Yes." Lin nodded to her.

"It's when the elves wiped out the Saurians."

"Wiped out?" Ford asked.

"Yeah," Daff said. "Off the map. They're extinct now."

"Very good, but not entirely correct," Lin said. "It's when the former King of Swords allowed a pogrom against the Saurians for trying to extend their territory into the mortal plane. They were not wiped out, but they were beyond decimated. Their ranks have never recovered."

Daffodil shot Isaac a look that said *ha!*

Had he offended her? He hadn't meant to. Had it been when he'd called her dangerous?

He held back a scoff and pushed himself down into his seat. Like being dangerous was a bad thing. In his world it was a compliment.

Isaac didn't want to be a Guardian, but if she did, there was no way skills like Daff's wouldn't be useful to them.

Lin could say what she wanted about noble intentions, but every one of the students would make a good soldier or spy.

"I thought the elves were supposed to be all about preserving life," Hex said. "It seems hypocritical."

No one looked at Vran. Everyone was pointedly not looking at Vran.

"It was," he said. "It was hypocritical, wrong, and completely stupid."

"I thought you didn't want to talk about it," Isaac said.

"I don't, but maybe I should. That's what no one wants you to know. The immortals, the races that control the Watchtowers . . . they're just people. They're as messed up as anyone else. They hide behind fancy words and magic, but give them a reason and they're just as petty and broken as everyone else."

Isaac shot his hand up.

"Yes, Mr. Frost?"

"What did the Guardians do during this war?"

Lin gave a little nod, and Isaac knew he'd scored a point, or he'd at least asked the right question for once. He was starting to get it, maybe. This was another kind of sparring match. If so, he could learn the moves. He could win.

"At the time, the Guardians were only drawn from the races in control of a Watchtower, meaning those in power. Some abstained from the action in protest. Others participated."

"That's horrible," Daffodil said.

"That's cops," Hex quipped.

"Historically, yes," Lin said. "At least often."

"If we become Guardians, what happens if we get an order like that?" Isaac asked. "Are we supposed to follow it?"

Lin cocked her head to the side.

He hadn't impressed her, but he felt like he was going where she was trying to lead him.

"No. Can anyone tell me why? Mr. Ford?"

The big guy barely fit into his desk. He thought for a long moment before answering.

"You just said it. The Guardians then were the same as the people in charge. We won't be."

"Exactly the king's intent," Lin said. "He's founded this school partly to sever the Guardians from the races that control the Watchtowers and diversify their ranks."

"What's the other part?" Isaac asked.

"To provide a place for those who need it."

"But don't the Guardians still answer to the throne?" Hex asked.

"The king has moved for them to answer to the Council of Races instead."

"That does sound more democratic," Daffodil offered.

"Yeah, but the tower races are on the council," Hex said. "Magical power has a lot of sway. If the elves, dwarves, and other races have the most magic, then they have the most political power."

"Like economics back home," Ford said. "He who dies with the most money wins."

"A fair analogy," Lin said.

"Though they're still dead," Isaac quipped.

"So the whole system is messed up," Ford said. "It's all haves versus the have-nots."

"As above, so below," Hex said quietly.

"Then what's the point of having Guardians at all? Get rid of them." Isaac turned to Vran. "And how do you guys still have kings?"

"Don't ask me," Vran said. "I don't get a vote."

He shrugged as though it had nothing to do with him, but the dean had said he lived with one of the court. There had to be more to the story.

"You can ask the king should you ever meet him," Lin said. "For now, I want you to focus on your next position paper. Six thousand words on the history of the Guardians and what you would change. How would you fix the system? Class is dismissed."

Isaac held in a groan as the others started packing up their notebooks. They filed out. Daffodil and Hex walked together.

He remembered the look on Daffodil's face. He hadn't made any friends today. He'd need to find his way back into their good graces if he was going to keep the ruse up.

Convincing them that he belonged here meant he had to put in the effort, which meant he had to do the homework.

It was all so incredibly boring.

Who cared about who killed who before he was born? He was going to kill people in the here and now.

"What's wrong, Isaac?"

Vran. He'd lingered behind, leaving them alone with Lin, who was erasing the chalkboard.

"I, uh . . . " He felt himself flush. "I don't know how to write a position paper, whatever that is."

"I guess it didn't go along with the lessons on stabbing?"

"No, not exactly," Isaac said.

"Well, it's just an essay where you take a position. Like, why great white sharks are the best."

"Are they though?"

"*Yes*," Vran said emphatically. "I can show you what to do. Want to meet at the library later?"

"There's a library?" Isaac asked, trying not to focus on Vran's dark eyes. His hair was big today, like a cloud of inky spikes around his head.

"Of course there's a library."

"Why would you help me?"

"Because you need it."

"Then uh, yeah. Sure."

Vran glided out of the room with a nod.

Isaac swallowed. He did not like this feeling, the sort of warmth that came over him when Vran spoke to him. It didn't feel like the kind of sensation an assassin should pursue.

Tick tock, Frost, he thought, and of course he heard it in the Old Man's voice.

6

A MAN MADE OF WIRES

Isaac expected stacks of moldering old books bound in worn leather, their titles written in ancient languages. He anticipated a smell not unlike the Graveyard, the scent of decay with a hint of rot. He kind of hoped for books chained to their shelves, bound in questionable hide, and scribed in as much blood as ink.

What he found beyond the tall wooden doors was a long metal counter and a sign that read *Absolutely No Magic in the Library: This Especially Means You, Vran!*

Beyond that were rows of steel tables and computers sitting in front of the rows of carefully organized shelves. What books he saw were new, often not thick, and their titles were printed in English.

"You look lost. Can I help?"

The man addressing Isaac wore a sweater vest over a shirt with rolled-up sleeves. He had glasses and a bow tie, which Isaac expected in a librarian, but his skin was copper and green, like circuit boards. His hair, polished wires, gleamed.

"Is this the library?"

"What else would it be?"

The guy took his glasses off and polished them with a little cloth.

"An office supply store?" Isaac suggested, waving at the computers. "I was just expecting something more . . ."

"Medieval?" the man asked with a laugh as he replaced his glasses.

"Yeah. No offense."

"Well, this is the library."

The wire man gestured to the broad, modern space.

"And you're the librarian?"

"I am. You can call me Jack."

"You're not a professor?"

"Nope. I'm on work study."

"You study work?"

"It means I'm a student."

"Oh, well, I'm here to meet Vran, to work on an essay."

Jack's metal face crinkled with annoyance.

"Is this about the sign?"

"Yes."

"Vran won't be teaching me about magic, just how to write a, uh, position paper."

Jack relaxed.

"You must be Isaac Frost, the newest admission," he said.

"That's me."

The guy, or whatever he was, smiled. "Robot" didn't feel right. Jack moved too smoothly, but his scent was pure metal and machine oil with a bit of aftershave.

"This must be for Professor Lin's assignment?"

"Yeah."

"Have a seat over there," Jack said, nodding to a table where several very new-looking computers were arranged.

A search engine was already open on the screen.

Isaac took the keyboard and typed in *history of the Guardians*.

"You know how to use a computer," Vran said, appearing next to Isaac in a wave of black clothes and mussed hair.

Isaac startled and narrowed his eyes.

"Easy," Vran said, lifting his hands.

"You shouldn't sneak up on me like that. I have knives, you know."

"Seen 'em," Vran said. "Murder Boy."

"Huh?"

"You've already got a nickname!"

"Thanks. I hate it," Isaac said, though in truth, he could take it to mean that the others were accepting him, that he was part of the group. That was a good thing.

"Do you have a nickname?" he asked.

"They tried Ocean Boy, but it didn't stick."

Isaac shook his head.

"But anyway . . . you can type," Vran said.

"The Undertaker made certain we knew about the mortal world and its technology."

"How?"

"Outings. He called them field trips."

"We have those too," Vran said. "Professor Lin especially likes them."

Isaac managed not to cringe. He hadn't enjoyed those sojourns, as crucial as they'd been to his training. "Do hers involve surviving on your own for days on end, stealing food, that kind of thing?"

"No," Vran said. "They're more educational in nature."

"How can they be educational if they don't teach you how to survive?"

Vran shrugged. "There's snacks sometimes."

"I like them already."

Isaac shivered from the memory of his first foray outside the Graveyard. He'd been alone for the first time he could remember.

He'd spent most of those twenty-four hours hiding in an alley, shivering from the cold as much as the fear. He'd stolen a muffin from a coffee cart. Chocolate, laden with big globs of melted chips—he could still remember the taste, how the sweetness had almost blotted out the sour smell of old piss that filled his hiding place.

He'd savored the pastry, licked the plastic wrap clean, and lain low, listening to every sound, watching every shadow, and scenting every approaching person until Kenji had come for him.

He'd scooped Isaac up and told him he'd done well, that he'd passed his test, and that it was time to go home.

Even then, Kenji's arms had been tattooed.

Each trip after that had been longer and more complicated. The

Undertaker set them to tasks: to steal a specific item, to spy on someone without getting caught, to learn a lesson.

Above all else, they were to survive.

Not every boy did.

Some had probably tried to run away. They'd likely learned that wasn't possible.

That was what he had to change. To save his brothers he'd become what he must, kill who and what he must. Then he and Kenji would be in charge.

Isaac forced the memories aside and studied the search results.

"That was easier than I'd expected," he said, eyeing the long list.

"Jack is a genius," Vran said. "He has the school plugged into all kinds of databases, many of them in the Spirit Realm."

"How?" Isaac asked.

"The school's a Watchtower," Vran said. "It's transplanar."

Isaac made a note to look that up later and focused on the first item he'd clicked on. The paragraphs were as long as a single page and written in a legalistic, formal tone.

"What is this?" he asked.

"It's translated from Elvish," Vran said, leaning closer to eye the screen. He wore jeans and a T-shirt with a few holes in it. Isaac could see small patches of his skin.

"The courts love their flowery speeches and adjectives," Vran explained with a roll of his eyes.

"When you're immortal you have time to use all the words?"

"Something like that."

"How am I supposed to do anything with this?" Isaac let out a long sigh. "This is going to take forever."

At least they weren't looking in actual books. That would take up the entire room, and he couldn't imagine having to sort through them.

"And how are we supposed to make centuries of history fit into six thousand words?"

"You don't need to include *everything*," Vran typed something into the computer in front of him. "See?"

Isaac scanned the words on the screen.

"You've already done the assignment?"

Vran smelled like the ocean, like sea salt and a bit of something else, something like pepper on the verge of burning. *There,* Isaac thought, *that was what his blood would taste like.*

"Yep. Just do what I did. Put together enough history to back up whatever position you're taking. You want examples that reinforce it."

"What position I'm taking?"

"What you said in class. You're pretty opposed to having Guardians at all, which is kind of dumb, but whatever. You want them abolished, to get rid of them." Vran made air quotes. "Lin wants us to talk about what we would do differently, so that part is easy."

"The whole thing is the hard part—and did you just call me dumb?"

Isaac's head already hurt from thinking about the task ahead.

"You'll have to explain what happens if there are no Guardians, find some historical examples where the Guardians weren't there that back up your argument against them. Prove that everyone would be better off without them."

"And why does that make me dumb?"

"Because it makes your job harder. The Guardians aren't always good, but you're going to have to dig through a lot of history to prove that they shouldn't exist. And your sources are mostly elven, so good luck with that."

"What did you go with?" Isaac leaned toward Vran's screen.

Vran jerked the mouse away and Isaac realized their faces were inches apart.

"Nope," Vran said, closing the file without breaking eye contact. "Do your own work."

"Please," Isaac said, chewing his lip when he paused. "I'm really lost here."

"Does that whole kicked-puppy thing work for you?"

"Usually." It always worked with Kenji, but only when Isaac had gotten his chores done or done well in his sparring matches.

"I'm more of a cat person." Vran narrowed his eyes. "But I'll walk you through it."

He opened his messenger bag and pulled out a spiral notebook and a pen.

Everything about Vran's clothes said mortal. Even his shoes, a pair of black boots, were scuffed. Everything was secondhand, worn, but the notebook was new.

He quickly wrote an outline. His handwriting was simple, straight-lined, and a little blunt, like he had to force himself to write in English.

"There." Vran ripped out the sheet and slid it toward Isaac. "Follow that, but do your own work."

"You know you're the least elvish elf I've ever met."

"How many elves have you met?"

"Just you and the scary lady, but you're not what I expected."

"Don't believe everything you read," Vran said, nodding back to the list of articles on Isaac's screen. "But you're right. I'm not like other elves."

Isaac wanted to pry more into Vran's background but knew better than to ignore the lifeline he'd been handed when it came to the assignment. Not to mention that if he asked Vran to share more about his past, Isaac would have to reciprocate. Treading into those waters could prove dangerous.

Isaac opened a file and started to type.

This wasn't anything like his homework at the Graveyard. Those tests had been mostly physical; when they were mental, they hadn't been about trying to argue a point but about solving a puzzle. This feeling wasn't unlike what his body went through after a heavy workout, only the strain was all in his head. Maybe that was the solution, to think of the paper as another sort of puzzle.

Vran slipped on a pair of huge pink headphones with cat ears on the band. They crushed a bit of his massive hair. The product had given up, and it had gone from spikes to curls. Lost in his own studies, he tapped out a beat with his pencil.

Isaac had lost all sense of time. He suspected it hadn't been hours, but it felt like it.

He stretched and saw Daffodil sitting at another table. Jack sat beside her, really close. They were speaking in hushed whispers.

"Hey," Isaac whispered to Vran, tapping him to get his attention.

Startled, Vran sat up, scowled, and slid his headphones to his neck.

"Is Jack Daffodil's boyfriend?"

"Yeah. He's nice."

"I don't have any classes with him. Do you?"

"No." Vran shook his head.

Isaac had the stray impulse to touch the hair curling around Vran's forehead and ears.

"I don't think he needs lectures and classes." Vran nodded to the metal shelves and computers.

"What about the gym and combat training?"

"He's got a note or something. No fighting for the librarian."

"I thought we all had to learn to fight, you know, together?"

"Not all of us," Vran said. "Jack's not going to be a Guardian."

"What's he going to be?"

"A librarian," Vran said slowly.

"Do we get to decide that now?"

"I don't think *you* get to." Vran shook his head.

"That's not fair."

"Take it up with Argent."

"But there are other classes?"

"I think so." Vran didn't sound certain, or he was hiding something. "Why do you want to know?"

"I just don't see anyone else, in the halls or whatever. There's all this space, but I only see our class and the professors using it." Isaac nodded to the high ceilings and the large, nearly empty library.

"There's the geese," Vran said.

"Yes, and the damn geese," Isaac agreed.

"There are other students."

"How do you know?"

"I met one of them, once. Why do you care so much?"

Isaac pointed to the ceiling, where some of the stones rippled like still water with a breeze crossing its surface.

"It's just . . . this whole place is like a dream. I'm worried I'll wake up one morning and find the floor gone."

"I'd try to catch you if you fell," Vran said.

"Can you fly?" Isaac asked.

"No. I said I'd try. I didn't say I'd succeed."

"How hard?"

"Would I try?"

"Yeah."

"Guess it depends on how much I like you that day."

Isaac stopped laughing when he saw his nearly empty screen. He could already tell that he had hours of work ahead of him, work he wasn't trained for, all to infiltrate a school he'd soon destroy.

"What's wrong?" Vran asked.

Isaac sighed and decided that a little truth would be easiest.

"I don't feel like I belong here."

"I'm not sure you do, but I felt the same way when they told me this was where I'd be going, and it's working out for me. Maybe it will work out for you too, *if* you do your own homework."

Isaac grimaced.

"To be honest, I think they're still figuring out what to do with you."

"Because I'm Murder Boy?"

"Yep." Vran nodded. "Trained killer isn't in the admission requirements."

"The dean said this place was remedial."

"That's one way of putting it."

Isaac couldn't really blame Vran for wondering if he'd fit in. He'd been surprised that it hadn't been harder to infiltrate the school, which might mean they were watching him. Vran went on missions. He was powerful, but he was also funny and more than a little pretty. As guards went, Isaac could have done worse.

Unless that was part of the plan. Vran might be an intentional distraction.

The elf's gaze had drifted back to Daffodil and Jack.

"What?" Isaac asked.

"They're cute together," Vran said.

Isaac had to agree.

Daffodil seemed happy, and if Jack was made of wires and circuits, then her touch couldn't hurt him. A man made of wires . . .

"Now why are you scowling?" Vran asked.

"Huh?"

"You're frowning again."

"Oh, it's just the paper," Isaac lied, waving at his screen. "I should get back to work. This is going to take me forever."

"Okay."

Vran put his headset back into place and returned to his own computer.

Isaac stared at his page of notes and forced his expression into neutral.

He'd been asking himself how you killed a man made of wires. He hoped it didn't come to that. The students weren't the target. He had to hope they wouldn't get in his way.

7
THE MISEDUCATION OF ISAAC FROST

It was just a paper—a grade—for a dumb class in a stupid school he wasn't even really attending. No one would even remember it. Still, Isaac's palms itched and he wished he'd worn his gloves.

He was just tired, that was all. He needed to get the job done. He'd worked too late on the paper to search for the labyrinth.

It didn't help that everyone was so damn helpful. Otherwise, he could have half-assed it and snuck off to get the job done. Maybe they were watching him, but he was starting to suspect they were actually nice, which made the inevitable outcome so much worse.

Either way, he was grateful that Jack had showed him how to format and spell-check the paper. Isaac had read it aloud so it made sense, at least to him. He hadn't shown it to Vran, feeling like the elf had done enough by giving him the outline and worrying that they'd argue over Isaac's position on the Guardians.

He kept thinking about that moment in the library and how Vran had casually touched his ear that first night. The feeling the memory brought up—a slight warmth in his chest—wasn't discomforting, not at all, and that was a problem.

"I've read your papers," Lin announced. "Some interesting approaches to the topic, especially yours, Mr. Frost. Would you care to share your thesis with the class?"

Isaac sat up straight as the others twisted in their seats to face him.

"Easy. Abolish the Guardians. Then they'd no longer be a tool of the royals and no longer able to take sides in a war. They can't hurt anyone if they don't exist as the council's private army."

"But how would you keep people safe?" Daffodil asked.

"I don't think they need it," Isaac said. "I think history shows that the Guardians are more trouble than they're worth."

"What do you mean?" Hex asked.

"I don't think they prevent crimes. They just enforce the, uh, status quo."

Hex nodded in consideration.

"You have a point that the Guardians have been tools of the royals in the past," Lin agreed.

"They still are," Hex countered. "This school operates with the king's approval. Even if we reformed everything, this place is only here because the king says so."

"Yeah, but you gotta start somewhere," Ford said. "I think it's cool that he saw a problem and wants to fix it. What would you do?"

"It's a valid question," Lin suggested, drifting between the desks. "The new king has given the Council of Races more say, or at least more time and consideration than his father did."

"Why not just make a clean break?" Hex asked. "You're already in the middle of a big change, so just get it done."

"Wouldn't that mean chaos?" Daffodil asked.

The students discussed it for a while, but Isaac had tuned out the debate and found himself watching Vran.

The elf sat half-slumped, half-draped over his seat. Isaac decided he was faking boredom. Something was going on behind those dark eyes. Isaac got the sense that Vran was watching the class the same way he was, like an undercover observer or a visitor from a foreign land.

Maybe it was the topic, the example of elven misrule that was abstract history to the rest of them, but Lin had said that Vran had been there.

"It's clear Mr. Frost has spurred an important discussion," Lin said, bringing things back toward order. "And it's clear some of you see value in his suggestion. Daffodil has a point. How would you handle law enforcement and peacekeeping?"

"You could abolish that too," Ford suggested. "It would be simpler to start over, without thousands of years of precedent."

"But that's got to cause a lot of other problems," Daffodil said. "If there are no laws and no punishment, then everyone would just do what they want."

"No, I mean like reform it," Ford said. "Make new laws that leave all the old stuff behind."

"Immortals have long memories," Hex said. "Hence all the grudges and turf wars."

Isaac couldn't tell if she was agreeing with Ford or not.

"So maybe not a clean slate?" Daffodil suggested. "But a reformation, where you keep what's good but simplify."

"What you're suggesting has been done before," Lin said. "In the mortal realm there are several examples, such as Justinian's Code."

"I say wipe it out," Isaac said, remembering the endless long paragraphs and pages of footnotes he'd scrolled through.

"You're advocating for anarchy?" Hex asked.

"Yeah, I guess so."

Isaac leaned back in his seat and crossed his arms.

"That's terrible," Daffodil said. "If there's no one to stop people from just doing whatever they want, that's what they'll do."

"Like what?" Isaac asked.

"Like steal stuff," she said. "Do you want randos taking your knives just because they can?"

"I'd stop them," Isaac said.

"And what if you can't?" Hex argued.

"I could," Isaac said. "And if I can't, maybe I don't deserve to have whatever they took."

"Basing your society on 'might makes right' gets you into *Lord of the Flies* territory," Hex said. "And some pretty nasty historical examples for both the immortals and mortals."

"Lord of what?"

"It's a book," Hex explained. "You really should read it. Maybe then you'd stop trying to reduce these complex issues to simple statements."

"Maybe you're making them too hard."

She scoffed.

Behind them, Vran had sunk further into silence. It took Isaac a moment to read the expression in his eyes. Kenji could look that way when Isaac failed some test, like the day he hadn't made it to the top of the knotted rope hung from the tallest tree branch.

Something in Isaac's stomach dropped.

Vran was disappointed in him. Worse, he didn't know why he cared what the elf thought.

"How would you address one species trying to take from another?" Lin asked. "Or one nation, one country?"

"If might makes right, then they'll just get what they want," Ford said.

"But it isn't right," Hex said. "Especially not to the people being colonized or invaded."

Hadn't she just been agreeing with him about the Guardians? Whose side was she on?

"Appeasement has been tried many times in both human and extraplanar history. It has rarely gone well," Lin said.

"Because once you give in to a bully, they never stop taking whatever they want?" Hex asked.

"That's one interpretation," Lin said. "Your next paper will focus on appeasement and its repercussions. I want you to include examples from the mortal and immortal planes."

At least Isaac didn't have to risk having an opinion.

Lin picked up her chalk and began outlining some examples on the board, listing World War II and the Cyclopean Attrition.

Hex took notes at a feverish pace, her pen slashing at the paper.

Isaac tried not to tune out the lecture.

He knew what the Undertaker would say, that might made right and that might often took the form of currency. The person who could pay the most could buy the strength they needed.

Isaac had no idea how many revolutions or coups the Undertakers had abetted or squashed over the years, but he guessed it was a lot. Even lines of succession had been pruned.

He thought of the coffins and the unmarked grave the Undertaker had been digging when last they'd spoken. It didn't matter who'd wanted the target dead or even who the target was. Someone had enough money to make it happen, and so someone else had been erased.

It didn't matter now. They'd never matter now.

For all of Lin's detail, the past was still the past.

No one could bring back the dead, not even the elves.

"I'm afraid that's all we have time for today," Lin said, bringing Isaac back.

"She makes it sound like we're in therapy," Ford remarked.

"Maybe some of us should be," Hex said with a sharp glance in Isaac's direction.

"What's that supposed to mean?"

But no one answered as they filed out.

"Frost," Lin said.

"Yeah?" he asked, worried he was in for a private lecture, or worse, more homework.

"You're clear to join the others at the gym today."

"Really?"

"Really."

Isaac bounded out of his seat.

At last. He let out a long breath as he stood.

He really needed to punch something.

He nearly collided with Vran when he reached the hallway.

"Sorry," Isaac said.

The elf shrugged and pulled his weathered backpack up onto his shoulder.

"Are you mad at me?"

"No," Vran said.

He picked at a bit of the black nail polish on one of his fingers.

"But you're . . . something." Asking put something weird and squirming in Isaac's gut.

"Yeah," Vran said. "I'm *something*."

"So, tell me," Isaac said, crossing his arms over his chest.

"I used to have a title, you know. It was a big deal. It meant I could get away with so much, but the people I'd allied with wanted to kill millions, billions. That's not an exaggeration, Isaac. They would have wiped out humanity as we know it and enslaved any survivors. Might can't make right. *It just can't.*"

"What happened? Who stopped them?"

"Have you ever heard the expression about bringing a knife to a gunfight?"

"No."

"The opposite happened."

"So what was your position?" Isaac asked.

"Sometimes smart beats strong," Vran said absently. "Which is why you want a council, to talk things out and think it through."

Isaac needed to learn that lesson. He'd failed today. He'd argued like an Undertaker. Next time he'd argue like a Guardian. Maybe that would earn him some trust. Maybe someone in the class knew more about the labyrinth.

"I wouldn't mind hearing about it, you know," Isaac said.

"About what?"

"Whatever you saw, whatever you went through. I can tell it's hard to hear them talking about it in the abstract."

Vran nodded.

"I'd like that. I would, but you're supposed to tell stories in order. And that's not how my story works."

"Why not?"

"A couple of reasons. Partly because I'm a sea elf. I'm water, and water follows water. It runs where it can. It doesn't follow straight lines."

"And neither do you?" Isaac asked.

"Adam would call that a rim shot."

"What's an Adam?"

"A friend," Vran said, but the way his eyes shifted made Isaac think there was more to the tale. Part of him sank a little and he reminded himself that he wasn't supposed to care.

"What's the other part?"

"I went somewhere I wasn't supposed to . . ." Vran trailed off and his expression grew distant. "It wasn't a good place, and it wasn't good for me."

Isaac shouldn't want to know, but he did. He suspected it had been Vran's alley, his field trip to somewhere scary.

"Tell me when you're ready," he said softly. "If you want to."

"Okay."

Isaac walked away. He wanted to know, right then he wanted to know, because he might not be around to find out later.

He hadn't even started his search for the labyrinth, but he knew he'd find it. Even though he hadn't found a way down, just going to class was teaching him the school's layout. He knew how to avoid the courtyard and the geese. He knew the fastest routes between his classes, and he knew the best doors when he wanted to visit the mortal world.

It wasn't always food courts. Sometimes it was a dusty Greek restaurant or a pub in Ireland with wooden beams and lantern light. Once he'd opened a door to someplace hot that smelled slightly gross with water running in a channel. Isaac had guessed Venice and closed the door.

Still, no way down, no labyrinth.

He was good at these sorts of tests. Maybe he wasn't smart like Hex or Jack, but he was dogged. He'd find a way.

He'd crack the code, and maybe, just for fun, he could solve the mystery of Vran along the way.

8
BLAZING HOT TEAMWORK

Isaac wasn't used to reading this much, thinking this much, and especially not sitting this much. That was the main difference between RCC and the Graveyard, aside from the presence of women. The Undertakers trained every day, the older boys pushing the younger to constantly improve.

There was always exercise if he found himself thinking too much or pondering that bright, warm place in his memory he could not visit. He'd run laps, spar with his brothers, do push-ups, or swim in the lake, though he avoided the last thing as much as he could.

RCC's gym was where it had been the last time he'd been there, which was usually the case with his classrooms and the hallways he used by day. By night the school liked to surprise him, twisting the corridors in strange directions, like stairways that stopped at the ceiling, never down, or paths that ended in a brick wall whether he went left or right.

"What, no dinosaur today?" Isaac asked as the other students filed into the gym.

"Apparently not," Hex said, though she watched the corners of the room.

"So what do we do?" Ford asked.

"We could spar," Isaac suggested.

"They usually don't have us fight each other," Shy said.

Damn, he was good. Isaac hadn't even known the invisible boy was in the room, and he had no proof, but he suspected Shy was grinning.

"Why not?"

"Because we're supposed to work together," Hex said. "You know, as partners. Why is that so foreign to you?"

"Because assassination usually isn't a team sport?"

Still, this was good. He still didn't have a measure of what the others could do in a fight. Gym time could help with that, as well as letting him blow off some steam.

"We won't be assassinating anyone." The dean walked into the room from the other end. "Our goal today is the opposite."

"What's the opposite?"

"Search and rescue."

She opened one of the arching wooden doors, and the smell of rain bloomed in the hall. The taste of murky water obliterated any trace of blood or sweat.

Sodden, glossy daylight streamed through the door. The scene beyond was too still, with roofs and treetops peeking out from a lake.

The class followed the dean through to a hilltop, a little island in the deluge.

Bits of wooden fences, grungy plastic bottles, and a host of refuse Isaac could not identify floated atop the too-still water.

"What is this?" Isaac asked.

"A flood," the dean said. "We'll search for anyone or anything alive and get them to dry land."

"Is this something Guardians do?" Isaac asked.

"It is now. The mortal authorities are working this way, but they're overwhelmed. They won't reach this village in time."

"What are we supposed to do?" Daffodil asked.

"We help whoever and however we can."

"There!" Ford said. "What's that?"

Isaac couldn't spot whatever he'd pointed to.

"Does anyone have a flashlight?"

"I can do better than that." Hex placed her hands apart, cupped like she held a basketball, and muttered something.

Her hands filled with silver light, a little moon. She released it and it flew to Ford. It drifted, slowly orbiting above him as he waded into the flood.

Isaac hesitated at the water's edge.

"Do you know how to swim?" Shy asked from somewhere nearby.

"Yeah, but I don't like it."

"Why not?"

There wasn't time to explain.

Isaac took off his jacket and boots. He left his knives atop them and followed Ford, who'd waded ahead.

The water was colder than he'd expected. He shivered at the contrast with the warm air on his shoulders.

Ford stopped moving. He focused on something that Isaac couldn't quite see in the dancing light of Hex's little satellite.

"What is it?" Isaac asked, imagining pale flesh and blue lips.

"A goat," Ford said, lifting it from the water. "I think it's alive."

He carried it toward the shore and a cooing, gloved Daffodil.

"Frost?" the dean asked. "What have you got?"

He closed his eyes and inhaled.

Water, lots of it, but yes . . . fresh and coppery, but bland. Human. Mortal.

"There," he said, pointing to a half-sunken barn. "Someone's in there."

"Are they alive?" the dean asked.

He narrowed his eyes and took another deep breath.

"I think so, but they are hurt."

The ground sloped downward. He'd have to swim.

"Shouldn't Vran be here?" Hex asked. "He's a sea elf."

"Yeah, isn't water like, their thing?" Ford asked as he waded back in.

"Vran is elsewhere, with the others."

Did the dean mean the other students, or was he just with the queen and the other royals?

More figures arrived on the hill behind them.

Doctor Cavanaugh and the other professors were setting up tents.

Everyone was here. The school was vulnerable, empty. It was the perfect chance to explore it, but how would he slip away unnoticed? All eyes were on him.

Ahead, the barn gave a loud creak.

Someone appeared at the window, spotted him, and waved.

"We've got to get them out of there," Ford said.

"I don't suppose anyone can fly?"

"No," Ford said. "Maybe we can build a raft for them?"

Isaac shook his head.

"We need this water to go somewhere." He called back toward the dean, "Where are the others? What are they doing?"

"They're tending to a forest fire in Oregon."

"Could we open a door to them?"

She cocked her head to the side.

"Why?" Ford asked.

"They need water. We need to move some," Isaac said.

The dean gave a little nod and he knew he'd passed another test.

"We need a door," Hex said.

"There!" Ford said, pointing to a house on the slope.

"It's too high," Hex said. "The water needs to run through it."

"No problem."

Ford trudged uphill and ripped the door off the house, jam and all. He carried it back to them.

He stood it beside Isaac.

"Be right back," Isaac said, stepping through to the school.

He explained what he was trying to do. It felt weird, talking to a building. The others remained outside, but Isaac could imagine them straining to listen.

He hoped RCC understood, stepped back outside, and closed the door behind him.

"We need to get it out to the middle, to where it's deepest."

"That water isn't clean," Cavanaugh said. "You shouldn't even be in it, let alone diving."

"Why?" Ford asked.

"Bacteria. Pathogens." Her angular features crinkled with the possibilities.

"Then let me do it," Isaac said. "I don't get sick, right?"

"I don't know that yet," Cavanaugh said. "I'm still running tests."

"I've got a better chance than the rest of you," he said.

"Are you strong enough to carry this?" Ford asked, hefting the frame in one hand.

"I will be if you let me taste you," Isaac said, pulling off his boots.

"Dude."

"Your blood," Isaac clarified. He took off his shirt and drew a knife. "I just need a drop."

"Fine."

Ford reached to prick his fingertip on Isaac's upraised knife. The big guy winced.

Isaac put the blade between his lips.

"That is pretty weird," Ford said as Doctor Cavanaugh approached with a bandage.

Isaac's vision went green, but only in one eye.

"Back at you," he said, striding forward to take the door.

Isaac hadn't gone swimming since that day, since Samuel, but he shook it off now.

It helped to have Ford's strength flowing through him. He wasn't even cold as he splashed out into the water, the door easily gripped in one hand.

He hoped the school understood what he was trying to do. Otherwise, he'd flood the place.

Isaac took a breath and dove, dragging the door down with him. It fought, wanting to remain buoyant, but he poured Ford's strength into his kicks. He couldn't see. Everything was murk and mud.

He hit the bottom and nearly rebounded off a sunken car.

The door tried to float upward, but Isaac wrestled it under a tire, lifting the car with ease.

Remind me never to take a punch from Ford, he thought as he surfaced long enough to take several breaths before diving again.

He shifted the door and opened it before it could fight him.

It sucked him inside. He knocked against the wall before righting himself. Lungs straining, Isaac swam. This must have been what it was like, to sink, to lose your vision. He could see colors, flashing yellow and orange, and wondered if that was normal for everyone drowning or if it was part of Ford's unique vision.

He found the closed door at the opposite end of the narrow hall and jerked it open with all his strength, all of Ford's strength, and was surprised it wasn't ripped off its hinges. Red light nearly blinded him before he spilled through it in a wave.

Tumbling, head over heels, Isaac knocked along, striking tree trunks and rocks until his hand found a purchase, a thick root. He gripped it and clung on as the water rushed by. Darkness closed in. His lungs burned.

Then he felt air. He took a few choking breaths. It tasted of ash.

The flood water rose in gushes and waves, splashing across the forest.

Everything sizzled. Everything steamed.

Then he heard the screams. They were like high-pitched screeches torn from narrow throats, like choking baby birds, like nothing he'd heard before. No person—no animal—screamed like that.

"What are they?" Isaac asked, clasping his hands to his ears.

"The trees," Vran said, approaching through the steam and smoke. "The forest is screaming."

The water ran from him, running and splashing toward the fire. The heat cooled, leaving Isaac soaked and shivering on the forest floor.

Vran's eyes had gone black, and the forking lines crossed his skin. Ash flecked his hair and clothes. He wore a long, hooded shirt.

He was still beautiful but older, like something from a weary dream. The screams quieted to pained murmurs.

"Did it work?" Isaac asked, finding his feet. "Did I help?"

The final whispers faded as Ford's blood left his system.

"You helped," Vran said softly. "We put out this part of it."

"But not all of it?"

Vran shook his head.

"It gets worse every year." He scoffed. "Stupid humans. It's their world. I'm not supposed to care."

"But you do."

Isaac was starting to get that.

Vran nodded.

"You need to get back before the dean docks your grade."

He cocked his head toward the open door.

"Yeah," Isaac grunted. "I'll, uh . . . see you."

"You did good, Isaac." Vran leaned in and quickly pecked Isaac's cheek. "Thank you."

Isaac flushed. He opened his mouth to say something else, but didn't have any words. He hurried back through the door and the flooded hallway. It was slick with mud and debris. Plenty of garbage and ooze piled in the corners.

"Thank you," he whispered to the school, patting the wall.

Too bad he still had to kill it.

Isaac climbed out of the door.

The wet washed the ash from his throat. His wet clothes clung to him and he fought back a shiver.

Still, he'd done it. He'd swam and dove to the bottom and his personal ghost hadn't risen to pull him down.

Water pooled everywhere. Hex had cast glamours on everyone who needed it, likely to ease the minds of the shocked people they helped to Cavanaugh's makeshift hospital. Ford and Daffodil were corralling a herd of muddy goats.

"You could have told me what to do," he said as the dean strode over to him.

"No, I couldn't," she said, looking between Isaac and the open door. "I needed to know if you'd lone-wolf it."

"So I passed?" he asked.

"This time. Now go help the others."

"Okay," Isaac said, smiling.

"And Frost?"

"Yeah?"

"You'll be cleaning up that mess," the dean said, nodding back at the hallway.

"I'll help," Ford said.

"Me too," Hex grumbled.

"Why?"

"Teamwork, Frost," Hex said with a long sigh. "That was the lesson, remember?"

9
KILLING PAIN

"You're weirdly good at this," Ford said, watching Isaac label a diagram.

The outline of the splayed dragon had been easy once Isaac figured that two heads meant two hearts even if the thing had a single digestive system.

"It kind of comes naturally when you've studied how to take things apart your whole life."

Daffodil made a face.

"Sorry," he said.

She nodded and went back to work.

His actions at the flood had earned him some trust. They still argued in class, but he tried to step more carefully and not show the outright disdain for the Guardians he'd learned from the Undertaker.

"I don't know if you should be," Daffodil said, looking up.

"What do you mean?"

"You are what you are. You shouldn't have to apologize for that."

"What's that supposed to mean?"

"Nature versus nurture, Isaac. You weren't born an Undertaker. You were raised one."

"Kind of." Ford glanced up from the bestiary he'd been idly flipping through. "You're the new guy. We're going to talk."

"I've been here a while now," Isaac protested.

"You're still the newest," Daffodil said. "And it's not a bad thing. We're just curious."

She waved a hand at her own books.

"We're here to learn after all, and you're special."

They all were, but he didn't mention it. He was trying to fit in.

Besides, his brothers were as diverse and unique as the class at RCC. The Undertaker didn't choose boys based on skin color or anything like that. Despite his prejudice against women, he only took in children he found useful.

Isaac had found more than a few of his brothers' species in the class bestiary, but no entry on Phages. There weren't even any entries on vampires, which confirmed what he'd always suspected: They were a myth, probably spawned from someone seeing a Phage in action.

The Old Man didn't talk a lot about his own nature, but Kenji had mentioned once or twice that he was undead. It made sense. He always smelled of magic, not wild like Vran's or almost chemical like Hex's, but something moldy and a bit rotten—necromancy, if Isaac had to guess. Maybe he'd been human, once, long before he'd learned to preserve himself through magic and alchemy.

Class ended and Isaac resisted the urge to bang his head on the desk. He still had his reading for Lin's next lecture.

He'd never get the job done with all this homework, but he'd never last long enough at the school to try if he brought too much attention on himself and didn't do the reading.

His last attempt to find his target, the school's beating heart, had led him in a small circle, back to his dorm room, again and again. Either the school was onto him or it was just messing with him.

He wanted a snack from the vending machine and wondered if the place would let him have one. Isaac rounded a corner and almost collided with Vran.

Dressed for action in jeans, combat boots, and a leather jacket, the elf bounced on his heels.

"What are you doing?" Vran asked.

"Nothing that can't wait," Isaac said.

Vran grinned.

"Good."

"Why?" Isaac drawled.

"We're wanted at the gym."

"Do I get to go hit something?"

"Maybe." Vran cocked his head to the side. "Why are you so excited about that?"

"My back still aches from scrubbing a ceiling," Isaac said, stretching. "And I have to read two hundred pages of *The Etiquette of Sentient Trees* before tomorrow. I'd really like to hit something."

"That does sound terrible," Vran said with a shudder of revulsion.

"The scrubbing or the reading?"

"Both," the elf admitted.

"And isn't it kind of wrong that it's printed on paper?"

"Probably," Vran agreed. "Come on."

He nodded in the direction of the gym. Isaac knew the way there now. The ceilings were arched in vaults marked in delicate wooden *X*'s, their cross points marked by light fixtures of black iron and amber glass.

"Is it another natural disaster?"

"Nope," Vran said. "It's a mission, so yes, I think you might get to hit something."

Isaac had no problem matching Vran's stride as they took a path he almost recognized.

"Is it always so random? The school, I mean."

Vran smiled and reached to trail fingertips over the stone wall as if in affection.

"It's not random at all, if you know how to walk it," he said. "It repeats."

"Sometimes," Isaac grumbled. "How do you do it?"

"It's like the ocean. It comes and goes in waves. You have to catch one."

"I don't get it."

"Okay, how about dancing?" Vran considered absently. "You have to find the rhythm."

Isaac pondered the comparison.

"Let me guess, you don't know how to dance?"

"No. I had lessons."

"Really? I didn't think the Undertaker would want boys dancing with boys."

Isaac shrugged, mostly because he didn't want to explain that they hadn't been social events. It might be needed to get close to a target, not to mention being good for coordination. They passed through an area where the light outside wasn't green. The sky hung sunny, bright, and mortal above them.

"Anyway, it takes time," Vran said. "To learn the school's rhythm."

"But you've done it."

Vran smiled.

Time wasn't something Isaac had a lot of.

The Undertaker wouldn't wait forever, but Isaac kept remembering the faces of the people in the flooded town, their gratitude and thanks spoken in a language he didn't understand. He couldn't deny that the students, wannabe Guardians, had done good there. He'd done good there. What would Kenji think about that?

They reached the door with the wire-crossed window he couldn't see through. Isaac pushed it open and found the scary lady waiting on the other side.

"Argent," Vran said, ducking his head in deference

Isaac decided Vran would never be a good liar. His face was too liquid, too expressive. He was afraid of this woman.

"We have a lead on the goblins," she announced.

"Will there be fighting?" Isaac asked, brightening.

"Quite possibly."

"Awesome. I could go for a rematch."

He punched his fist into his open palm.

Argent gave him a look that said she was not impressed.

"You found her?" Vran asked.

"We found her *ex*," Argent said. "He runs a bar in the Decay."

"What's that?" Isaac asked.

"I see your studies are going well."

"Astral Geography and Cosmology is next semester," Vran told her.

"It's a dip in the Spirit Realm, one of the lowlands," Argent explained. "Sometimes they sink low enough to separate and become their own demi-plane."

"It's an Underworld?" Vran asked, voice shuddering.

"No, Vran," Argent said gently. "Not yet. I'd never send you back there, not unless there was no one else, not unless I had no other choice."

"Okay," he said quietly.

So that was Vran's alley. Part of Isaac wanted to know about it and part of him didn't.

"It is, however, a sight," Argent warned.

"How so?" Isaac asked.

"There are lots of mushrooms and dead things."

"When do we leave?"

The two elves looked at him.

"I grew up in a graveyard," Isaac said. "Death doesn't frighten me."

"She would if you met her," Vran said.

Isaac filed that away too. He needed to move, to do something. The flood and fire exercise felt far too long ago.

"So . . . now?" he asked.

"Now is good." Argent tapped a finger to her cheek. "But you'll need to look the part."

"How?" Vran asked.

"Rougher. Tougher."

He reached up and mussed his hair with his hands.

"Cute," she said. "But I was thinking something more drastic."

Cold washed over Isaac, and once again he was taken by the sense that a drop of her magic could freeze him solid. Whatever he did here, when he did it, he needed to be far away when Argent found out.

The cold passed and Vran had changed. Instead of a disaffected rock star, his appearance was closer to a street tough, with a leather jacket, faded black jeans, and a bit of dirt on his face.

Jagged black lines covered the right side, like a tattoo.

Isaac found his own clothes unaltered.

"You don't need it," Argent said. "Try not to talk too much, Vran. You'll give yourself away."

"Okay." He still had the jitters. "But you'll be watching, right?"

"Not this time. I have other business."

"But—"

"For the king."

I'll keep you safe, Isaac silently promised, remembering the times when Kenji had said the same to him. He tried not to remember the time he'd said it aloud. Voicing it felt like a risk, like he might fail again.

"Can you open a door, Vran?" Argent asked.

"There's no water here."

"You don't need it. You're past that."

"I'm . . . I don't know."

Vran shrank. He shuffled from foot to foot.

"You've done it before," she said.

"Why can't *you* do it?" Isaac asked her.

"Because above all else, this is a school. Vran is here to learn, Frost, just like the rest of you."

Vran closed his eyes. His body tensed. He grimaced, like he was trying to lift some incredible weight.

"What's wrong?" Isaac asked. "Is it too far?"

"Too near," Vran muttered.

The air grew damp and briny. This was the same magic that had swirled around Isaac in the ruined house. He could hear the things, the whispering shadows, and forced himself to not step away from Vran.

The elf's face changed from younger to older, then back and forth in quick succession, like several versions of him were laid atop each other, all occupying the same space. The lines on his skin darkened. They grew like roots or bare branches in winter.

An outline formed, a portal lined in purple light.

Then Vran made a choking noise. He opened his eyes and the door faded.

"I can't," he said with a gasp.

"It's all right," Argent said with a gentleness that surprised Isaac. "You're trying. Keep practicing."

She opened one of the random doors lining the wall, exposing a sky darker than the Spirit Realm's emerald twilight, true night tinged in purple.

"In you go."

"You're really not coming?" Isaac asked.

"I wouldn't send you if I thought it was too dangerous. Well, I wouldn't send Vran. Follow his lead, Frost. He knows what to do."

"Get captured?"

"Not this time. Get *information*. Don't engage. Track and report. See if the goblin has the same blood as the others. You should be able to do that by scent alone, right?"

"If I can get close enough."

"Good. Once we're certain, we'll bring him in. In and out, boys. Be careful."

Isaac followed Vran through the door.

And they were elsewhere. The way back closed as if it had never been.

"What was that?" Isaac asked.

"What?" Vran asked.

"You changed when you tried that spell."

"Oh, yeah. That happens sometimes."

He started walking, not even taking in their surroundings.

"Hey," Isaac said, catching up. He took Vran by the sleeve of his jacket. "Do you want to tell me why?"

Vran slumped.

"No."

"That's okay," Isaac said.

He felt a prickling in his chest not unlike the needles of the tattoo gun. It was the opposite of the tingle he'd felt when Vran had kissed him on the cheek. He didn't like it.

"It's not because I don't trust you or anything," Vran said. "It's because we don't know why. Argent and the king have people working on it."

"It's bad then? Does it hurt?"

Isaac chose not to dive into the question of whether or not Vran trusted him. He wasn't ready for that answer, and after all, the elf really shouldn't.

Maybe they shouldn't be here together. It wouldn't be good for Isaac to get attached . . . but he'd already made that silent promise. Maybe this time he could keep it.

"I don't want to talk about it, at least not now," Vran said. "Let's just focus on where we are and what we need to do."

They took in the Decay.

"She said there'd be mushrooms," Isaac mused. "She wasn't kidding."

Purple, gray-veined, they rose like a forest, taller than houses, than most trees. Spiderwebs as thick as bridge cables hung between them. They shed spores like snow, colorless flakes that drifted and swirled through the air to pool across the ground like miscolored snow.

Above, the sky was a darker green than in the Spirit Realm, but there were stars.

All Isaac could taste was rot. The crescent moon of the Spirit Realm hung above them, but it was waning, not waxing. Tinged in purple, it was black at the edge.

The school had put them on a low path, a road hollowed into the earth where the mushrooms loomed like walls on either side. Isaac felt for his knives, made certain they'd come along, but did not relax when his hands found them.

Vran caught a spore on his tongue and promptly spat it out.

"Good thing you're not allergic," Isaac said. "Wait, is this stuff safe? Is it poisonous?"

"Argent wouldn't send us somewhere like that."

"Not you, maybe. And don't forget that she almost let those goblins drain your blood."

"But she didn't." Vran held up a finger. "I wasn't in any trouble until you showed up."

"Uh-huh."

"Which way?" Vran asked.

Isaac scented the air. Rot, yes, but something tangy laced the edge. Woodsmoke.

He pointed.

"That way."

They walked for a while.

Isaac tried not to fixate on his companion, but eventually gave up and asked, "Why are you at the school?"

"Like she said, to learn."

"But you're allowed to leave whenever you want."

"Sort of." Vran ducked his head. "I'm on probation, remember?"

"Yeah," Isaac said.

"Why are you asking anyway?"

"Because I want to know." Isaac meant it and wished he didn't.

Vran smiled and Isaac flushed.

"Come on," he said. "I think there's a town ahead."

"What makes you say that?"

"I can smell blood."

Vran's eyes opened wide.

"Not a lot of it," Isaac assured him. "Just a butcher shop or something . . . a little bit of this and that. Typical town stuff."

They'd moved closer to the hills, and the mushrooms grew thick enough to serve as buildings. Yellow dots swayed among them, glowing steadily enough that Isaac took them to be lanterns.

The residents had carved caverns into the purple-gray fungus. Walkways spiraled up their stalks. Some of them rivaled RCC's keep in height.

"Do we know the name of the bar?"

"No," Vran said. "But how many can there be?"

"In a place as depressing as this?" Isaac waved at the landscape. "I'm guessing a lot."

"I guess we have to find it then."

Isaac sighed.

"It's another test, isn't it? She's testing me."

"Probably. Almost everything at RCC is some kind of a test."

Isaac tasted the air in little sips.

He sifted out the unfamiliar, the races he hadn't been exposed to.

Rot. Rot. More rot. Woodsmoke. Something else, a faint trace of earth and acid.

Ale, he decided. Alcohol.

Isaac led Vran into the streets running between the stalks. Here and there were hollows, natural squares and alleys. Blood had been spilled there, a quiet murder or two, in the places shaded by the caps above.

There. Something familiar, a sour, leathery flavor he knew.

"I think I found him. This way."

"So you're like a shark?" Vran asked.

"How so?"

"You can smell a little blood from far away."

"Yeah. Now that I've tasted goblin blood, I can find our guy."

"What else can you smell?"

"It's as much sense as smell," Isaac said.

He'd never tried to explain his power before. No one at the Graveyard had ever asked how it worked even though he'd learned to use it on his brothers, trying on their powers to master his control and not be overwhelmed or too disoriented to fight when he ate their blood and changed. He'd learned to identify them blindfolded, playing hide and seek, testing and pushing the range of his senses.

Isaac remembered what Vran had said about dancing and wondered if he liked music.

"It's like a single note in a song, or in this case lots of songs, some louder than others."

"But you've heard it before, since you tasted the goblin's blood?"

"Yeah. It makes it easier to find again." Isaac cocked his head to the side, trying to sort through the scents, to find the goblin in the blend. "It would be easy if he were bleeding, and harder if somebody else was."

He kept losing the goblin then finding him again, like a fish leaping in and out of a stream.

At least the streets were quiet. Shadows moved in the windows and doors that made up the dwellings above them, but a lot of noise or proximity would have made it harder.

Isaac kept tasting and testing the air as he led Vran up a spiraling, rickety walkway of planks held together with rope.

The trail wasn't strong. He had to pause a lot to sort it out. It was as much instinct as sense, but it strengthened as they neared the top of a particularly high stalk.

Isaac peered out across the valley, to the ridge of hills beneath the purple-tinged moon.

"Is that . . . what is *that*?"

It was bigger than anything he'd ever seen, anything he'd imagined. The hillside was shaped like a sleeping man, a stone giant stretched across the horizon.

His skin was pale like the fog in the Graveyard, like moondust.

The giant's arm lay crooked beneath his head, like he might be sleeping, but Isaac had no doubt he was dead. The mushroom forest flowed like spilled blood from his belly, from a great gash in his side.

"I think it's a god," Vran said, voice hushed, like he might wake the landscape and doom them all. "A dead god."

"They can die?"

"Anything can die. Though sometimes they just shed their skin, or so Professor Lawless says. This might just be his old body."

"Professor Lawless?"

"She teaches the Astral Geography class. You'd like her. She has an eye patch."

"I really need to take that class." Isaac's eyes traced the long scar of a canyon across the landscape. "It looks like he crashed here."

"Yeah, something probably killed him." Vran scanned the caves cut into the stalk.

"What could do that?"

"Another god." Vran shrugged like this was all normal, a typical night on patrol for an aspiring Guardian.

They climbed higher, and the walkway swayed, though Isaac did not grasp the taut rope that acted as a rail.

"There. Is that it?"

Vran pointed to a cave where several figures sat inside, casting happy shadows in the golden light of the open windows.

Isaac took a last look over his shoulder, in case the giant corpse had stirred. It hadn't, but he wouldn't mind getting out of here. He started to ask Vran how they'd get back to the school, but the elf had already stepped into the bar.

10

INTO THE DECAY

Vran paused on the other side of the door. He bounced a little on his feet, looking excited.

"Have you ever been in a bar before?" Isaac asked.

"Would you believe me if I said yes?"

"No."

"Well, you're right," Vran admitted. "You?"

"No." Isaac took in the bar. "It's not what I expected."

He tried to compare it to what he'd seen on the bits of TV he'd caught. Gritty, dim places full of rough-looking people, they were usually quiet enough to have a conversation. Sometimes there were fights.

This place didn't look like any of those.

The bar itself was carved from pale, polished stone. It might be bone. Isaac wondered if they'd taken it from the body of the dead god and if he'd ever want it back.

The chairs and tables were flexible, smaller mushrooms of various heights and a few swing-like contraptions hanging from the ceiling where huge fireflies hovered, lazily congregating in pairs or trios. They cast the dancing light Isaac had seen from outside. He gave up trying to decide if they were fixtures, patrons, or employees.

The spores drifted in from the open windows, dusting everything. No one appeared to mind, though a dark blue gnome snapped a paper coaster over his pint glass to keep them out of his beer.

Isaac brushed his shoulder clean. He almost reached out to do the same to Vran's black locks, but resisted.

"I don't see any goblins," Vran whispered. "Is he here?"

Isaac tasted the air.

"There's definitely a goblin in here," he said. "No idea if it's our guy."

"So let's mingle." Vran headed for the bar, where a woman in large square glasses served drinks.

Isaac followed. This was more like it, more his element. He'd take it over reading and writing papers any night.

The bartender hovered a few inches off the floor, suspended in the air by a pair of shiny, diaphanous wings sprouted from her back. Isaac could scent her blood, something sweet and gauzy, like cotton candy. It clashed with her disaffected expression and her wine-red eyes.

"What'll it be?" she asked, jerking her head to the racks of bottles.

"I don't know," Vran said. "What do you like?"

Isaac could see what Argent had meant about Vran needing to keep quiet. The elf gaped. He was too wide-eyed and excited to belong here.

Isaac caught himself wondering how far down the swirling marks Argent had painted on the right side of his body ran and struggled to push the thought away.

The bartender gave a little sigh and muttered something about tourists before mixing a shaker of liquids and ice. Her wings hummed as she shook the canister. The concoction came out apple green as she poured it into a martini glass. Then she topped it off with an eyedropper of something yellow. The liquid came alive, turning a bright pink filled with swirling points of light.

Vran was already reaching for the glass.

"What is it?" Isaac asked.

"A Fairy's Flight," she said with a shrug. "Vodka, a little elderberry, and the memory of a first kiss."

"Whose kiss?" Vran asked.

She shrugged.

"Whoever was dumb or desperate enough to sell their memory."

Vran sipped and pondered.

"Is it good?" Isaac asked.

"Yeah. It's sweet. I like sweet."

Vran passed the bartender a shark's tooth.

She bit it and tucked it into her register, an old brass and copper machine. She started pulling out change, a handful of baby teeth.

"Keep it," Vran said, waving her off.

Isaac led Vran farther into the bar's curving depths.

"Don't you want one?" Vran asked.

"One of us should keep a clear head. We don't have any backup this time, remember?"

"I thought you were used to working alone?"

"I was *trained* to work alone," Isaac said.

"And now you're not."

Vran took another slow sip and smiled.

"Fine." Isaac made a gimme gesture. "At least let me taste it."

Vran slid the glass across the bar.

The sweet flavor overlaid the sharp blandness of the vodka.

Then Isaac's lips tingled, just a little—the memory of the kiss, he guessed. It was even sweeter, and it made him flush a little.

He'd never been kissed, never kissed anyone, and wanted to as someone else's memory moved through him, spreading a warm but jittery delight through his chest.

Isaac watched the light of the fireflies flicker over the mushroom gills that lined the ceiling and wondered how this would feel to someone on the other side, someone who hadn't been kissed in years.

Sometimes he felt very old, far more than whatever age Doctor Cavanaugh thought he was, and sometimes he felt like an idiot whose life had never really begun.

It took him a moment to realize that Vran had wandered away, likely following the notes of music winging through the space like fluttering moths.

Isaac wound his way around the core of the stalk and found a little stage carved into an alcove.

A woman with curling brown hair sang a song about loss and love. Isaac could taste her sorrow in her scent.

He scented a hint of magic mixed with her blood. Whatever it was, it ran through her band too.

It was faint like she was faint, like she was a candle that had nearly run out of wick but just kept burning, all the way down.

"What are they?" he whispered.

"Lost Ones." Vran sounded sorry for them. "Humans who wandered into the Spirit Realm. They ate or drank something they weren't supposed to."

"I've never understood that," Isaac said. "How it works I mean."

Vran finished his drink and set the glass among other empty bottles and pints. Gnats sipped at the sticky aftermath.

"I don't either. Not exactly. It has something to do with resonance, that if you take in life from another plane, then it mixes you up, changes you. You can't quite go back to being who you were before."

Is that what happened to you? Isaac was working up the courage to ask the question aloud when Vran tugged his sleeve and nodded at a figure sitting at a low table near the window.

The goblin was dressed in an old-fashioned style that Isaac would call dapper. He wore a vest, tie, and a flat hat as he listened to the band with rapt attention.

Isaac tasted the air.

"That's him."

Vran leaned to stare at the goblin.

"Don't look," Isaac said.

"He's smaller than his ex-wife. Is that usual for goblins?"

"I've had four biology classes, Vran."

Isaac watched the goblin out of the corner of his eye.

"What do we do now?"

"We've tracked him down so now we go tell Argent."

"Are we certain he's the right one?" Isaac asked.

"Can you tell somehow?"

Isaac concentrated on the scent and tried to sift his memory of the kids, the goblets. It was definitely a push, another test of his powers. He hadn't had any of the kids' blood. He hadn't had any of the dad's. Maybe if Isaac could nick him somehow . . .

The goblin stopped tapping his foot and faced them. He fixed on Isaac and his eyes went wide.

"Damn it," Isaac said. "He's going to bolt!"

The goblin leaped out the window, showing more agility than Isaac had expected, clearing it easily and landing with a thud on the walkway outside.

"Come on!"

Isaac headed for the door.

The goblin darted down the ramp in a blur of green.

"We only want to talk!" Isaac called.

"The hells you do," the goblin shouted. "You're a freaking Undertaker."

"Not anymore!" Vran screamed. "He's nice now. I promise!"

Don't make promises you can't keep, Isaac thought as he blinked at the lights when they hit the street.

Isaac should have known that the Old Man's plan of putting the word out that he'd run away would work a little too well. The goblin at the house had heard of him. Isaac should have assumed that her ex would know about him too.

They'd entered one of the squares, a market full of stalls and wagons. The makeshift shops sold everything from fruit to candles to magic wands. The fireflies were here too, tethered and leashed in clusters like buzzing, slightly unhappy party balloons.

Massive blue spiders pulled carts driven by all sorts of figures.

"Go left!" Isaac called. "Let's try to head him off."

Vran listened for once.

The goblin ran, dropped, and slid under a wagon packed full of gibbering, living jack-o'-lanterns who had more than one comment about the chase. Isaac came around it, but found he'd lost the trail. He turned back and forth, trying to spy their quarry. He didn't see Vran either.

The market's back half was a warren of narrow little streets and ways.

Isaac tasted the air, trying to pick out the goblin's scent among the riot of clashing smells. Incense. Flowers. So much sweat and too much blood, too many kinds.

He ran through a series of stalls selling devilish-looking masks that winked and taunted him as he passed.

The taste of goblin blood bloomed in the air like ink dropped into water.

Isaac ran that way.

"No," he said. "Damn it."

The goblin lay face down, motionless, in an alley entrance.

A figure crouched over him to pull a throwing knife from the goblin's back. He wore a sleeveless shirt, exposing the inked feathers covering the corded muscles of his arms. Yellow eyes shone in the depths of his hood.

There could be no doubt that the goblin was dead.

Kenji did not miss.

Isaac tried to keep his eyes off the goblin and on his brother.

"Hello, Dove."

"What are you doing here?" Isaac asked.

"A job, obviously."

Kenji stepped over the corpse to face him.

"Isaac?" Vran called from somewhere nearby.

"This way."

Kenji grabbed Isaac by the upper arm and dragged him into the alleys. Isaac's older brother was broad-shouldered and long-haired. Isaac caught his scent, thick red wine and something smoky.

"You're going to blow my cover."

"We have a few minutes until he finds you," Kenji said. "Let him worry. Make him miss you a little."

So Kenji had been watching them flirt. No surprise that Isaac hadn't sensed him. He'd never tasted Kenji's blood and never seen it spilled. He didn't even know what Kenji was.

"Who wanted the goblin dead?"

"Some client." Kenji shrugged. "Does it matter?"

Isaac had known better than to ask. A good Undertaker didn't want or need to know. He just took the money and did the job.

"Have you checked in with the Old Man?" Kenji asked, a flicker of something, concern maybe, shifted his honey-colored eyes to a darker shade of gold.

"Not for a while."

"Why not?"

"Because I don't want to blow my cover."

"That's not a good idea, Dove. Have your fun, but don't make him think that you're not up to getting it done. You know how that will go."

"I *am* getting it done, but it's going to take time. What's the rush anyway?"

"I don't know. The client is antsy. They want that school gone."

Kenji would never tell Isaac, even if he knew the answer.

He hadn't survived this long without knowing when to play by the Old Man's rules. There was more than one reason he was the heir apparent and why Isaac trusted that he could take the Undertaker down when it was time to make their move.

Isaac had always imagined the day when Kenji would take over. Kenji had hinted that Isaac was his favorite, that they'd run things together. Isaac just needed to prove himself, to earn enough feathers, and survive until the time was right.

"I've got this," Isaac said. "Really."

"Okay, but don't keep him waiting long. And check in with him. Eyes on the prize. Someday."

"Someday," Isaac echoed.

Kenji sank back into the shadows.

Isaac had too many questions.

He needed to know why Kenji had been here, why the goblin had to die. The jobs shouldn't be related, but if someone had hired the Undertakers to keep the Guardians from finding out who was draining magical blood and what they wanted with it, then Vran was in danger.

Vran, who Isaac kind of wanted to kiss to feel that nervous tingle with.

Shit, Isaac thought.

He dashed out of the alley, hoping to look like he was still giving chase. Short of breath, he skidded to a stop.

Vran crouched over the goblin's body, his expression sad.

"What happened?" Isaac asked.

"I don't know. I just found him here."

Isaac's heart sank as Vran's shoulders slumped.

Isaac hoped Kenji hadn't left a calling card to mark the kill.

It served as a warning, that the Undertakers weren't to be messed with—that they'd kill anyone, anywhere. It would make things so much worse if Argent learned they were involved.

"What's in his hand?" Vran asked, reaching to uncurl the dead goblin's fingers.

Isaac already knew.

Vran glared at the raven's feather, and things became a lot more complicated.

11
A DOOR MADE OF KEYS

"What is this place?" Isaac asked as they walked through the old building.

"Liberty House," Vran said. "It's the school's mortal anchor, the main one."

They'd left the Spirit Realm for the mortal plane, and Vran wore a glamour to make him look human. His ears were round, his skin more pink and free of the forking lines. Isaac preferred his true appearance.

Workers rattled about the halls, hammering, sawing, and making repairs.

"The main one?" Isaac asked.

"There are a few, but this is where Argent keeps her office."

Isaac grimaced. This would not go well.

He wove around a ladder. Someone was painting and plastering the oppressive cinderblock walls.

"On the mortal plane?"

"Sometimes we need to keep an eye on things."

The queen stood in front of a door. Like Vran, a glamour hid her true nature. Isaac could have passed her on the street and never known she was anything but mortal. Dressed in a steel-colored suit and a burgundy silk blouse, she looked formidable, like a lawyer ready to do battle in court.

She waved them into the office behind her.

"And occasionally we need to act, to alter mortal police records or evidence. That sort of thing."

"I thought Guardians were supposed to follow the rules," Isaac said. "That doesn't sound very lawful."

"Morality across the realms is grayer than any of us would like, Frost. We do what we must to protect them. Sit. Both of you."

It wasn't like the dean's office.

This was modern, free of the wooden shelves and books, with a clean desk and stiff chairs for the guests. Her computer was one of those sleek, one-piece sorts, with a big, curving monitor.

Argent took the office chair behind the desk and leaned forward. Folding her hands, she rested them in front of her.

"Now tell me, what in the lowest hells happened down there?"

Vran shot Isaac a look.

Isaac made a *go ahead* gesture.

Vran explained how they'd started off, searching for the goblin, trying to blend in. Isaac added details, making sure Vran got it right, but not too right. She didn't need to know that they'd been flirting. They ended at the goblin, at finding his body.

Isaac tensed. She couldn't know, couldn't see through him. He hadn't spent long talking to Kenji.

Argent leaned back, fingers still laced, as she considered their story.

"And that's all you saw?" she asked, her gunmetal eyes fixed on Isaac.

"He was dead when I found him."

Vran sounded sad. He could never be an Undertaker, not if he could mourn someone he hadn't known, hadn't met. Even then, grief didn't get you anywhere. It didn't help. It didn't bring them back. Isaac knew that all too well.

"With no sign of who or what killed him?" Argent asked.

He had the distinct impression that she'd rather have a weapon in her hand and appreciated the barrier of the desk between them.

"No," Vran said. "Not until we saw the feather."

Argent settled back into her chair, but Isaac didn't relax. He started when someone dropped a bucket or something outside in the hall. It rattled while his heart raced.

"And you lost Isaac for how long?" Argent asked Vran, eyes flicking to his.

This could be it. This could be the moment when he died.

"Like, five minutes? Maybe less. Maybe more," Vran stammered. "I don't know. We were running. It all happened so fast."

"Hand over your knives, Frost."

He chewed his lip.

"I'll only ask once," she added in a crisp tone.

Isaac let out a breath, slid them free, and laid them atop the glass desktop, hilt toward her.

"Why did they kill him?" Vran asked.

"I don't know," Isaac said. Argent's expression didn't change. "I don't, *really*, but someone must have wanted him dead."

"Someone who could afford an Undertaker," Argent said. "Someone who wanted to make sure he couldn't tell us what he knew."

She stared at Isaac's knives like she could melt them with a glare. He resisted the urge to snatch them back.

"What do we do now?" Vran asked.

Isaac kept quiet. He didn't know whether chiming in would help or hurt his case. She hadn't asked him any questions, whether or not he'd killed the goblin. He figured she'd be able to tell. At least she could see that his blades were clean.

When the silence went on too long, Isaac asked, "Do we have any other leads?"

Argent considered him, and it felt like she was measuring every atom of his being.

"I want to know as badly as you do."

Hopefully the truth would save him.

Was there really a client, or was the Old Man playing some other game? Maybe he just wanted to thwart the Guardians, make it easier to operate across the planes, but Isaac didn't think so. The Undertaker never made a move without a goal, without an objective, and he never worked for free.

"I have an idea," Argent announced. She leaned back in her chair, never taking her eyes off Isaac.

"I'm not going to like this, am I?"

"Probably not." Her mouth almost twisted into a smile. "Let's go talk to Shepherd."

Vran cringed.

"Will I need those?" Isaac nodded to his knives.

"Possibly."

"Can I have them back?"

"Definitely not."

They followed Argent out of her office and deeper into the building.

They passed a collapsed wall. The landscape outside was flat and covered in yellow grass. The ground, where he could see it, was ruddy, not unlike the soil in the Graveyard.

Isaac shivered. How near were they to the Undertaker or his brothers?

Hopefully, far away. He did not like to imagine them close by. Kenji had gotten as close to Vran as Isaac could stand.

Make him miss you a little.

Kenji knew Isaac too well. He'd been watching them, and he knew, had seen how Isaac was around Vran. He'd seen what Isaac hadn't wanted to admit to. He liked Vran, and that was a complication this job didn't need.

Argent led them down a flight of stairs and things bent, twisting sideways. They were back at RCC.

Then she led them down again.

This was it. A way below, and they'd just walked him to it. He just had to find it again and he could complete his mission.

The hallway smelled familiar. It resembled any of the school's modern passages, but the door at its end was new and made of keys.

They covered it, welded together, a mix of modern and antique. A few blockish ones were stamped with numbers of statements like *Do Not Copy.*

If he was lucky, the school would remember him and let him return here on his own.

Argent led them through. It vanished once it closed, leaving only a cinder-block wall behind them.

Electric lights, linked by wires, buzzed along the ceiling. Their bare bulbs cast the stone walls and floor in harsh yellow light.

If there were prisoners, Isaac could not scent them.

All he got from the air was a bit of damp and something electrical, like singed rubber or plastic.

Argent led them through the halls, taking turns with surety.

He watched for the guards, the things Hex and the other students had whispered about, but saw nothing.

They came to a thick iron door, the kind with bolts and a slot for someone to peek through.

Argent knocked.

"Come in," a man's voice called.

The door opened to a cold room with vaulted ceilings that gleamed with white metal.

The dead goblin lay face down on a steel table, still dressed in his vest and breeches. His hat was missing, and Isaac found that sad. He was glad he couldn't see the goblin's eyes.

A man stood beside the body, examining it with intense focus. He wore a lab coat and surgical gloves, the kind the Undertaker wore when he prepped a body for burial.

The man looked up from the body as they entered, giving Isaac a view of his face.

What the hell?

Isaac shirked back and wished Argent hadn't taken his weapons.

The man, the creature, was a patchwork of people, sewn together. His eyes were pools of blue light. He had two different pieces of mustache, several different pieces of beard.

None of the fragments that made up his face quite met, and more blue light leaked from the seams. He had no clear scent but a dozen, all mingling like some stew of mortal components simmering in a type of magic Isaac didn't recognize.

The various bits of the creature's face curled in a patchwork smile at his reaction.

"You can call me Shepherd, and as for the question you're dying to ask, I'm a demon."

"Demons are real?"

"Yeah, but they're not what you think," Vran said, though he also kept his distance.

"No one ever is," Argent said in a bored tone.

"Cause of death is obvious," Shepherd said, gesturing at the body and its blood-stained clothes. "A single stab wound to the back, expertly placed."

"Can you talk to him?" Argent asked.

"Isn't he, uh . . . dead?" Isaac asked.

Shepherd gave an uneven shrug as if to ask *So?*

"Possibly. He hasn't been gone that long."

He had a strange accent, nothing Isaac could place. Maybe it came from being made up of so many people. Maybe that was the accent in whatever hell he came from.

"Well, get on with it then," Argent said.

The demon took off his glove. His hand was another patchwork, each finger a different shade. A few of the nails were painted, one red, one pink. He jammed his middle finger into the knife wound.

Vran made a gagging sound.

Shepherd stared into the distance, his blue eyes shuttered as he concentrated. He made a slight growling sound, like a dog discontented with its meal, and twisted his finger as if digging for something. He eventually withdrew his hand and shook his head.

"It's no use," he said. "He's crossed too far for me to call him back."

On one hand, this was good. The Undertaker's client had gotten what they'd wanted. The goblin was silenced. At the same time, Isaac needed to earn back enough of Argent's trust to divert suspicion. There was also the matter of his own curiosity, the building need to know *why*.

"Can I try?"

"The blood is dead," Argent said. "Can you work with that?"

"I don't know."

She cocked her head to the side.

"I am here to learn, aren't I?"

"All right then. It's not like you can hurt him."

Isaac turned to Vran. "Don't watch, okay?"

"Why not?"

"Because it's kind of gross."

"So?" Vran asked.

"I don't want you to see me like that."

"Okay."

Vran scoffed and faced the wall.

"What's the big deal?" he muttered. "I've seen worse."

Argent rolled her eyes.

Isaac dipped his finger into the stab wound. The flesh was cool, the blood thick and frigid, almost gelatinous. It felt a bit like the mochi ice cream Kenji had bought him on one of their field trips outside the Graveyard.

He wondered if all dead blood was like that.

Unlike the mochi, the blood did not taste sweet when Isaac popped his fingertip into his mouth.

This wasn't the blood of the living. This was thick and not quite bitter. Lifeless.

Cold seeped into his throat, which felt suddenly dry.

He almost asked for water but held his tongue still, kept the drop of blood perched upon it.

He closed his eyes and felt at the edges of the taste.

They'll kill her. They can't find her. Oh, gods, the boys!

Then he was running. He leaped out the window.

The goblin's thoughts stumbled together, a rush of panic and worry.

Ex or not, he'd clearly cared about his former wife. He cared about his children.

Damn it, Bella. I told you not to. Didn't matter how good the coin was.

"I have a name," Isaac said. "Bella."

He ran into the market and seized with pain, straightened and fell.

His last impression was the hard ground of the market meeting his face. The dusty spores clouded around him as he made impact.

Then nothing.

"He never saw it coming," Isaac said. "He didn't see who threw the knife."

"We need more," Argent said. "Where would she go? Where is she hiding?"

Isaac pushed himself into the blood. This wasn't like the power he borrowed. This fought him—no, not fought, not exactly. It didn't have the life, the strength to give him what he wanted, to tell him anything more, but he saw how he could pour a little of his own into it, how he could fuel it.

Isaac had never tried anything like this before. He'd never been trained to use his abilities this way.

"Isaac?" Argent asked.

"I'm trying," he said.

Where? he asked the blood, the last bit of the goblin's memory. *Where would Bella hide?*

He could feel the secret, the memory. Whatever bit of the goblin remained curled around it. He'd taken it to his grave, intending to protect his family.

Please, Isaac pled, trying to pry it loose. *We have to get to them first.*

The memory didn't budge, but maybe Isaac had another way to unlock it.

He rooted around inside himself, in his veins and their memories. He had to hurry. The dead blood was almost gone, burning away, flaking away like ash. Whatever remained of the goblin was fading fast.

There.

The final, fleeting taste of Bella's blood, the drop he'd tasted the night he'd met Vran. He offered it like a key to the panicked beat of the dead man's final moment.

The taste of Bella's blood slid into the memory and it cracked opened like a door on long rusted hinges.

She's smart. She'll go where they'll never look for her . . .

"I have it," Isaac said, knowing that he did.

He just had to take it in, to remember it, like an idea that woke him in the middle of the night. He had to remember, to write it down.

He wrote it in his veins.

This felt different than when he caught a scent. This was something deeper, but Isaac knew he could follow this trail across the worlds, could follow it anywhere.

Then the dead blood was gone and he was suddenly empty, all of his own strength gone, burned away in the effort of what he'd done. The trail went with it.

He had no time to protest as a wave of dizziness tried to sweep him off his feet.

Opening his eyes, Isaac vomited harder than he ever had before.

What would Vran think of that?

He didn't have time to ask as the wave carried him away.

12
DEAD MEN'S TALES

Isaac floated, warm and prone, at the bottom of a lake. He could see the surface but lacked the strength to reach for it, to kick upward and wake.

Something cold wrapped around his ankle, a hand. In the dark, in the mud and reeds lining the bottom, a pair of eyes glared at him, green and angry. The figure pulled him closer, and cold ran through Isaac's body like lead poured into his veins.

It was the goblin.

He didn't speak. He just glared at Isaac, held him tight, held him down, anchored in the murk.

I'm sorry, Isaac mouthed.

His stomach tightened to something hard and round, like he'd swallowed a baseball, like its weight could keep him there forever, even if the goblin let him go.

The goblin didn't say anything. He didn't absolve Isaac. He couldn't. The dead couldn't forgive. They couldn't do anything, not anymore.

Besides, it was Isaac's fault, wasn't it? Kenji wouldn't have been there if they hadn't gone into the Decay.

He closed his eyes, let himself settle into the mud. The reeds were sharp against his skin, but this was where he belonged. Then, just like that, the goblin released him.

Isaac sat up and took a heaving breath, like he had to remember how.

"It's okay," a voice said. Vran. Isaac knew him as much by scent as sound. "You were dreaming."

He took several heaving breaths.

His throat burned, dry and scratched, like he'd been coughing for days. He caught Vran's scent, only Vran's, and relaxed.

He was safe, still in RCC, the school he had to kill. They hadn't kicked him out. He hadn't failed his mission, not yet.

"Did we win?" he asked. It came out gravelly.

"You puked. Like, a *lot*."

Vran almost sounded impressed.

"Yeah—that was not fun."

And not how he wanted Vran to see him.

Isaac took in the room. The bed was identical to his own, but not his own.

Rocks and seashells littered the shelves and desk, collections of this and that: a pile of coins, something in a jar that glowed, a single drum with a pair of sticks, and a ball of dried mud with crow feathers stuck into it.

"Whose room is this?"

"Mine," Vran said. "It was closer than yours so I brought you here."

"You carried me?" Isaac asked.

"You're not that heavy, though I might have banged your head on a doorway once or twice."

Isaac felt his skull for bumps and didn't find any.

"I can't tell if you're joking."

"Then I guess you'll never know."

Isaac still wore his tank top but not his jacket.

His arms weren't green, so he hadn't absorbed any of the goblin's traits when he'd eaten the dead blood.

His stomach flipped at the memory of the taste. He would have vomited again if he'd had anything left in his guts. He studied Vran and his collection of curiosities.

"I didn't think you slept here, at the school I mean."

"I don't."

"But you have a room?" Isaac asked.

"Why not? It's a big school."

"How big?" Isaac asked.

"I don't think anyone can say, not exactly. It changes all the time. It's still new, still settling. Buildings do that."

"Not like that they don't." Isaac nodded to where the wall rippled and warped like lake water in a breeze.

"Well, Watchtowers are more than buildings. They cross the Spirit Realm, across all their layers. They're anchored to mortal structures, like a jellyfish on a string, but they do drift."

"And this one is new so it's still getting used to its leash?" Isaac asked.

"See? You get it. Maybe a few head bumps are good for you."

"Maybe. A few more and I'll pass that quiz when the time comes," Isaac said.

"Maybe I did you a favor and knocked some sense into you."

"Maybe." Isaac rolled his shoulders. "She still has my knives, doesn't she?"

"She does."

"What does that mean?" Isaac asked.

"I think it means you're on probation too."

"No more missions?" Isaac asked.

"Probably not, but you still have to go to class, and Lin's next essay is almost due."

Isaac groaned.

"Have you even started it?" Vran asked.

"Here's the thing," Isaac said. "I don't really know how to write an essay. Don't look at me like that."

"You did okay last time."

"Because you helped me. Writing really isn't my thing."

"But you could probably kill someone with a pen?"

"Easily. I could probably do it with just the cap."

"You make it sound fun."

"More fun than homework."

Isaac was already calculating the best place to stab someone.

Vran shook his head as Isaac stretched and took stock.

He felt sore, but everything was still attached.

At least he was still here, could still complete his mission. He'd miss his knives, but there were plenty of pen caps around.

Then again, essays and tests—a wall of boredom lay between him and victory. Kenji had been right, he needed to call home.

Isaac balled up his fists and spied a well-worn paperback on the nightstand.

"*The Last Sun*?" he asked, picking it up.

"Yeah. It's Adam's favorite book."

A little wriggle of something squirmed in Isaac's belly. It displaced the roil left from being sick but didn't feel much better.

"Who is Adam?" he asked. "To you I mean. You said he was a friend."

"He is, but he's also kind of like a big brother." Vran moved to sit, placing himself near enough to Isaac that he could feel the coolness of his skin.

Isaac let out a breath.

A big brother. He could live with that. After all, he had one too.

"What now?" he asked quietly, leaning close enough that their shoulders brushed.

"I think you should brush your teeth before Argent gets here." Vran knocked Isaac's shoulder hard enough with his that Isaac tipped over.

Isaac pulled himself to his feet.

"When is she coming?"

A knock sounded at the door.

"About now," Vran said.

"Great."

Isaac stumbled to the bathroom and found his toothbrush atop a folded change of clothes but doubted he could get away with showering. He settled for scrubbing at his teeth and took a bit longer than absolutely necessary.

He needed time to clear his head. He needed to think and focus so he did not give himself away.

Voices echoed through the bathroom's thick, wooden door. The queen did not sound happy.

"Okay," he whispered, spitting and rinsing in the sink.

He opened the door to find Argent and Vran facing off, each with their arms crossed.

The queen radiated annoyance.

"Well?" she demanded. "Where is she?"

Isaac lifted his hands.

"I've only got one card to play here, and that's it," he said.

Argent narrowed her eyes.

Isaac couldn't taste her magic and that felt far scarier than what he'd sensed when he'd first met her. This was a predator, a hawk or an owl, ready to dive for a mouse.

"You're on thin ice here, Frost."

"I am going to tell you."

"Then do."

"I just don't want you to cut us out, especially Vran. He didn't do anything wrong."

"Neither did you," Vran said.

"He's right," Isaac said. "I was in the wrong place at the wrong time."

"We wouldn't be having this conversation if I thought you'd killed him. You tasted dead blood to earn my trust, did you not?"

"I did," he admitted, not happy that she'd seen through him.

"Then earn it." She held out her palm as if asking him to hand something over. "Tell me what you know."

"She's back in the mortal plane," he said. His stomach gave a fresh turn when he remembered the dead goblin's worry, his panic for his children. "He figured you wouldn't look for her there twice."

"Earth is a big world," Argent said. "You'll need to be more specific than that."

"Let us help and I'll tell you where she is."

"Why is this important to you?"

"It's not, not exactly, but I ran away from the Undertakers. If they're involved, then I want to stop them."

She didn't look like she was buying it. Then again, he couldn't tell. The queen's face may as well have been stone as she asked, "What else?"

Isaac let out a breath.

"The blood . . . what they're doing." He shook his head. "I want to know why, who's behind it, and what they're doing with it."

"Why do you care?"

"It's blood. It may be—I've never met another Phage, have you?"

"Once," she said. "And not for a very long time."

"I want to find them," he said, realizing it was the truth. "I want to know where I come from, where I *really* come from."

Argent considered his words.

"Fine. Tell me what you think you know."

"And you'll let us help you catch her?"

"I won't be sending you alone again, but yes, I'll include you if possible. If I deem it safe."

Her stress on the last word made him want to ask for whom, but Isaac decided he didn't want to know the answer.

And maybe, with backup like Argent, Bella and her children would survive.

It couldn't be a coincidence, the way the Undertaker had sent him in to disrupt Vran and Argent's sting. He'd set back the Guardians' efforts *and* gotten into the school. Two birds with one stone. It was a brutal efficiency, very much the Old Man's way.

"I hate to break the tension, but we've got class," Vran said.

"Which class?" Isaac asked.

"Lin's."

Isaac muttered a curse under his breath.

"So?" Argent asked.

Isaac described what he'd learned, every detail of the trail to Bella, what he'd seen in the goblin's memory.

"I'll let you know when we've found her," Argent said.

"Can I have my knives back?"

"Say please," she said over her shoulder as she walked away.

"Please."

"No." Her eyes narrowed to slits. "Now go learn something."

"That went well," Vran said after they'd started walking to class.

Isaac was tempted to argue but had to agree. Argent hadn't expelled him or incinerated him. Both were wins.

They slipped into their seats just as Lin was starting.

Isaac felt strangely unarmed. It wasn't just his knives. He didn't have pen and paper.

Hex and Daffodil remained cool to him. His help with the flood hadn't improved things there.

Ford grinned though. At least someone other than Vran was happy to see him.

"As you know, this school is new," Lin announced. "But it is not the only school for practitioners. Who can tell me which institution is the most influential?"

Hex raised her hand.

Lin nodded to her.

"The Elven Academy?"

"That is correct," Lin said. "Alfheimr's Academy has a long tradition of training the nobility in etiquette, magic, and politics."

"They don't let anyone else in, right?" Ford asked. "Only elves?"

"Also correct. They usually favor the scions of elven nobility."

"They're snobs," Vran said, not looking up from whatever he was doodling, some spidery-looking sea creature.

"They wouldn't take you either?" Hex asked.

"Not anymore, and I wouldn't go if they invited me."

Did that mean Vran wasn't a noble anymore? If not, how did he rank living with one of the court and hanging out with the queen?

Someday Isaac was going to pin Vran down and find out more about the guy. Hearing how the thought sounded, and picturing it, made Isaac slump in his seat.

As much as he hated the homework, at least Lin's class was teaching him how to navigate the other worlds and their politics. Maybe it would give him some clue into the elf who'd become the focus of his thoughts.

You're only visiting, he reminded himself. *On borrowed time.*

Still, knowledge could be a weapon. Even the Old Man would agree with that.

And Vran might know where the heart was. Isaac knew that was an excuse. He'd been shown a way down. He just had to find it again.

And Kenji knew. He'd seen how Isaac was with Vran.

Still, maybe he could sell it as gathering intel, useful stuff for the future.

Knowing how the elves and their systems fit together had to have value. He'd even uncovered one of the Guardians' secrets, that they interfered with the mortal authorities from time to time. That might be something they could exploit. He didn't know what Kenji thought about the Guardians. He didn't know how he intended to deal with them when he was in charge.

"As you may also know," Lin continued, bringing Isaac back to the moment. "The King of Swords himself sponsored our school's founding."

Daffodil's hand shot up. She was wearing a lot of pink today.

Lin nodded at her.

"Didn't he go to the Academy?"

"He did, yes," Lin said. "Which is partly why I think he wants us to be on good terms with them."

The class stiffened, looking worried. Isaac tensed, suspecting he was not going to like what she said next.

"Thus we have been invited, cordially, to attend their autumnal ball."

"What is that?" Isaac asked.

"A dance and a party," Lin said.

"A party, thrown by elves?" Isaac asked.

He couldn't help but look at Vran.

The look on the guy's face was confusing. Isaac couldn't read if it was dread or excitement. It might be both.

"When is it?" Daff asked.

"The autumn equinox," Lin said. "Very soon, so we'll begin focusing on elven protocol, history, and manners."

Vran groaned.

"Why?" Isaac asked. "We're not elves, at least not most of us."

"To prepare you," Lin said. "You will not just be representing RCC, you'll be representing the king. In fact, your behavior at the ball will be worth a significant amount of your grade."

"You can't just change the syllabus," Hex said.

"Take it up with the dean," Lin said.

"Why wouldn't they take you?" Ford asked Vran, circling back. "You're an elf, aren't you?"

The class paused. Isaac did not stare at Vran. He pointedly did not stare at Vran.

The others were looking at the elf, their faces curious. Ford didn't sound like he'd meant it to be cruel.

"Why do you have to be so blunt?" Hex asked him. "It's none of your—"

"Because I'm a Lost One," Vran said, cutting her off. "Because I went where I wasn't supposed to go, and I swallowed the water there. A lot of it."

Isaac didn't know what he was supposed to do. He had the urge to say something, do something, to make the wormy feeling in his stomach go away.

It wasn't unlike the moment in a fight when you were given an opening. He could retreat. He could go for the kill.

He thought about what Kenji would have done, but he wouldn't have done it here, in front of the others. He would have come to Isaac later, hugged him, and told him it would be all right. He would have come when most of the awkward exposed feeling had gone away.

Isaac wanted to do something. He wanted to hug Vran, maybe?

He focused on the blackboard and whatever Professor Lin was saying instead.

13

GRAVITY'S JUST A THEORY AND IT CAN STILL KILL YOU

Professor Lawless did indeed wear an eyepatch.

"There are many theories regarding the planes of existence," she said. "The purpose of this class is to explore them and, if possible, give you the basic foundation of those theories in order to explore more safely and perhaps prove a few theories of your own."

"Hence, Planar Theory?" Isaac asked.

"Precisely," Lawless said.

"We know all this," Hex said. "Why do we have to go over it again just for his sake?"

"She's right," Isaac said. "Not to mention, I can't be ready for this. I can't even do algebra."

Lawless hummed.

"The Queen of Swords felt that Mr. Frost would benefit from some advanced studies in this area, especially after his recent mishap."

"So we're being punished because he messed up?" Hex asked. "We're not even allowed to go on missions and he gets to what, just blunder through them?"

Isaac cringed. It was bad enough losing his knives and having the dead goblin haunt his dreams. Having the entire class aware of what happened felt like an extra punishment.

He didn't have to ask how Hex was doing. She had one of her

notebooks out and open to a page filled with equations and sketches of circles and lines—things he did not understand at all.

"I don't think a review of the fundamentals or the purpose of the class as a punishment," Lawless countered.

"You said the queen wanted me in this class," Isaac said. "I thought the dean was in charge of the school."

Lawless narrowed her good eye.

"She is, but the royals have their opinions, and we take them into consideration when we have to."

Isaac straightened in his seat.

"Am I the only one who thinks that's kind of controlling?"

"Save it for social science and history," Hex said. "We're here to learn about the planes."

"Hex is right," Lawless said. "We need to assess your knowledge and close any gaps. The other students have already shown sufficient understanding of the topic thus far."

Isaac sunk into his seat. He didn't even have Vran to look at.

Apparently, world walkers were exempt from the basics.

"Any questions, Mr. Frost?"

"Why is it all theoretical?" he asked. *And if it is, how can you teach it to us?*

He managed to keep the second question to himself. Perhaps he was learning something from Lin's lectures after all.

"We don't understand how it all fits together," Lawless replied. She used a pointer to direct his attention to a mural of elaborate circles drawn on the wall. Each was labeled. The school was there, in the layer marked *the Spirit Realm.*

"But the elves own this school," Isaac said. "Can't they clear it up for you?"

"Own is inaccurate," Lawless said. "Sponsor is closer to the state of things. Even then, there are places even they can't or won't go."

Lawless pointed down to the various Underworlds.

There. That was where Vran had fallen, the place he feared.

"But why don't they share what they know?"

Isaac leaned back in his seat and crossed his arms over his chest, feeling pretty certain from her expression that he'd scored a point.

"Did your own mentor not prepare you for planar travel?" the professor asked. "After all, the Undertakers operate everywhere, do they not?"

"He would have when the time came."

"Maybe you wouldn't have screwed it up if he had," Hex grumbled.

"I heard that."

"You were supposed to."

"Perhaps," Lawless said with a little smile that Isaac did not like. "But even if the immortals were to share their knowledge, we should work to prove it for ourselves."

"Trust but verify," Hex said.

"Precisely," Lawless agreed.

Isaac didn't doubt the Old Man would hold back knowledge to keep himself at the top of the hill. Hells, he could even admire the shrewdness, not that Isaac knew of anyone other than Kenji coming for this crown as king of the assassins.

It made sense that the elves would hoard what they knew and that the professors would want their own share of that advantage.

"Since we're reviewing the basics, what is the most important consideration in planar travel?"

"Resonance," Daffodil said.

"Exactly, and what does that mean?"

"We're not supposed to eat the food," Isaac said.

"Yes, Frost, but do you understand why?"

"Not at all." He remembered the band he and Vran had watched perform in the Decay and the woman's soulful, lonely song. "But I know it can make you a Lost One."

"Each plane's magic has its own frequency," Lawless said. "In some ways, the philosophers who posed a belief in the music of the spheres weren't wrong. An apple from Earth has a certain resonance. Another apple, from another plane, will have a completely different resonance. Consume enough magic from another plane and your own frequency would shift. You'd no longer vibrate at the same resonance as your home plane. You'd become trapped between, not quite fitting into either."

So that was what had happened to Vran, why he wasn't with the other elves at their school for snobs. Did he want to go there, be with his own people?

It felt like something someone should want, like something Isaac should want, but he'd never met another Phage. He'd never known another home but the Graveyard or another family but his brothers.

He wanted to talk to Vran about it, but just the idea of the conversation felt dangerous, too personal.

Eyes on the prize, Dove.

He heard the admonishment in Kenji's voice.

He wanted to ask Vran what he'd wanted, but the question felt personal, too personal.

Still, he was curious.

"How much does it take?" he asked. "How many apples before your frequency shifts?"

"I'm not certain anyone knows," Lawless said. "And it's not as though anyone is keen to volunteer as a test subject."

"Could you fix it?" Isaac asked. "If say, someone drank water from the wrong plane, couldn't they just drink a bunch more from the right one and they'd start vibrating at the right frequency again?"

Hex was looking at him funny. No, maybe not funny, just perhaps with a speck of . . . respect maybe?

"The shift appears permanent," Lawless said. "You might take in more of your original harmony, but the frequency won't reset. You'd be changed forever, caught between."

"That can't be right," he said.

"Why not?" she asked, raising a perfectly sculpted eyebrow.

"I'm a Phage. I take in blood from all sorts of races, from all sorts of planes, but it burns out. I don't keep the powers of whatever I tasted forever. I'm not a Lost One."

He paused, thinking.

"Am I?"

Lawless narrowed her one eye at him, and he felt a bit like a rat in a cage.

"What is your home plane?"

"I—I don't know."

"Then it sounds like an excellent study. We should test you."

"You're going to take more blood samples, aren't you?"

"I doubt that will be necessary. Jul—I mean, Doctor Cavanaugh, likes her needles. I'm certain she has enough for both of us."

"Pity," Isaac said.

Hex shot him a confused glance.

"Free cookies," he said with a shrug.

"Each of you is expected to complete a research project before the term is over," Lawless said. "It must have a practical, measurable component."

"You want me to measure myself?"

"Innuendo has no place in my classroom, Mr. Frost."

"Huh?"

Hex sighed.

"She means dick jokes."

"Ah."

"You're already behind, Frost," Lawless continued. "I'd cut the humor and focus. Using your own resonance as a test subject may help you make up lost ground, and it might help you learn more about yourself, such as where you're from."

"I've never done a study like that," he said.

"I'll help him," Hex offered. "If he helps me back."

He narrowed his eyes at her.

"How?"

"I need some assistance with my project," she said. "Bring your knives if you can."

Isaac perked up until he remembered that he could not. An improvised weapon would have to do.

"Why?" he asked.

"Because I might need some muscle and Ford already said no."

"Too busy with my own project," Ford said happily.

"Deal."

"Excellent," Lawless said. "I'm excited to see what you find, especially the temporal implications."

Isaac had felt like he was on the right track, and then things went over a cliff.

"Temporal?"

"Lost Ones are not just lost in the planes, but time, which is why they cannot go home again. They return far from when they departed while most plane walkers report that little time passes while they're elsewhere."

"Is that why there are dinosaurs here?" Isaac asked.

"Exactly," Hex said.

Lawless nodded in agreement.

"Things long extinct in the mortal realm and native to that plane wandered into the Spirit Realm or were brought here. As such they survived the events that killed their species on their native plane."

"But it's not the same," Isaac said, thinking of the geese. "There's some weird sh—stuff here."

"It's possibly multiversal," Lawless said.

"Or metaphysical," Hex added.

Lawless nodded reluctantly.

"I don't like that theory as much, but it is possible that dreams or belief help to shape this space."

Isaac thought of the waving walls.

"Do you mean the school?"

"The Spirit Realm," Daffodil said.

"That's my project," Ford said proudly.

"How are you going to measure dreams?"

"Sleeping a lot," Ford said. "If I dream of a pizza and I wake up to find a pizza, then I can prove it."

Hex rolled her eyes. She was clearly the star student. Isaac didn't know how he could help her, but he was more than intrigued about the idea of finding out more about his people.

He'd meant it when he'd told Argent he wanted to know more about the Phages, about where he came from. More and more he had the feeling that it was tied to that memory he couldn't force to surface, to the warmth and light from some time long ago.

Had the queen added him to this class to cure his ignorance for missions or because he'd said he wanted to know about his people?

Something akin to affection for her threatened to surface in his chest.

Was that why she was so forgiving with Vran? She had a soft spot for a Lost One, at least an elf. He doubted the same applied to him.

"Can we all just nap through our assignments?" he asked.

"Mr. Ford's analysis might allow us to prove an archetypal model," Lawless said with a sigh.

"But you don't like it," Isaac said.

"I think the theory has some merit," Lawless said. "We cannot discount anything until it is proven and measured, but no, I don't know if attempts at lucid dreaming are a valid avenue."

"Can we go back to the time thing?" Isaac asked. "Are you saying that no time passes while I'm at the school?"

"Not exactly. RCC occupies a focal point in the planes."

She used her pointer to aim at the mural again. The school was like a spiral seashell, or a drill bit, going up and down for a good distance into the planar layers.

"As a Watchtower the school has a different temporal weight than most transplanar structures."

"Which is what I'm working on," Daffodil said proudly. "Measuring how time gets warped the further you get from the campus."

Isaac really was behind.

His head hurt, but he was starting to get an idea or two as he studied the mural.

The Decay was listed, just beneath the Spirit Realm. The Graveyard wasn't mapped, but maybe it was like that, a Hollow. It was outside of time, sort of, so it had to be connected to the Spirit Realm.

Thinking of it now, trying to remember it, it felt like a dream, with fuzzy edges and uncertain details—but seasons had passed, hadn't they? Or had that merely been weather?

Had the sky ever been any color but gray?

If Lawless was successful, if she found a way to measure the Spirit Realm, how long would the Graveyard remain a secret? How long could the Undertakers hide?

If the Old Man knew about this, then maybe there was no client. Maybe he was taking the school's existence personally, saw RCC as a threat.

The Undertaker liked to brag that no one could find it, could find them. Maybe that was because they were out of time as well as space. If so, what did that mean for Isaac or any of the boys? It might mean that any family they had was long dead, extinct like the dinosaurs on earth. And like the dinosaurs, it might mean that any chance of finding them lay here.

14
COPING MECHANISMS

"A change of schedule for you, Frost," Professor Lin said when her class ended. "You're to head for necro-counseling."

"Necro-counseling?" he asked. "What's that?"

"You'll see," Vran said.

"Is this a punishment?" Isaac asked.

"Go see Shepherd," Lin said tersely.

"Alone?"

"Alone."

It couldn't be that easy. They wouldn't just hand him access to the labyrinth. This had to be another test.

Figuring he was being watched, he hadn't searched for the heart since they'd returned from the Decay.

"I don't know the way," he said.

"I'll walk you there," Vran offered.

"You won't be late?" Isaac grabbed his backpack.

"Never."

"Thanks," Isaac said.

He wasn't happy about another meeting with the demon, especially not by himself, but Shepherd dwelled below. Isaac could pretend to get lost. He could say that the labyrinth had confused him. He could find what he needed to. He didn't have his knives, but a pen might do. Today might be the day he finished the job.

Vran didn't lead Isaac anywhere special.

He had a brighter air today. The lines on his skin were almost too pale to see, and his hair was spiked with product, looking more tamed and less like a cloud of squid ink.

They walked until Vran took the sleeve of Isaac's jacket, tugging him toward a stairwell that Isaac had never noticed.

Had it always been there?

Isaac didn't like to think of himself as that distracted. The Old Man would have beaten him for missing such an important detail.

If it was a glamour, it was better than the ones he'd seen Hex weave.

Vran's senses had to be sharper than Isaac's.

Or the school trusted him more.

The door made of keys waited, open just a crack, at the bottom of the stairs. Yellow light spilled from inside.

Isaac didn't sense anything strange about it, no magic, no malice. It was simply a door made of keys. He should be able to find it again.

"Thanks for walking me," he said. "I've got it from here."

"Are you sure?"

"Yeah."

Vran nodded and walked away.

Isaac took a breath and pushed the door open.

He liked Vran, but he had to get on with this. The Undertaker wouldn't wait much longer. Isaac needed to update him on his progress, and he needed something to show for the time he'd spent.

Isaac hoped he didn't lose his way as he passed the door to Shepherd's office.

The power lines, running bulb to bulb across the ceiling, guided his way.

If he'd had his knives, he could have tried to scratch markings into the walls, a pattern to follow.

The school was full of doors, but these halls had only bricks. If this was a jail, where were the cells? Where were the prisoners and the guards everyone dreaded so much?

Isaac followed the lights, walking from tiny sun to tiny sun, connecting the dots in the darkness. They reminded him of the constellations he'd drawn with Samuel when they were learning how to navigate by the stars.

As always, Samuel, one of the few humans in a brotherhood of the monstrous and fantastic, had been behind in the lesson.

Isaac tried not to think of him. He tried to never think of him.

Isaac pushed the memory away, packed it down. This wasn't the time for ghosts.

Something whispered from behind. Isaac reached for his knives but of course they weren't there.

Murderer, a voice said.

Killer, another added.

No, chimed a third. *Not yet. Would be. Wannabe.*

Isaac spun back and forth, watching for whoever taunted him, and found no one.

"Shy?" he asked. "Is that you?"

But there was no hazy boy shape, no scent of any kind.

Ahead, the farthest light went out.

"I grew up in a tomb," Isaac announced. "I'm not afraid of the dark."

That was the first test, the first thing the Undertaker subjected them to.

Isaac froze in place, just like he had back then, just like he always did. He tensed, senses alert, as one by one the lights went out and the darkness marched toward him.

He could hear something in the darkness, even if he could not see or scent it, and tried to quiet his own breathing. He knew to freeze like this, but Samuel had always cried.

Something in the darkness sniffled, reminding Isaac of when they'd been dumped in winter woods, lost and shivering, the constellations their only guide.

The lights kept going out. The buzzing dimmed.

Isaac shook his head. He would not run. He would not give in to fear.

An Undertaker was the thing to be afraid of.

But are you an Undertaker? one of the voices asked.

Would be, another echoed. *Wannabe.*

Killer.

The darkness overtook him, and it was complete.

He could retrace his steps but had no guarantee the school would not change the path.

A hand brushed the back of his shoulder. It trailed cool fingertips down his arm, the pressure slight enough that he could almost convince himself he was imagining it.

An Undertaker does not run.

The thing on his arm reached his wrist, like it might take his hand.

This was just another test. He'd passed them all before. He'd passed the hardest one.

What does he want?

A feather.

Blood.

What do you think he's sorry for?

"Samuel," Isaac said.

He hadn't meant to answer.

Samuel . . . the voices hissed liked a chorus.

The memory came unbidden, uncalled. He sank into it, like a pool hidden by rotting leaves, like an open grave he'd run straight into.

They were learning to swim, taking turns diving into the deep pond behind the hill.

Isaac had yet to take his turn.

Samuel was there, like always. The younger boy always followed him, always wanted to be where Isaac was.

Slight, pale, with hair darker than Isaac's, they could have been blood brothers.

Samuel stood atop the rocks, shivering in his shorts.

"Are you going to go next?" he called down to where Isaac watched.

"You go," Isaac grumbled.

It would be nice if Samuel stayed down, if he got lodged in the soggy sunken branches at the bottom. Then Isaac would be free to try and join the older boys. Like Kenji. That was what he wanted, to be like Kenji, to be that quick and cool.

"Okay! Watch me?"

"Sure."

He didn't know why Samuel's clinging to him grated so much. They were best friends, at least they were if you asked Samuel, but lately the other boy asked question after question. *What do I do? What should I say?*

It was like he couldn't do anything if Isaac wasn't there, wasn't watching; like a clock without a battery, he'd stop completely if he wasn't in Isaac's shadow, but it was Isaac who felt run down, dragged down, like the other boy's endless energy came at the expense of Isaac's.

"Watch me, Isaac!" Samuel called. "I'll show you I can do it!"

Movement caught Isaac's eye, and he realized that Samuel had climbed still higher, to the very top of the rocks. If he jumped from there, he might hit the bottom. He really might never come up.

Isaac screamed a warning, but it was too late.

Samuel leaped. He fell. He slapped into the water.

Isaac ran for the edge of the pond, but Samuel didn't rise.

Isaac could let him go, just let him drown. He'd be rid of the whining, the crying—Isaac leaped into the pond, splashing his way toward the center of the ripples. It wasn't far. He'd been right there.

Isaac took a gulp of air and dove. He couldn't see through the murk.

He came up, yelled for help, yelled and yelled.

Then he took another breath, held it, and dove.

He stayed until his lungs burned.

When he came up again, Kenji was there, along with some of the others.

"Samuel," Isaac gasped, slapping the water. "He didn't—come up."

Kenji dove in.

He didn't surface for a while. He stayed down so long, so much longer than Isaac could have, so much longer than Samuel could have.

When Kenji rose again, he shook his head, long hair whipping back and forth.

"I can't find him."

Let him go, a voice said. It was so small, but it came from deep within him. *Just let him go.*

Watch me, Isaac.

He hadn't been watching. He'd been annoyed, hadn't wanted to be there, or hadn't wanted to be there with Samuel. He'd wanted to be alone.

Now he was.

Kenji took another breath and dove again. He came up quicker than Isaac had expected, Samuel in his arms.

Kenji lay the boy on the ground, and Samuel coughed, spitting up pond water.

"Did you see, Isaac?" he asked, voice weak.

"Yeah. I saw," he said. "I watched."

He felt the tears try to fall, but he forced them down, forced them not to come.

He'd refused to cry then. He couldn't remember the last time he had cried, if ever, after that, but he cried now, in the labyrinth beneath the school. He wiped at his face.

"Isaac," a voice called. "Isaac."

It was like a light, like a window had opened.

He was lying on the ground, outside Shepherd's open door. The pale glow from inside pooled around him and gave the demon a saintly halo.

"What? Where?" Isaac sputtered out his questions and sat up.

The memory was gone, but the clammy feeling of the cold water remained. The tears, and the dead weight like a cannonball in his chest, remained.

"You wandered," Shepherd said. "And the gaolers took you."

"What are they?" Isaac asked, remembering the dissonant chorus, the angry voices. He'd been there. It hadn't been an illusion or just a movie he'd been playing back in his mind. He'd relived the moment, that terrible day when Samuel hadn't come out of the water.

"They aren't unlike me," Shepherd said.

"Demons?"

Shepherd nodded, the pieces of his face not quite uniform in their movement.

"They're—terrible." Isaac couldn't think of a better word.

"Yes, they are, but they don't usually bother the innocent."

"Then I guess I'm not that innocent." Isaac tried to draw the cloak of his confidence back around himself as he stood.

Shepherd gave him a look that said he wasn't buying it.

"Do you want to talk about it?" he asked, looking over his shoulder, following Isaac's eyes to the warm light of his office. "I could make some tea."

"Not really," Isaac said.

"It is why you're here, Frost, to talk."

"Are you really a counselor?"

"No, but I've eaten three of them."

Isaac scowled.

"Sorry, that was a little demon humor."

"Funny."

"I'm still getting the hang of jokes."

Shepherd gestured for Isaac to step into his office.

"But you know all about it don't you?" Shepherd asked.

"Humor?"

"Eating people."

Isaac shook his head.

"Not people, not *flesh*, just a little blood here and there, as a treat."

"Sit. Please." Shepherd gestured to the chair opposite his desk. He circled it and sat.

Isaac didn't mind having some furniture between them.

The gaolers were nasty things. If Shepherd were their cousin, then he could likely pry into Isaac's mind in a similar way.

He forced himself to keep his face even, to not betray what he was feeling.

He'd cried.

They'd made him cry.

They'd pay for that. He'd find the school's heart, and he'd kill it. After this, after today, he'd enjoy it.

The anger soothed the ache.

"Lin said I was here for necro-counseling."

"Yes. Many believe that a person's main issues stem from our parents, that unresolved trauma haunts us, if you will. You're an orphan?"

"All the Undertakers are."

"Why is that?"

The Old Man said it all the time.

We are your family. This brotherhood is your family. You have no other.

They were unwanted. They'd be hunted anywhere else. Only among monsters would monsters like them be safe.

"It's to keep us from having other loyalties, other ties."

"And yet you left. You ran away?"

"Yeah."

Shepherd nodded. This was it. If Shepherd could read his mind, he'd know Isaac was lying.

The demon let out a breath.

"I conceived of necro-counseling as a means of helping students like you resolve issues with their parents."

"Wait—you mean their *dead* parents?"

"Exactly."

Isaac was pretty certain he'd heard Hex talking to Daffodil about her mother. She'd even sounded fond of the woman. The idea was so foreign to him that the conversation could have been in another language. The thought of it, having someone like that in his life, made his stomach flip. It wasn't unlike how he felt when he considered how Vran would react to learning Isaac's true purpose at RCC.

"What if their parents aren't dead?"

"Well, then we kill them, of course."

"That's another joke . . . right?"

The demon sighed.

"It wasn't funny, was it?"

"More than the last one. Keep practicing."

"Sarcasm is not a replacement for a personality, Frost."

"If you say so."

"Anyway, if the parent is living, then a therapist can give the family the tools to communicate."

"But if a student can't talk to their parents about their issues, you hold a séance?"

"Nothing quite so ceremonial or ritualistic, but I have access to the dead in a way that most do not. Would you like me to try to find them for you?"

"Who?"

Isaac asked it mostly to buy time. His chest tightened.

"Your parents."

Isaac pressed himself against the back of the chair.

"I—I don't know."

It had never occurred to him that he could talk to his parents, that somewhere out there, they might still exist. Who were they? What had they been like? Why had they given him up?

The memory, the vague, gauzy thing at the bottom of his mind tried to surface. He could taste sunlight and something chalky. There was an overall sense of warmth, a woman's smile—then nothing.

Isaac hadn't mourned his parents, not really, but there had been times when he'd dreamed of what it would be like to live a life with them, a completely different life. He never let those dreams go too far because he couldn't see how they ended, and because there was no point. His life was his life. His brothers were his brothers, and no matter what lies he told, an Undertaker never got to leave.

"If you decide, let me know," Shepherd said gently.

"You're not going to make me?"

Lin had told him to come here. She hadn't sounded like he had a choice.

"Of course not. Therapy only works if you engage with the process. If I force a reunion, I could traumatize you. We're here for the opposite of that."

Shepherd reached for the pile of folders on his desk and opened one.

"You know, you are quite the talk among the staff."

"Why?"

"None of us have ever met a Phage before. Doctor Cavanaugh has the results of your tests. I'm happy to say you are perfectly healthy."

"That's good, right?" Isaac asked.

"Yes, almost suspiciously so. She also confirmed that you're immune to blood-borne pathogens. It makes sense, considering that otherwise, every use of your power could expose you to incredible risk."

"Cool. Good for me."

"Can you remember the first time you used it?"

"My power?" Isaac shook his head. "No—I don't know."

He'd never really tried to think that far back, at least not in that direction.

"Was it with your family or with the Undertakers?"

Ah. This was like the way the Old Man handled a test, a sneak attack from the direction you weren't looking.

Isaac had always tried to force the memories of his early childhood to surface. Blood remembered. Blood didn't forget, at least it *shouldn't*, but all his attempts to reach back that far had failed. His own blood was useless to him.

"I don't know," he said. "I can't remember. Any time I try to look that far back, I just can't. It's not there."

"Have you tried walking yourself backward, seeing how close you can get?"

"You mean like sneaking up on it?"

"If you prefer that terminology."

Isaac considered it. It was the Undertaker's approach to the problem. Maybe he could see what he wanted to if he didn't look directly at it, if he came to it gradually.

"We could try talk therapy, working our way through what you do recall. With time we may be able to tease more of it into view."

Isaac nodded.

He liked the idea of finally knowing, of having answers, but time wasn't something he had a lot of.

He had a school to kill, a literal deadline.

What he needed was to get out of here and get back to work before the Old Man came calling—or worse, sent Kenji to do what Isaac hadn't.

"Is Isaac Frost your real name?"

"No," he answered absently, imagining the havoc one of the older boys would cause if they came to the school. They wouldn't care about anyone. They'd simply reach their objective and eliminate anyone who got in their way.

"The Undertaker gave it to me."

Cold as ice, the Old Man had said. *I'll call you Frost. Isaac Frost. Would you like that, Dove?*

"Why Isaac?"

"There's a Bible in the Graveyard, in the chapel where we had our meals. If a boy doesn't have a name the Undertaker picks one from that."

Surely that wasn't some deep secret, but with the Undertaker you never knew what might set him off.

Shepherd scribbled a note and asked, "So you don't have another name?"

"Not that I know of. I've never been called anything else."

There was *Dove,* but he didn't think Shepherd was talking about nicknames. All the boys were a dove until they earned a feather.

Some of them, like Samuel, never would.

"Could you talk to anyone?" Isaac asked. "Anyone who has died?"

Maybe, just maybe, he could say he was sorry.

"Theoretically," Shepherd mused. "But it takes a blood connection for me to bridge the living to the dead. I don't suppose you have something I could work with?"

Isaac shook his head.

He clenched his fists. He wasn't used to all this sitting around, all this talking. He needed to hit something, to stab something.

No wonder the Guardians were so ineffective if this was how they spent their time.

"Are we done? I have a lot of studying to do."

"We can be done." Shepherd nodded and it took a moment for the bits of his face to all align with the motion. "Let me know if you change your mind about contacting your parents."

"I will," Isaac said, standing. "Thanks."

He hurried into the hall and paused.

The yellow lights stretched into the darkness.

He could try again, face the guards again. He'd be better prepared this time, but no, not now. He felt wrung out, like he'd run for miles.

He knew the answer to Shepherd's question.

Of course he wanted to know, maybe even needed to, but he wasn't ready.

Coward, he thought, and he heard it in Kenji's voice.

15

DEATH BY FIELD TRIP WOULD REFLECT POORLY ON THE SCHOOL

Professor Lin opened the door at the end of the hall. She dug her hands into the pockets of her long skirt and asked, "Is everyone ready?"

"If it's not another disaster zone, then yes," Hex said. "Otherwise, I want galoshes."

"It is not," Lin said.

Isaac wouldn't have minded another flood or fire. Other than quick food outings, he hadn't left the school since they'd gone to the Decay. He could use some action.

Still, he couldn't help but ask, "What happens if we say no?"

"You fail the class," the dean said, approaching their group.

She wore high boots and a stiff jacket that had probably come from a military surplus store, the kind some of the older boys in the Graveyard favored.

"Behave, Mr. Frost," she added. "Or did you forget that you're already on probation?"

"Yes, ma'am," he muttered. "I mean, no. I didn't forget."

"Excuse me, Dean?" Ford asked her as she shouldered a long rifle. "Why are you coming with us?"

Isaac didn't know the make, but the gun had an antique style with a hexagonal barrel and a heavy hammer. Intricate patterns were worked into the polished metal.

"In case you need me," she said.

"Why would we need you?" Hex asked. "Where exactly are we going?"

But the dean was already walking through the door. Lin followed.

Isaac exchanged a glance with Vran.

"Should we be worried?"

"I think you're paranoid," Vran said. "Cute, but paranoid."

He followed their teachers with a shrug of his shoulders.

Hex waved her fingers, made a claw of her hand, gathering her magic.

Isaac went after her.

The air tasted like winter, far colder than the forever spring of wherever the school resided.

They'd come out through a half-collapsed barn, the only building in sight. Beer bottles and trash lined the interior, hinting of teenagers who'd come out here to party. Isaac wondered if any of them hadn't made it back.

Isaac winced as something cold pricked the back of his neck.

"Snow," Vran observed, reaching to catch a flake on his palm.

He drifted away from the group, his posture stiff, his expression sad.

Isaac didn't know if he should follow or not.

The cold reminded him of the Graveyard, of the crypts when winter came. They were taught and told to survive anything, including the elements, including sleeping in stone houses with only each other and a few blankets for warmth. Isaac shivered at the memory of the long nights and cold so intense that his teeth clattered.

He hugged himself for warmth and took in the landscape.

There was little cover here, few trees or hills, but at least he didn't see any reason for the dean to have brought her gun.

"Where are we?" he asked.

"You tell me," Lin said.

It didn't look like much, just endless fields and a few trees.

"Hex?" Lin asked. "Professor Lawless tells me you have been practicing forensic magic?"

Hex nodded.

"Why don't you show us what you can find?" Lin asked.

Hex let out a long breath and held up her hands. The other students, who'd fanned out to explore, drifted back toward her. All except Vran. The elf, wearing a black trench coat, the hem in tatters, stood at a distance, stiff as a scarecrow.

Hex made a loop with her thumbs and pointer fingers and peered through it. Isaac wondered what her blood would taste like. Her power wasn't one he could use. Spell craft was just that—a craft. Power like hers was useless without the knowledge or practice to wield it. Still, it wouldn't taste like any other human's. Magic was a rare trait, and it spiked the blood. Every practitioner had a unique scent.

"Why are we here?" Ford asked the dean. "Couldn't you just tell us about it?"

"Some things are better experienced," Lin said. "No matter how well I explain it, it cannot compare to observed experience."

"But it's just grass and mud," Ford said.

"And kind of cold," Daffodil added, huddling against Jack.

The librarian wore a long coat of soft tan wool. Did he even feel the cold? Isaac wondered if he'd chosen it for Daffodil's sake.

"Aren't you exempt from this kind of thing?" Isaac asked him.

"Practical experience isn't the same as reading about something," Jack said.

Hadn't Isaac made that very point to the dean once?

"You weren't at the flood."

"No, I was at the fire. I can take a lot more heat than the rest of you, and smoke doesn't bother me."

Lin cleared her throat to get their attention.

"This is a field exercise," she said. "Use your abilities. Each of you brings something unique to the class. Each of you contributes something."

"What are we looking for?" Daffodil asked.

"The past. I want you to tell me what happened here."

"It's like spooky CSI," Ford suggested.

Lin nodded.

Vran walked through the field, tickling the palms of his hands on the tips of the grass stalks. He stared into the distance, no doubt seeing details or realms Isaac never could.

Ford closed his eyes and cocked his ear toward the trees lining the thin strip of water running alongside the field.

Isaac remembered the screams in the fire.

"Can you talk to them?" he asked.

"The trees? Yeah. Kind of. I mean, I can hear them, but they don't hear me back."

"Have you tried?" Lin asked.

Ford narrowed his eyes like he thought she was mocking him.

"You're here to expand your knowledge, Mr. Ford," the dean said. "Of everything, including yourself. Each of you has a place here, a point."

"All right," he groused. "But no laughing."

Ford lumbered off toward the creek. Isaac had to admit that RCC's approach had some advantages over the Undertakers. They explored more sides of the students' powers, looking beyond combat. Something they found that way, something unexpected, could give them an advantage in battle.

Always surprise your enemy if you can, the Old Man was fond of drilling into them.

Daffodil pulled Jack along by the hand, frowning as she scoured the landscape with her eyes.

Isaac understood. It wasn't like he could bleed a field and taste its memories.

Your eyes can lie, Kenji had said once. They'd gone outside to spar in the dark.

Kenji had struck him, gently, over and over with a staff while Isaac learned to scent his opponent and to listen. It took him hours to go from dodging to deflection to scoring a point.

Isaac closed his eyes and breathed deep.

He tasted loam and recent rain. Despite its pure appearance, the snow that trickled down tasted of plastic and chemicals. Most water on the mortal plane was laced with something acrid that should not be there.

The wind whipped over them, sending all of them closer together.

Isaac shot the dean a dirty look for not telling them to wear heavier clothes. The others weren't like him. They weren't used to tests like this. Vran had frozen in place, his coat billowing around him like a storm cloud. Did he feel the cold at all, or was the garment just for show?

Isaac wondered how the elf would take it if he tried to climb inside the way Daffodil did with Jack.

Isaac couldn't even pretend that there would be some tactical reason for it. He just wanted to.

The wind died down and left behind the taste of blood. Old, faint, but unmistakable.

Isaac couldn't name the flavor.

Crouching, he scooped up a handful of dirt and sniffed it as the clumps fell from his fingers.

There.

Blood and magic, like specks of glitter in a pile of dust.

"A battle," he said. "A lot of people died here."

"Not a battle," Vran said. "A massacre."

"It has been called both," Lin added. "Well done, Frost. Your senses are remarkable. It was forty years ago, but I thought the sheer quantity might leave traces you could detect."

"I can't scry back that far," Hex said, sounding annoyed.

"You're doing better than me," Ford groused, kicking the dirt. "I got nothing."

"Did they talk to you?" Isaac asked.

"Sort of. They're really self-involved. Like dude, I get it, squirrels are the worst. Tell me something useful."

"I can't poison my way into the past," Daffodil said.

"That is why you're a team," the dean said from the edge of their group. "Sometimes, you must rely on each other."

"This is where the elves ended the Christmas War," Lin said. "Though Vran is right. It was not much of a contest."

She waved to indicate the creek.

"The Saurians crossed through freshwater. They made their portals here, intending to gather and march on the nearest mortal town. Who knows what happened next?"

"The elves were waiting," Vran said. "*We* were waiting."

He sat on the ground and picked some half-dead flower. Running it between his fingertips, he crushed it to flakes and powder.

"The King of Swords brought the blizzard. Everything was ice, and Saurians don't do well with the cold. It slowed them, made them easy targets."

"The elves just cut them down?" Daffodil asked.

"It was like a game to them." Vran shrank inside his coat.

Isaac didn't know what to do. He wanted to try and comfort Vran, but didn't know how the elf would take it, especially in front of everyone. Isaac took a few steps that way and stopped.

"The elves . . . we're supposed to revere life," Vran said. "But I think there's something beneath all that, something we try to hide, like an undertow. They could have stopped that day. They could have killed a few of the Saurians as a warning to the others. They could have captured them, but the king sent the cold back through the river, to the Saurian villages. He froze the water. He froze their egg clutches. It was genocide. I don't know if he meant it or if he just got carried away."

Vran trailed off and dropped the naked flower stem.

No wonder the Old Man hated the Guardians so. No wonder he hated the ruling races, if this was how they acted, how they used their power. The Undertakers might kill for payment, but at least they were honest about it. They didn't try to pose as something noble and better than everyone else.

"But that was the old king, right?" Daffodil asked.

"That is correct," Lin said. "The former King of Swords was challenged by his son and was defeated."

"You mean he killed him," Isaac said.

Why did they have to dance around it? All of Lin's lessons about etiquette so often came down to that: a mask for what had really happened.

"He shot him," Vran said. "The prince shot his father with a mortal gun."

"And then he decided to open a school?" Isaac asked.

"Yes," the dean said.

She'd been at the periphery of their conversation, circling and eyeing the horizon. He wondered who she watched for. The Saurians? The elves? The battle had been long ago. Surely, they weren't going to surprise the students now.

The client then. The Old Man wouldn't send the Undertakers against the students. Isaac was already on the inside, but that didn't mean the client wouldn't try to stack the deck with another party.

Shit.

He hadn't thought of that. The Old Man was nervous about the timeline. That could mean other freelancers were in play.

No wonder the dean had brought her gun.

The Decay and the dead goblin had put her on alert.

The others weren't up to fighting assassins. Isaac needed to keep his eyes peeled, to watch the river, to watch his six and stop tracking Vran's every move. He wished he had his knives.

He met the dean's gaze. She didn't say anything, but he got the sense that she knew he knew.

Did she believe that was the point of him being at the school?

It made sense. You caught a thief with a thief. You caught a killer with a killer—with *him*. If he were really one of them, he could help them protect it.

"The new king realized the Guardians were part of the problem," Lin said, continuing her lecture.

"But he killed his father to take the crown," Hex said. "That's hardly the sign of the moral high ground."

Vran shook his head.

"The old king wanted to kill everyone on the mortal plane. He could have done it too. He had to be stopped."

"Bloodlust," Isaac said quietly.

Some of the boys got it. It could be useful, to a point, but the Undertaker tempered it, beat it into shape. They were trained to kill, but only when they were supposed to.

There were whispers in the crypts at night, about the ones who liked it too much, who enjoyed it and killed when they weren't supposed to, who went rogue. Mad Dogs, the Undertaker called them.

He never sent the brothers after them, at least not alone. He went himself and took only the best, the ones like Kenji.

Still, the boys whispered at night about the killers who got away, the ones they never caught. Isaac wondered what it said that these were the ones the boys talked about and not the ones who simply tried to run.

"They all died here?" Daff asked, eyeing the ground like the ghosts of the Saurians might rise and haunt them.

"And on the Other Side, where they had their homes," Lin confirmed.

"It's horrible." Daff cuddled closer to Jack.

"The old King of Swords was a primordial power," Lin said. "His entry into the conflict ensured the Saurian march came to a quick halt, but the price was high."

"Not for him," Vran said. "He didn't pay anything."

"That is not entirely true," Lin said. "The monarchy was nearly absolute, but the will of the client races and their impression of the crown were able to temper his actions from time to time. Actions such as this lessened his sway over them, which allowed his son the opportunity for a smoother transition of power."

Vran scoffed.

"What if he hadn't done it, though?" Shy asked.

He was a blur in the thickening snowfall, an outline Isaac could almost see clearly. He wore a ballcap and a long-sleeved sweatshirt. He was shorter than Isaac, closer to Hex's height.

"Chicago is only about a hundred miles from here," Lin said. "If the Saurians had been allowed to march, they would have exposed their existence to the mortal world, and they would have caused many deaths. That was their intention."

"It's the nuclear question," Jack said. "Does one bomb stop the war and save lives or does it just speed up the slaughter?"

"Even if it stopped a war, it doesn't mean they deserved to be wiped out," Hex said. "The king killed their babies."

"Agreed," Lin said. "And these are the questions we're here to ask. It's also the subject of your next essay."

No one groaned, but the class murmured their discontent.

"This is college. I'll remind you that none of you—well, most of you—don't have to be here. That said, I want you to consider when overwhelming force is appropriate. Is it ever, even in war?"

"It's not the same, though," Isaac mused. "The King of Swords wiped out the Saurians, almost completely. The Allies didn't bomb all of Japan."

He was proud that he could cite something historic.

"The loss of life was still immense, Isaac," Lin said. "Was it justified?"

"I don't know," he admitted.

"That's a good start," Lin said. "We'll spend a little more time here. Write down any observations you have, anything of note, before we move on."

They wandered, in pairs or solo.

Hex wore an especially grumpy demeanor. Isaac didn't know if it stemmed from the moral debate or that her magic hadn't provided the answers she wanted.

Ford stuck to Shy's side, as far as Isaac could tell, while he worked his way toward Vran.

"Why is the dean here?" he asked. "And why does she have a gun?"

"I don't know," Vran said.

"Are they still sending you on missions?"

"No," Vran said. "Why are you asking me about these things?"

Because it was easier than trying to grasp the enormity of Vran's lifespan, that what was ancient history to the rest of them was just his childhood.

Isaac expected Vran to wander off, but he just stood there, as if in challenge, though Isaac could not say to what.

Was he still upset about the goblin? Or was he sad because he'd gotten in trouble too?

He wore his older face. Isaac wondered if his state as a Lost One was like a sickness, if it wore him down and made him cranky from time to time.

Isaac didn't know how to ask, to pierce Vran's defensiveness. He just stood there until the dean announced that it was time to go.

Lin nodded and opened the barn door.

"Where are we going now?" Ford asked.

"You'll see," she said, waving him to step through.

The air changed. It was warmer here, more like summer.

They remained at the river, but a wider and cleaner version. The barn had vanished, as had the smell of toxins. Mud and sweet water filled Isaac's nose.

Balls of dirt bound with sticks lined the bank. They had doors and windows. Smoke rose from their central chimney stalks.

Figures shuffled between them. They kept their distance, not responding to the students' arrival. They were taller than Isaac had expected, taller than Ford. There weren't many of them, maybe just a few dozen total. They were preoccupied with the river and the long, flopping fish they dredged from it.

"Can they see us?" Hex asked. "Should I cast a glamour?"

"No need," Lin said. "They know we're not a threat."

The scene felt dirty and kind of sad. So the Other Side wasn't all magical schools and dinosaurs.

"Why are you showing us this?" Isaac asked.

"What is the purpose of a Guardian?" Lin asked.

He hated it when she answered a question with a question.

"To guard," Hex said. "To protect."

"And yet too often Guardians have been political pawns," Lin said. "We're not the only ones having that discussion. It's happening throughout the planes, especially among the races who make up the council."

"And you are part of that conversation," the dean said.

"Is that why we're not being trained by Guardians?" Daffodil asked.

"The king wants a new breed of Guardian," Lin said. "Your class is intended to act as a break with the past and a bridge to something new."

And not everyone is happy about it, Isaac thought, eyeing the dean's gun.

"Will they make it?" Vran asked, nodding to the village.

"We don't know," Lin said. "The elves are helping. The king is helping, but you cannot restore a species overnight."

Vran opened a door in the air and stepped through.

"He probably wants to be alone," Hex said when Isaac moved to follow.

Isaac shook his head.

"If he did, he would have closed it behind him."

16
SURF'S UP AT THE END OF THE WORLD

Isaac froze in place, letting his eyes adjust to starlight and its gleam on the ocean stretching ahead. Water like a dark void, similar to Vran's eyes, roiled and splashed.

The doorway behind him was a pair of pillars with a lintel, a bit of the marble ruins that dotted the lowest points of the purple hills stretching toward the sea.

The beach sand sparkled silver in the endless starlight. The moon was little help. It hung limned in sunlight, an eclipse.

Vran sat on a rock, staring at the water.

Isaac moved nearer.

"What is this place?" he asked.

"It used to be called Starlight's End," Vran said without looking at him. "I like it here."

"It's beautiful."

Vran scooted to the side, made a little space, and Isaac took it as an invitation.

They studied the sea together, listening to the white-capped waves.

The eclipse seemed permanent, that or it moved so slowly that the light didn't change. Isaac wondered if this place ever saw a sunrise. If it didn't, it suited Vran's style all the more.

Isaac wanted to put his arm around the elf, to pull him close the way he'd seen Jack do with Daffodil, but it was an unfamiliar feeling. Not hot—not cold. It was like standing on the edge of the jump into the Graveyard's pond. He'd gone there many times after what had happened to Samuel. Isaac had teased himself with the idea of leaping in, of seeing how far he'd sink, how long it would take for someone to wonder where he was.

This feeling was a bit like that, like standing on an edge. He liked and did not like it.

"Are you all right?" he asked finally.

"No," Vran said. "It was stupid."

"What was?"

"The war, killing the Saurians. All of it."

"Lin said you were there."

"I was a kid then," Vran said. "And I watched my elders revel in it. They were so eager, so excited, like an outing or a party. Is that how it was for you, living with the Undertaker?"

"No. Killing is just the business. He'd never celebrate it."

"I can't decide if that's worse or not."

"Me either."

"We both ran away," Vran said.

"You left your family?"

"Yes, and then when I got a title, my court started in on the same stuff. *Idiots.*"

"You don't like dumb people, do you?"

"I don't mind dumb people. They can't help it." Vran edged a little farther away. "I don't like smart people who make dumb decisions. They should know better."

"Lin shouldn't have made you go there, made you see that place."

"Yes, she should have. Everyone should see places like that, hear the stories, the history. Maybe then they'd remember. They could see when it was coming and stop it from happening."

"'Those who don't know history are doomed to repeat it'?" Isaac quoted.

"It's so much worse than that." Vran groaned. "Elves *know*. We're immortal. We should remember. We do remember, then we make the same mistakes anyway."

"Maybe people are just people, Vran. Maybe nobody is better than anybody else, no matter how long they live."

"Maybe."

They sat in silence for a while. Isaac's eyes traced one of the black lines down Vran's neck and into the collar of his T-shirt. This one had a dissected heart on it and read *Bad Luck*.

"You're staring," Vran said.

"Yeah."

"Why?"

"I never know how to take you. It's like there are all these versions of you. I'm never quite certain which one I'm meeting."

"It's not hard, Isaac. There's the me who wants to just go back to watching humans and trying to understand them. There's the me who wants to help everyone, and the one who doesn't want to help anybody."

"So why don't you do that? Why be at the school if you don't have to? The Guardians . . . the immortals. Their fight doesn't have to be your fight. It isn't mine."

Vran met his eyes.

"I have to stand for something. We all do, even when they think we don't. I tried not participating or just walking away. I tried just watching. It didn't solve anything."

Isaac didn't know if he should press for more.

A tightness in his chest told him he should ask, but something held him back.

Was this just getting to know someone and becoming friends? Was it something else? He had no way to measure it. His brothers were a constant. They'd always been there. He didn't have to figure them out. He only had to protect them, to earn enough feathers that he'd be ready when Kenji made his move and took over the Graveyard. He understood that.

This was hard, so much harder when the people you met didn't all have the same upbringing, the same background information.

They sat in a calm place, but Isaac did not feel calm. He felt like he was walking on ice, like cracks could open beneath him at any moment. If they swallowed him, this moment, this chance at *something* he couldn't name, would vanish.

"You have to stand for something, Isaac," Vran said, breaking the peace and putting another crack in the ice beneath him. "If you don't, then I . . . I just can't if you don't."

"What do you mean?" Isaac asked. "Can't what?"

"You keep talking about not having principles or taking sides," Vran said. "That it's somebody else's fight, but that's still taking a side. You get that, right?"

"Was that what running away was?" Isaac asked. "For you?"

He barely remembered to add the last part, that he was supposed to have run away from the Undertakers. He could remind Vran of that lie but didn't want to. Surely even the Undertakers couldn't reach him here.

"I used to be like that, you know," Vran continued. "Not caring about anything, or at least I told myself that's how it was."

"What changed?" Isaac asked.

"I grew up. I started caring about one person and it changed everything for me. I started caring about the world."

"Why?"

"Because I saw how he cared." Vran scoffed. "It's like he infected me."

Isaac had to wonder if that was what was happening to him, because the problem wasn't that he didn't care. The problem was that he wasn't who Vran thought he was. He never could be, could never live up to any kind of ideal.

He couldn't run away from the Undertaker. He couldn't hide here forever. There wasn't a way out. Many had tried, and he knew how those stories ended.

"I don't want to be a Guardian, Vran," he said. "I don't want to enforce someone else's idea of right and wrong. I don't want to control other people."

"So what do you want?"

Isaac chewed his lip.

This was getting messy. It felt messy.

"I don't know what I want to be," Isaac said. "But I know I don't want anyone telling me what or how to think. I just want to be free."

Saying it aloud felt like a confession, and it hurt more than a lie would have.

"Don't we all?"

"Why can't you be?" Isaac asked. "Look at this place. You can go anywhere, literally, travel to any world you want."

"No, I can't."

"Why not?"

"Because the people I care about, and the people who care about me, aren't just anywhere. They're back there, at the school and in the mortal world."

Isaac thought of Kenji, of how he'd been the one to check on Isaac when he'd broken his arm, bringing him food when he'd sulked in his crypt.

"I think I can understand that," he said. "They're your family."

"Yes," Vran said. "The one I chose."

They sat in uncomfortable silence for a while longer.

"The other ones . . . the sea elves. They aren't good people, are they?"

"No," Vran said. "They're not."

"Then I'm lucky that you are."

"You don't know that. You don't know the whole story, my whole story."

"I'd like to," Isaac said quietly, because even though there wasn't anyone else around, it felt like another confession.

His skin felt very tight. The sound of the waves was distant now. The only real sound was the blood in his ears, the rush of it in his veins.

"I could show you," Vran whispered.

Isaac didn't have to ask what he meant. He could scent the blood on the air the instant Vran bit his lip. Isaac could taste that strange swirling *something* that he'd first sensed just before they'd met, the wild thing always beneath the surface when Vran was near him.

Now he was offering to show Isaac everything, his memories, his past, in a drop of blood and a kiss, a real kiss.

Isaac had wondered about this since that night. He'd thought about it at least once a day, usually in class, when he should have been taking notes or plotting how to find the school's heart.

All he had to do was lean in, press his mouth to Vran's, and let the memories take him in a flood. He'd know. He'd *know* Vran. No one had ever offered this to him, trusted him like this. Every taste he'd won from a brother had been in combat, stolen when he'd had the chance to get the upper hand.

Isaac had the crazy idea that they could run, together. Maybe, just maybe, they'd make it, but Vran wouldn't go. He was bound to the people he cared about.

It was all there, a kiss away—and Isaac wasn't ready.

Isaac couldn't do the same, couldn't offer himself like that. He wasn't who Vran thought he was. He was a liar.

Isaac let out a shaky breath. He tried to steady his voice when he said, "We should get back."

17
BRO CODE

Isaac threw himself onto his bed after class.

He couldn't get the look on Vran's face out of his head. It hadn't been just disappointment. He'd hurt Vran, and realizing it put something in his chest, something hard and spiky that he didn't have a name for.

He groaned. This was stupid.

None of it—the school, the students—was supposed to matter.

He needed to get the job done and get out of here. He needed to get down to the basement, face whatever tortures the spirits threw at him, and continue his search for the school's heart. He picked himself up to do just that and started when a knock sounded at the door.

Isaac swung it open to find Ford standing on the other side. The jock wore a glamour to hide his wooden half.

Isaac decided he preferred Ford without his disguise.

"I'm going for pizza. Do you want some pizza?"

"Why are you asking me?" Isaac asked.

"Because I think you had a fight with your boyfriend and pizza might help."

"Vran's not my . . ."

Was Vran his boyfriend? What would that require? Someone had to ask someone? Was that what he wanted?

Shit, he was bad at this. Isaac truly had no idea what he was doing.

"I don't know what he is."

Ford crossed his massive arms over his chest.

"Well, he's something to you and you're sulking. Pizza always helps, so . . . pizza? I'll buy."

Isaac nodded.

He could tell himself that it would be good for the mission to garner sympathy and get closer to another student, but the truth was that Isaac was hungry. Eating might take his mind off that moment by the ocean and the purple islands, which would be a bonus.

"How did you know?" Isaac asked, pulling on his jacket and following Ford into the hallway.

"That you liked Vran?" Ford laughed. "You two always watch each other, especially when you don't think the other knows about it. That and the way you chased after him on the field trip."

Isaac felt himself warm.

"No, I mean that I might need . . ."

"Pizza?" Ford asked. "You came back alone and were upset. At least Jack thought so. He told Daff. She told Hex. Hex told me."

Isaac did not like that his emotions were so obvious to them. He was slipping. He hadn't even noticed them watching him.

"It's a small class," Ford said with a shrug. "There's not much else to talk about and you guys are the topic du jour."

Isaac flushed a little as Ford paused at a certain door.

"We'd like to go for pizza, please," he said.

He opened it and they stepped through onto a street lit by yellow lamps.

The air smelled of fresh rain and garbage. Buildings in the distance, towers of glass and steel, blotted out the night, but here everything was shorter, made of old brick.

"Where are we?" Isaac asked.

He'd never get used to the way the school dropped them in different places at different times. Day—night—it all ran together. At least the Graveyard was consistent.

"Chicago," Ford said, looking both ways before crossing the quiet street.

"Does the door matter?" Isaac asked.

"What do you mean?"

"We passed several before you picked one."

"I don't know if they do," Ford admitted. "But I like to use different ones for different things. That's the pizza door."

"Why?"

"I dunno. It just feels like the pizza door."

Isaac thought back to when he'd tasted Ford's blood. He hadn't tried to read any of the troll's memories, but he could remember his senses, the way the trees had spoken to him. Maybe Ford could hear the school, had a better sense of its nature.

"What's behind it when it doesn't lead to pizza?"

"With RCC, who knows?" Ford asked. "A broom closet? A mad scientist's lab? Maybe it's the dinosaur locker room."

"Dinosaur locker room?"

"You know, where they hang out when they're not in the gym."

He led Isaac into a dark cavern of a restaurant and past a sign that said *Seat Yourself.*

They settled into a booth.

The place, rough stone walls and deep-red carpet, reminded Isaac of the big house at the Graveyard. This smelled better though, with odors from the kitchen wafting through. His stomach grumbled.

"Pepperoni?" Ford asked, looking at the menu on the plastic table tent.

"Sure."

Isaac wasn't picky.

Pizza had been a rare treat, something they'd gotten with Kenji on their forays into the mortal realm. Samuel had said it was a smart food for them, because you could eat it with one hand and fight with the other. Kenji had laughed and agreed. It had been a rare, original insight.

Isaac realized that he'd missed this, eating with someone, with his brothers.

"You didn't invite the others?"

"I tried to ask Shy, but couldn't find him," Ford said. "I didn't ask the girls. I think they might be pissed at you."

"Why?"

"Vran's kind of everyone's little brother," Ford said with a shrug. "Which is funny, since he's older than all of us put together. They're protective of him."

"And you're not?"

"Sure I am," Ford said. "But I thought you could use some pizza."

Isaac smiled.

"I could. Thanks."

Ford nodded.

A waitress came and took their order without any of the usual fake friendliness so many servers exuded. Isaac appreciated the honesty of that.

"I like this place," he said.

"Me too," Ford said, taking a sip from the water the waitress had left. "It's funny how water tastes different everywhere you go."

"Does that mean they don't like me?" Isaac asked. "The girls?"

"It just means they're taking his side," Ford said with a long draw from his straw. "They know him better."

"No. They like him better."

He got it. He liked Vran too, but now he didn't see a way back to the easy place they'd been before. He'd rejected a precious gift—Vran's memories, his past.

He couldn't offer the same, and he didn't want to.

It would mean telling Vran the truth, all of the truth, and Isaac wasn't ready for that. He thought back to his conversation with Shepherd, and how he'd run away from the chance to look back, to know about his parents.

"What did you guys fight about anyway? Was he mad that you went after him?"

Isaac didn't know how to answer that. How did he explain? Vran liked his secrets. It wouldn't do Isaac any favors to share anything Vran had told him.

"I don't know. Do you have anyone? Do you ever fight?"

"Girls aren't exactly lining up," Ford said. "Not like they were before I sprouted bark. Which is sad really, I can bench like five hundred pounds now."

He flexed a massive arm, but Isaac didn't miss that his smile had dimmed.

"I'm sorry."

"It's okay, I mean, mostly," Ford muttered. "The school's all right, you know? It's just not the college experience anyone thought I'd be having, me especially."

"I never thought I'd go to school at all."

"No?"

"No."

He'd been trained to kill, trained and trained, but the Old Man hadn't sent him on a job before this one. He'd held Isaac back.

I don't need a raven for this job. I need a dove.

Had that been it? Had he just been waiting for the right job or was there another reason?

"How'd you get into the school?" Isaac asked. "Was it like the others? I know Daff accidently poisoned her prom date."

"Nothing dramatic like that. I was sleeping and I woke up with all these cramps, like I'd worked out really hard without stretching. I went to wash my face and when I checked the mirror, well . . . I'd hulked out." Ford wiped a hand down the half of his body covered by the glamour. "At least half of me had. My parents freaked out and pulled me out of school. They told everyone I was in a car wreck and homeschooled me for the rest of my senior year. They were so sad when it happened, when I changed."

"Why?"

Ford paused so the waitress could drop off their food. She put the pizza on a little wire stand so it floated over the table. It smelled so good. Isaac watched Ford grab a piece.

He continued his story between bites while Isaac ate uninterrupted. "They had their own plans for my life. They acted like I'd died, or like I'd been crippled. They were so relieved when the dean came knocking and offered me a place at RCC."

"Do you know why it happened?"

"Something about recessive genes," Ford said. "Somewhere way back I had a troll in the family tree. I guess. Science stuff is more Jack or Hex's department. And it's not like I can fix it."

"Would you want to?" Isaac asked. "I mean, be normal if you could?"

Ford's glamoured brows furrowed as he considered the question.

"I don't think so," he decided. "It's part of me, and even if I could, it's not like I can go back to how it was. High school's over and my parents showed their ass."

He sank a bit and chose another slice.

"I don't know what to say," Isaac said.

"You don't have to say anything. It is how it is."

The hot food was melting some of the hardness in Isaac's stomach.

He'd never considered that being an orphan might be easier.

He couldn't imagine wanting to be rid of your kid, especially a kid like Ford. He was a good guy. Nobody had a problem with him. Isaac couldn't imagine anyone having a reason to, and he couldn't imagine someone putting out that light.

"Anyway, I don't date anymore," Ford said. "I don't think it's the same though, dating girls and guys, especially when the guy's, you know."

Ford held an upraised finger to each side of his head.

"Yeah . . ." Isaac agreed.

He wasn't sure being an elf had anything to do with it. The problem was Isaac. He wasn't who he said he was, and there wasn't any way to tell that to Vran.

They drifted into an awkward silence as they ate. Isaac was having a lot of those lately.

He felt like quicksand, dragging down the mood, like he'd drained the life from the half troll.

"Thanks for getting me out of my room. I'm not good on my own," he said, meaning it.

It was almost funny. As assassins, they worked alone. He was trained for that, but life—when there wasn't a job—that was social. They sparred and argued and took care of each other, except for when they didn't.

Isaac didn't like being by himself, even if he wasn't any good at connecting with others.

"Did you have a lot of friends in high school?" Isaac asked.

"Yeah, especially on the football team."

It made sense why Ford had sought him out. He must be lonely too.

"What do you do when you're not studying?" Isaac asked.

Ford brightened again, smiling a little too quickly for the glamour to keep up. For a moment, his cheek was made of bark and his one eye sparked green.

"Video games. I didn't leave my room for a week when Jack figured out how to get me an Internet connection. Has he hooked you up yet?"

"No. I've never . . . I've seen the games, you know, in store windows."

Ford's eyes widened.

"Dude. Seriously?"

Isaac nodded.

"Didn't you grow up with nothing but boys?"

"Yeah," Isaac said.

"Man, that's like child abuse." Ford straightened and shot a dazzling smile at the waitress. Isaac could see how he'd have no trouble getting dates, but he appeared to have adjusted, that he liked who he'd become.

She stalked over to them, her expression a little warmer than before.

"Can we get another pizza to go?" Ford asked. "A large supreme along with some napkins and stuff?"

"Sure," she said.

It came and Ford paid.

He led Isaac back outside, holding the box tight in both hands, the little bag with the plasticware and napkins looped over his wrist. The wind cut through them.

"This way," Ford said.

The alley could have been any of the ones Isaac had slept in, and he eyed it warily.

It would not help his mission for one of his little brothers to spot him, especially if they were to name him or beg for help.

Isaac didn't see anyone but would have sworn he felt eyes on them.

He tensed, watching the shadows as Ford placed the pizza at the door to a zipped-up tent.

"I'm leaving a pizza," he called. "It's hot."

"What kind?" a voice called back after some rustling.

"Supreme. I hope that's okay."

"Sweet," the woman called back.

Isaac heard the zipper opening as they retreated.

"You do this a lot?" Isaac asked.

"Yeah."

A whole pizza. Free.

Isaac tried to imagine what it would have meant during one of his field trips. He tried to picture how his brothers would take it, alone and scared in the world.

Ford led him away, back toward the door they'd come through.

"Now what?"

"Now it's time for *Madden*," Ford said, putting an arm around Isaac's shoulders and hugging him close for a moment. "You have a lot of catching up to do."

18

SPAM FROM BEYOND THE GRAVE

Isaac burst through the office door and closed it behind him.

"I want to know," he said.

"And a good morning to you too, Mr. Frost," Shepherd said.

"Sorry."

He didn't really mean it.

"Why the sudden change of heart?" the demon asked. He turned his office chair back and forth.

"It's not really that sudden," Isaac said, reaching to scratch the back of his head. "It's been weighing on me since we talked about it."

Shepherd hummed.

"They might not be easy answers," he said. "You might not like what you find."

"I know."

"So why the urgency? Why now?"

Isaac took a breath and tried not to look at the empty steel table where the goblin's body no longer lay. Only the faintest trace of blood in the air told him the corpse had ever been there.

"It's just . . . I think it's time. I don't want to run away from it anymore. It's like I've been carrying this thing, this weight, and I wasn't even really aware of it. It didn't bother me or feel heavy before. Now it does."

"Your time at the school is changing you," Shepherd mused. "You're growing up, or at least outgrowing some of the defenses you arrived with."

"That doesn't sound like a good thing," Isaac said.

Defenses kept you safe.

"Oh, but it is," Shepherd said, leaning forward. "We develop defense mechanisms because we need them, but when we outgrow them, they hang around, like old land mines, and sometimes they hurt us. Sometimes they cause us to hurt others."

Isaac thought of the beach at the end of the world and grimaced.

The demon took a sip from his teacup.

"Is that empty?" Isaac asked.

Shepherd frowned.

"I was hoping you would not notice."

"Then why do it?"

"To make myself more relatable. Is it working?"

Isaac shrugged.

"Do you think you're ready to let go of some of your defense mechanisms, Isaac?"

"Sure," he said, though he wasn't certain they were the problem.

The problem was that he liked a guy, and talking to Ford had solidified what Isaac already knew. Isaac needed to know where he came from before he could trust Vran or anyone else to tell him about their past. They had an advantage he didn't. They knew about their families.

It was a blind spot, something that could creep up on him if he let it, and he'd already had too many surprises since he'd arrived at the school.

"What does it take?"

"Nothing you're unfamiliar with, just a little blood. Do you want to do it now?"

"Yes, please."

If he didn't commit and get it over with, he might chicken out.

"Give me your hand."

Isaac reached out.

He was used to cutting himself. He was used to cutting others, but it was different to have someone else draw his blood.

He expected a knife or ritualistic-looking dagger, but Shepherd simply pricked Isaac's fingertip with a pin and squeezed a drop into his palm.

"That's it?" Isaac asked.

"That's it. The magic is sympathetic. It doesn't take much to make the connection."

Shepherd rubbed his palms together.

He didn't close his eyes, but Isaac wished he had.

They filled with the same light that glowed in the cracks of his skin. Images flickered there, skulls mostly, though occasionally Isaac saw faces. He couldn't look away.

No one familiar came into view, which was a relief. He did not want to see the dead goblin. He did not want to see Samuel.

Several moments passed and Shepherd snapped out of whatever trance he'd been in.

"There's no one there, Isaac," he said. "I'm sorry."

"I don't understand."

Shepherd sighed.

"I'm saying that either your parents are still alive or they've been dead too long for me to reach them."

"Do you need more blood? Something else?"

"No. That was enough. They're simply not there."

"You're wrong," he said. "You have to be."

Shepherd shook his head.

"I do not know much, Isaac Frost, but I know death. If their spirits had passed through in any recent time, I would be able to summon them. Therefore, they must be alive or they died long ago."

"I—I—" Isaac stammered.

"There is someone close," Shepherd said. "Not a relative I think, but . . . a friend? They're trying to reach you."

"No," Isaac said. "I don't want to talk to him."

"I thought you wanted to know about your past."

"He doesn't have anything to do with my family." Isaac stood up. "I think that's enough for today."

He walked out of Shepherd's office.

"Set an appointment next time!" Shepherd called after him. "I'm a very busy thing, you know."

Isaac didn't bother to respond.

He could try to seek the heart again, but no. He needed other answers.

Marching upward, he found his room, shut the door behind him, and pressed his back against it.

He had to know. He had to buy time; he also had to approach this with care. The Old Man did not like being questioned, and he wouldn't like Isaac demanding answers when he hadn't brought results.

Letting his breath even out, Isaac sat, closed his eyes, and put his finger to his mouth. He bit, pulling another drop from the finger Shepherd had pricked.

Vran could go anywhere, walk between worlds. Isaac could only travel here and, even then, only in spirit and for a little while.

The Graveyard came into focus as it pulled him toward it. It was hazy, less clear than the last time. Perhaps time away was weakening his connection to the place. Perhaps that was just wishful thinking.

The buildings lay ringed in fog, hidden, which wasn't unusual. Isaac approached slowly, trying to note details, to see it as an outsider might. It was, in many ways, just as much of a school as RCC, though less structured and more focused at the same time.

They didn't attend classes, didn't have a bell, but they gathered for lessons. In the distance, he could see rows of his brothers practicing their fighting forms or pairing off to spar. Something in Isaac's chest pulled tight. Yeah, part of him missed this. Part of him still belonged here.

"What's taking so long?" the Old Man demanded without any other greeting.

Isaac didn't start. He was used to the Undertaker sneaking up on him. It did bother him that he hadn't seen it coming.

"There are defenses," Isaac said. "A maze. Demons. *Actual* demons."

"Are you giving me excuses, boy?"

This was the tone he used when punishment was coming, usually a beating or a snipe hunt through the grounds, a miserable run to hopefully avoid his brothers, who had to try their best to find him. Getting caught was humiliating, and came with a beating. Failing to catch him meant missing a meal.

"No sir. They're *trials*, but I'm getting through them."

"Then why are you here?"

"They're asking a lot of questions. I need answers to keep my cover."

That was the best lie Isaac could come up with. It was also the best kind, the sort that mixed the truth in.

"What sort of questions?"

"About where I come from."

The Undertaker straightened. Made taller by his top hat, he loomed.

"You come from here."

"I mean about Phages, about my parents."

The Old Man's anger drained away. He let out a long, sympathetic sigh.

"Come inside, Dove," he said, gently nodding toward the chapel.

The largest of the buildings, where they had their inside lessons, their meals, and sometimes slept, huddled together, when the winter became too strong for even them to survive.

The chapel was empty as they entered. He read the sign hanging over the tables where they ate.

No family but killers. No memories of the dead.

Isaac thought back to his conversation with Shepherd.

Speaking to the Old Man was like that, navigating defenses. You never knew when your steps would lead to kindness or an explosion. That they'd gone into the chapel was a good sign. It meant the Undertaker was feeling fatherly. He was often gentler in the chapel and brought them there for any talk he considered delicate.

The Undertaker settled onto one of the long wooden benches at the tables where they ate and gestured for Isaac to sit across from him.

The place still smelled of the eggs and potatoes the boys cooked each morning for breakfast in the massive pots and pans that filled the kitchen.

"What do you need to know?" the Undertaker asked.

"Are my parents still alive?"

The Old Man regarded Isaac for a moment.

"What does it matter? They didn't want you. They traded you away. We want you. This is your family. What kind of Guardians are they training there?"

"Traded?"

"A life for a life, Dove. That's the deal I offer certain clients. They could have paid another way but they chose to give you to me."

The Old Man had a point, unless one lie led to another.

The Graveyard was home, the only home Isaac knew.

The hard part was that he couldn't imagine where else he'd go. The school wouldn't want him once they knew why he'd come there, but maybe, just maybe, he had a home out there, a family.

What would it be like, to show up at their door, an adult, fully formed? Would they look at him the way Hex and Daff did, with suspicion? He'd been trained to kill. Who would want a son like that?

"If this is the kind of nonsense they're teaching, then maybe we should leave them be," the Undertaker said. "They'll bring themselves down with this sort of weakness. Are you even sparring?"

"Not really. They aren't focusing on it, not like we do."

"That will make fighting them easier, when it comes to that."

"Is that what the client wants? I thought we were only supposed to take down the school."

"That's the contract, for now, but if they're training Guardians, then we'll be fighting them soon enough."

"But *why*?"

Isaac paused. It had just slipped out. He wasn't to ask questions.

He expected the Old Man to strike him or at least shout, but what he said was, "Because the elves have a new king. The old one only cared about the immortals, but this one is an idealist. He's butting in, training mortal Guardians. The old one ignored us. This one will come for us eventually."

"Is there a client?" Isaac asked and knew he'd gone too far.

The Old Man's eyes went cold, stony.

"Get it done, and learn everything you can."

"Yes, sir," Isaac said. "But . . . my parents? What do I tell them?"

"Tell them your parents are dead," the Undertaker said. He eyed the window and the rows of graves outside. "That's the best and easiest thing."

But was it true?

19
LET'S GO PUNCH SOMETHING

Isaac couldn't sleep. His conversation with the Undertaker hadn't given him nearly enough answers. It certainly hadn't helped with what he most wanted to know. The only thing he'd really gained was some insight into the Old Man's motivations. He wanted dirt on the Guardians. He expected to fight them someday, and there probably wasn't a client.

It was a change, one that scared Isaac. Part of the Undertakers' survival was their anonymity, that they struck from the shadows. If his brothers went head-to-head with the Guardians, they might be exposed. He wondered how many cells lay beneath the school. He wondered about the fate of the inmates he hadn't seen or sensed, and he thought of the danger if Argent gave the Graveyard her full attention.

Isaac dressed and headed into the halls.

The school felt different, more settled, even if the emerald twilight never changed. Maybe it slept when the students did.

The lights were on in the library.

"Isaac?" Jack asked, looking up from a laptop. "What time is it?"

"Late. Do you mind if I try to look something up?"

"Not at all," the metal man said. He looked as he usually did, a sweater vest and bow tie, with a little pin of blue, pink and white stripes on his vest. "What are you looking for?"

"I need to know about Phages, where we come from. How we work. That sort of thing."

"May I ask why?"

"It's for Lawless's class project."

For once, lying wouldn't be easier.

It was a relief, actually. Lies piled up. They were hard to keep track of. He already had too many things to keep track of.

"But it's not just about that."

Jack raised a copper eyebrow.

"I don't know anything about my family," Isaac said. "I thought they were all dead, that I was an orphan, but now I'm not sure."

"Does this have anything to do with the Guardians' investigation into the goblins?"

"You know about that?"

"It's all one network." Jack gestured at the computers.

"Yes, I mean, if someone is draining magical blood, it makes sense that it might have something to do with Phages, with people like me."

Jack considered what Isaac had said, had confessed.

"You have the opposite problem that I did."

"How so?"

Jack smiled.

"I always knew who I was. I just didn't get to be him until I got here."

Isaac didn't know what to say, so he nodded.

"We're lucky," Jack said, leading Isaac to one of the computer desks and gesturing for him to sit, "that there's a place like this, somewhere we belong."

Isaac scoffed and tapped the space bar on the keyboard to wake the machine up.

"You don't think you belong here?"

"I didn't choose to come here. The queen brought me in. She *arrested* me."

Just because he had made sure it happened didn't mean there wasn't some truth to it.

"You haven't exactly made any daring escape attempts," Jack mused, looking back at the screen.

Isaac watched his reflection scowl in the monitor.

He shouldn't have said anything. He should have pretended he was thrilled by his sentence at the school, but the truth was, it grated. It wasn't the students, or even the classes, though he could have done without the homework.

It was, he decided, the mask. Pretending, lying, was getting old.

What he'd said to Shepherd was true. The weight got heavier the more he became aware of it.

"Nothing," Isaac said, looking at the search results.

"Can I drive?" Jack gestured at the keyboard when Isaac didn't respond.

"Sure."

Isaac leaped from the chair.

The librarian sat and pressed his fingers to the keyboard. He didn't type, but some of the wires in his hands and forearms brightened to canary yellow.

The screen flickered, pages scrolling, information sorting.

"There isn't much," Jack said, pushing back from the screen.

A few links were left.

Isaac had known it wouldn't be as easy, that there wouldn't be pictures of his parents looking sad and forlorn, yearning for the baby they'd sold, but he'd hoped for more.

Then again, why would they be looking for him? He hadn't even thought to try and find them, not until now. He'd been content with what the Undertaker had told him and they'd gotten whatever it was they'd wanted, whoever they'd wanted, dead.

"I'm sorry, Isaac," Jack said. "I don't see any references to a Phage home plane or any kind of settlement."

Isaac peered at the screen.

"What is there?"

"Most of it you already know."

Jack stood up and gestured for Isaac to sit.

"But for what it's worth, blood isn't everything."

"Easy for you to say . . ."

He was a Phage. Blood meant everything.

Isaac read what there was and left the library.

He didn't want to read anymore. He didn't want to study or lie in his bed looking at the ceiling. He wondered if Vran were still mad at him and if he could go find out.

Isaac turned a corner and ran into Hex.

"What are you doing up?" she demanded.

Several tools and rolled-up pieces of paper jutted from her overstuffed backpack.

"Couldn't sleep." He pointed a finger at her gear. "You?"

"I'm working on my project for Lawless."

"At . . . whatever time it is?"

Hex shrugged.

"Might as well start the day early." She narrowed her eyes. "You know, you're supposed to be helping me with this."

"Happy to," Isaac said. "Like I said, can't sleep."

"Here."

She thrust the backpack at him.

Isaac took it, if only to hopefully win back a little ground with her.

"So what's the plan again?" he asked.

"I'm going to measure the school's boundaries and its rate of change."

"And you need me to carry the backpack?" he asked.

"Partly. I also need someone to keep the geese away when we're in the courtyard. Think your lethal combat skills can handle that?"

"Probably."

"You don't have your knives."

He shrugged.

"I'll get creative. What's first?"

"I want to look at one of the outer walls."

She started walking and Isaac followed. It beat lying in his bed and thinking about everything until it was time for class.

"Does the temperature ever change?" he asked when they'd entered the courtyard.

Hex hummed.

"Good question. I don't think it does. What made you think of that?"

"The place where I was raised has seasons, but barely. I was wondering if it or the school were closer to the mortal world. It's fall there, but this feels more like spring."

"The Spirit Realm changes. It is quite volatile at times. The Watchtowers, however, are anchored in the mortal plane, and usually show less variance. This pocket plane of yours is then also likely anchored in a similar fashion. Perhaps a comparison of it to the Spirit Realm should have been your project."

"Maybe."

He certainly wasn't getting anywhere with the history of the Phages.

The geese kept their distance as Hex stopped in front of one of the outer walls. Isaac scanned the shape of the keep and tried to decide if his room was somewhere in the shifting stones and emerald light binding it all together.

"Why is it a castle?" he asked.

"Huh?"

"I mean, I get the whole magic school vibe, but the mortal anchors are modern or at least modernish, and most of the classrooms don't feel like a monastery or anything like that."

"Ask the elves. They chose the anchor points."

"There's more than one?"

"Yes." She gestured for the pack and he handed it over. "Liberty House in Oklahoma is the main one. They built the tower there, but there are anchors everywhere."

"What are we supposed to do?" He nodded up at the wobbling wall.

"I'm going to mark the stones." Hex took a grease pencil from her kit. "You keep watch."

"Okay."

Isaac reached out to touch the wall, expecting cold, but the stones felt warm. He gave one a gentle push, and the wall bowed inward like it was made of rubber.

Why a castle? Because it was defensible, unless there were massive holes in its walls.

RCC was unstable enough that if someone attacked the school, they'd have no trouble breaking through.

Hex moved to the outer wall and began scratching letters and numbers on the stones surrounding an especially bright patch of green.

They weren't even, not like bricks. Some were jagged, others smooth.

"Are you measuring their shapes too?"

"Why?"

"I think they change," he said. "These stones are irregular, but the ones in the keep are uniform."

Hex nodded and started taking pictures with her phone as she walked around the side of the tower.

Isaac squinted.

"They get more uniform the further they are from the glow."

"You're right, Frost. I guess those senses of yours are good for something besides murder."

One of the surly, glowing waterfowl waddled nearer.

Isaac glared at it.

Stabbing might be out, but a swift kick would do the trick if it came to that. Punting one of the birds would certainly vent some of his frustration.

"I'll see if Daff has noticed it," Hex said. "She's trying to measure time. I'm hoping we can figure out the rate of change when we compare results."

Isaac almost quipped that yeah, he'd been there when they'd told him what they'd chosen as projects, but he remembered that he was trying to play nice.

"Whose idea was it to put a school in a Watchtower anyway?"

"The king's," Hex said. "He combined it with the rebuilding of the eastern tower."

"That's got to be why it's so unstable, right?" Isaac asked. He pushed a section of the wall and watched the bricks float out, then back into place.

"Yes. The magic is still settling into place."

Hex watched the bricks spin and slowly drift back into position.

"But not all of it," Isaac said. "The floors don't do that."

He stomped.

"Neither does the ground."

He was more than a little worried that the base of the walls fluctuated. It wouldn't take much to collapse them.

We'll be fighting them soon enough.

"That's the question, what makes RCC special?" Hex made a note in her journal, a black-and-white book covered in numbers and notes. "There are other Watchtowers and other magical points of interest, but they don't work like the school."

"Because it's new?" Isaac wondered. He grabbed one of the stones and held it. It didn't fight too hard, but it pulled at his grip, as if wanting to get back into position.

"Possibly," she conceded. "We're missing something."

He let the stone go and it swam through the air, wobbling its way back into place.

"The professors don't know?"

"I'm not even sure the royals know," Hex said. "But I'm determined to find out."

"Why? I mean, it's interesting, but if even Lawless doesn't know . . ."

"They built this place out of a crumbling building and a fount of transplanar magic. Half the time it's more like a moody teenager than a building."

"Growing pains," Isaac said, thinking of how some of his brothers could get, how he'd been, during those years.

"Perhaps," Hex considered. He could almost see the calculations running through her head.

The school itself never felt unfriendly, just the guards in the labyrinth, but Isaac had to wonder what would happen if it sensed his purpose. What would happen if it had a resentful mood swing?

"It has to be measurable."

Hex counted and took more notes.

"Why? I thought magic was all willpower and chaos. You know, like how Vran does it."

"Maybe for him, but for me it's not that different from science or math. It's still willpower, but it needs focus, channels. That tells me that it can be measured, that it's not all chaos."

"How did you get here?"

"Why do you want to know?"

Isaac shrugged.

"I've asked everyone else. Well, almost everyone. I can never find Shy."

"I don't think he even bothers with class most of the time," Hex said.

"And it's only fair. You all know how I got here."

Hex paused for a moment.

"I have a son, Langston. I was trying to complete some of my schoolwork, and he wouldn't stop crying. I kept thinking that I just needed a moment, some quiet. My head was killing me. Then it felt like something snapped and . . . silence. I'd stopped time. It had frozen. Nothing was moving. Nobody was moving, including Langston. I panicked, worried that it wouldn't start again, that he wouldn't start again."

"That's terrifying," Isaac said, because it was. "How'd you escape it?"

"I realized that the formula I'd been writing had something to do with it. I read my notes and had no idea what I'd written. I'd been working on the proof, trying to solve it. I erased what I'd written and time started moving again. The Guardians brought me in later that day."

"So, you're dangerous too. That's why you're here."

Hex scoffed.

"I want to be here, Frost. I get to study things nobody back home even knows exist. This is where I belong."

"So I'm the only inmate?"

"You keep making comments like that, but they don't exactly keep you in handcuffs. You're not stupid. You don't have to spend so much time proving to us that you aren't. I think your real problem is you don't know what you want."

"Maybe not," he agreed. "Was Langston okay, after time started again?"

"Yes, though he stopped crying. He knew something had happened. That's another reason to be here, to learn what I need to in case he has the same abilities."

Isaac nodded, but he was thinking about how the more he talked to the students, the more he heard how much they needed this place.

He had to wonder if he could really do it, if he could take it away from them. If he didn't, the Undertaker wouldn't hesitate to send someone who would, someone who may not care about what happened to whoever got in their way.

He was starting to think that the best chance they had was for him to finish the job himself, but then he'd be the one to take away the home they'd found.

"We can go," Hex said, snapping him out of his thoughts. "I want to check these measurements against Daffodil's notes."

"What exactly are you trying to find, anyway?" he asked, lifting the backpack.

"The school, as a Watchtower, might be its own little plane, like a pocket dimension. I want to prove that time and space warp the closer you get to it."

"You think time moves differently here?"

"I suspect that we'll find the Watchtower is anchored closer to the mortal plane so time moves closer to what we're used to, that there's not as much slippage as, say, in Alfheimr."

"But a pocket plane *could* have a time difference?"

"Yeah," Hex said, looking back at him as they left the school. "Why do you ask? You look worried."

"Not worried," he said. "Just thinking."

"And pretty hard judging by your frown. About what?"

"My project," he said. "And about how long."

"For who?"

"If someone were lost, how much time would pass for their family, for the people they left behind?"

"There's a theory of an axis, that time and space turn on it throughout all of the planes." Hex's brown eyes narrowed in thought as she paused. "If your pocket plane was far from the center, time might be completely distorted."

"And if they grew up somewhere like that? What if it was years, or a couple of decades?"

"I don't know. I'm not a physicist. It's quite likely that time in their home plane moved at a completely different rate. When I froze time,

I stepped outside of it, but my heart was still beating. I was still living. I suspect that if I'd stayed there a year I'd have come back a year older. We know that some planes change the deeper you go. A human who left the edge of them for even a few days might return to earth centuries later, like travelers in a spaceship moving past the speed of light."

Isaac squeezed his eyes shut and let out a long breath.

"What's this about, Frost? You look rattled."

He let out a long breath.

"Maybe that's it then."

"Maybe what's what?" she asked.

"Maybe the reason I can't find any other Phages is because I was raised in a pocket plane."

"Oh," Hex said.

Understanding dawned and with it something he'd never expected to see from her, a flicker of pity.

Maybe the Graveyard was so far away that centuries had passed.

Maybe the Undertaker hadn't been lying.

Maybe the Phages, including his parents, had been dead so long that even Shepherd couldn't find them.

20
I FEEL PRETTY

Lin finished her lecture. Isaac had tried to pay attention, he really had, but he continued to strain at the endless bits of history and how they connected to elven etiquette and legal protocol.

He liked the debates about the Guardians better. They made his head hurt, but not in a bad way.

This was all far more boring, but he snapped to attention when Lin said, "I'll remind you that the ball is tonight, and that you'll be representing the school. We'll leave through the courtyard gate at the sixth bell. Be prompt."

Everyone stood and packed their books.

Isaac faced Vran, mouth open to say something, but the elf fled before he could get a word out.

"That's still not going so great, huh?" Ford asked.

"No."

Vran remained distant, and he'd made it clear that he really didn't want to talk to Isaac.

The most he'd give was a nod in greeting. Vran always wore the hood of his sweatshirt up, hiding his hair and most of his face. He spent their shared classes taking notes in the spiraling Elvish language and drawing sharks in the edges of his pages. Sometimes the sharks were eating people, and he suspected the spiky-haired stick figure was meant to be him.

"So, are you ready to party at elf prom?" Ford asked.

Isaac hadn't really thought about it. It didn't hold much appeal, especially if Vran wasn't speaking to him.

"What are you wearing?" Ford asked.

"I don't know, this I guess?"

"That would make a statement," Ford said, taking in Isaac's usual jeans and leather jacket.

"What are you wearing?"

"I found a sick vintage suit," Ford said, squaring his shoulders. "It even fits over my arms."

"You're excited about this," Isaac said. "Why? I thought prom was a high school thing."

Ford shrugged.

"It is, but I didn't get to go to my senior prom, you know, because of the whole tree thing." Ford pointed to his mismatched face. "A lot of us didn't."

"I'll just skip it," Isaac said.

In truth, that would be best. The school would be empty. He could take another crack at the labyrinth.

"You do and Lin will fail you, if she doesn't kill you. 'Sides, I'd thought you be into it."

"Why?"

"It's a ball, thrown by elves. They'll go all out, and it would be a good chance to try and get a certain someone's attention."

Ford nodded toward the door Vran had fled through.

Isaac stared in that direction for a breath.

"You might be right," he agreed.

"Usually am, bro."

"I'll come up with something," Isaac said.

"Cool," Ford said, walking on. "See you there."

He didn't have the money for something fancy. He didn't even know where to start.

Sure, he could dance, but a party thrown by elves was another level.

Isaac needed help, but Undertakers weren't supposed to ask for backup.

Then again, Guardians *were*.

Letting out a long breath, Isaac started walking.

He found the right door—at least he hoped it was the right door—and knocked.

Hex opened it.

"I need your help," he said.

"With what?" she asked, crossing her arms and blocking the entrance.

"This dance thing."

She rolled her eyes.

"I'm not practicing with you, Frost, especially if you're wearing combat boots."

"Not with that," he said. "Well, not the dancing, but the boots, sort of. I don't have anything to wear."

"Because you only wear that?"

"Yeah."

"And you didn't prepare at all? You waited until the last minute."

"Correct."

Hex stared at him for a long moment, gave out a long sigh, and pulled a cell phone from her pocket. Her fingers danced over the buttons.

"Who are you texting?"

"Daff. This is her department and we're going to need help."

"With what?"

"Your hair for starters."

She stepped back and lifted a hand, waving for him to come in.

The walls of her room were lined in bookshelves. There were probably more actual books here than in the library. Here and there were pictures of a little boy. He had Hex's scowl but also her expression of wonder and curiosity.

Isaac took in some of the titles.

"Read much?"

"Yes."

"For fun?"

She sighed.

"I should be at Howard, or some other HBCU, getting my master's, but I came here instead."

"Why?"

"Didn't we just do this? Where else was I going to learn about magical theory? It's not in any of the curricula back on Earth."

Isaac knew she was smarter than him. That wasn't a surprise. Scanning the books and realizing there was no fiction on the shelves, he felt the gap widen.

An uncomfortable pause passed as Isaac drifted from shelf to shelf.

"Have you read all of these?" he asked.

"Not in their entirety," she said with a shrug. "They're mostly for research."

He could see that. Colorful tabs were stuck to many of the pages.

"You'll be teaching here soon."

"Probably."

"Hi!" Daff called from the open doorway.

Hex let out a sign of obvious relief that Isaac was tempted to mirror.

Daff set down a large bag, the sort Isaac might have used to carry weapons to the sparring field.

"What did you bring?" he asked.

"*Everything*," she said, pulling out a pair of scissors and a comb. "I've got to admit, I was hoping I could get a chance to practice. Jack's hair is just wires. It doesn't grow."

"Practice?"

"It's a hobby," Daff said.

"Should I be worried?"

"Nah. I'm wearing gloves."

He'd meant about keeping his ears but swallowed the impulse to say it aloud.

"You're holding in something snarky, aren't you?" Hex asked.

"How did you know?"

"Your face did a thing."

"A bit like you had a stomachache," Daff added.

"I'm trying," Isaac said. "You're doing me a favor here."

"We really are," Hex said. "A big one."

"Be nice," Daff chided her. "He's trying, so can you."

Hex scoffed.

"Go wash your hair, Isaac," Daff said. "It will be easier to cut if it's wet."

He shrugged out of his jacket and headed for Hex's sink.

She had a lot of stuff, things like hair oil that he didn't recognize. There were several bottles of shampoo, all in various stages of empty.

"Use the green bottle," Hex called, anticipating his confusion.

He returned to find Hex's desk chair in the middle of the room and Daff ready with a plastic sheet that could have come from one of his body disposal lessons.

"What?" she asked. "Haven't you ever had a haircut before?"

"Yeah," he said. "Of course."

He didn't know how to explain that the Undertaker had lined them up and cut them all at once, buzzing their hair with a pair of electric clippers. It had been utilitarian and quick.

No one had ever tried to make him attractive. Once, one of the boys had brought lice back from his street lessons, and the Undertaker had shaved their heads, one by one. He'd nicked more than a few of them and the scent of so much blood, so many types and flavors, had given Isaac a headache. It had been like wandering through the aftermath of an explosion in a spice aisle.

"Have a seat," Daff said. "I promise I won't hurt you."

It could be a prank. Maybe she'd make him look stupid, but he'd asked for help and decided to accept his fate.

Daff put the cape on him and started working quietly, smiling or scowling as she focused, running the comb through his hair and snipping away.

She finished and dried it with a towel before applying something from a tube, running her gloved fingers through his hair.

Isaac couldn't see Hex but she was working on something in the corner of the room. He could hear her scraping chalk along the floor.

"What do you think?" Daff asked, holding up a mirror for Isaac to see.

Isaac had never tried to apply the standards he had for beauty to his own features.

She'd shortened the sides to a buzz but left the top long enough to hold the swoops and spikes the product had added.

"I like it," he said.

"Really?"

Isaac nodded. "Really. Thank you."

"I'm glad," Daff said. She blushed a little.

"My turn, Cinderfella," Hex said as Daff took off the cape. "Step into the circle please."

He studied the complex ideogram she'd drawn. He didn't know any of the symbols, but they looked more like math than magic to him.

"You're not going to turn me into a toad or anything, are you?"

"Only because it would be a waste of Daffodil's time and talents. Now move. We have to get ready too."

Isaac stepped into the circle, and Hex bent to scratch at the runes she'd drawn, completing whatever incantation she'd prepped.

Something warm and fleeting, like the brush of tall summer grass, rushed up Isaac's body. His clothes warped and rippled, the threads unweaving and coming back together.

"Ooh," Daff purred. "I like it."

"It's a basic transformation spell." Hex bent to wipe away a bit of the circle with a cloth. "You can come out now."

Isaac took in his reflection.

"Are you sure about this?" he asked.

"Yes," Hex and Daffodil said together.

"You look hot," Daffodil added.

Hex nodded grudging agreement.

"The binding should last until midnight. Then you'll be a pumpkin again."

Isaac stretched to take in the effect.

Hex had changed his jeans and jacket into black velvet. The pants were tight, on the edge of uncomfortable. His shirt had grown sleeves and become a purple button-up.

Self-consciously, he reached to undo the second button. You could just see the top of the tattooed heart on his chest.

It wasn't a glamour. These polished shoes didn't have the same weight as his boots.

Daffodil cocked her head to the side.

"What about some eyeliner?" she asked. "A little blue would make those pale eyes pop."

"Makeup?"

"Yeah."

"Not for me," Isaac said.

"You can call it guyliner if it would help," Hex said.

"Nah, I'm good."

"I think Vran would like it," Daff stressed.

Isaac hesitated.

"Nah," he decided. "But thank you."

"See?" Daff asked. "I knew he could be nice."

"You're welcome," Hex said.

Daffodil gave her a questioning look, and she added, "You want to reinforce positive behavior."

"You two make me sound like a puppy."

"You're more like a stray cat," Hex said.

Isaac narrowed his eyes. He wasn't certain, but he thought they might be insulting him.

Hex sighed.

"We like you, Isaac. We're just not sure how to take you sometimes."

"What do you mean?"

"Like that whole bit about saying the Guardians should be abolished."

"But you agreed with me."

"I said you had *some* good points," Hex stressed. "As I've said, many times, the rest of us want to be here, and I don't think we know how to deal with someone who doesn't and constantly reminds us of it."

"Or calls us dangerous, and the school a prison," Daff added.

Isaac let out a breath.

"I don't *not* want to be here."

"Does that have anything to do with Vran?" Daff teased.

"Don't answer that," Hex said. "We don't have time for boy talk. We'll see you at six."

She closed the door in his face.

21
LIFE'S A DANCE

Ford gave Isaac an approving nod when he reached the courtyard.

Isaac wasn't certain what "sick" meant, but in this case, Ford had been talking about a suit of burnt orange and heavy shoes of brown leather. He wore a white shirt and a green bowtie.

"Admit it," Ford said. "I rock this."

"Yes. Yes, you do."

Isaac was immediately glad that he'd made the effort and asked for help as the others drifted toward the gate.

Daffodil wore a dress of shimmering pink velvet with long skirts and gloves to match. Jack's vest and bow tie matched her though his suit was black. Her hair was swept up into a complicated weave tempered with copper wires.

Hex's appearance reflected her power.

Her usual skirts and black lace had been replaced with layers of glossy black that flickered with faint traces of silver limned in gold. They were moons, Isaac realized, slowly phasing from full to new as she walked.

Her hair was braided with traces of silver beads, and her lips were colored a deep blue. She wore gloves like Daffodil's, the kind that reached her elbow. They were dyed to the same color as her lips.

Isaac opened his mouth to say something nice but froze at the sight of Vran.

"See?" Daffodil said, leaning toward him to whisper, "*Guyliner.*"

Isaac could not argue.

Black didn't describe the depth and sprays of distant stars worked into the fabric or the rippling gloss layered atop it.

Vran was dressed in midnight.

The suit jacket framed his shoulders and squared them. He'd buttoned it but wore no shirt beneath, exposing a long V of pale skin that Isaac's eyes immediately traced.

Vran's hair curled around his head in swirls, but the soot that lined his eyes sparkled with a trace of blue. It matched his freshly painted fingernails. The lines forked over his face and neck, dark cracks in porcelain. Isaac was struck with the sudden need to follow them, to trace their path wherever they might lead his fingertips.

Vran stepped forward, reached out, and ran the sleeve of Isaac's jacket between his thumb and finger.

"Not bad," he said before turning to Hex. "Your work?"

"Yeah."

"It's a good spell," Vran said. "You're getting stronger."

"You look . . ." Isaac stammered.

Like a dream. Like Isaac's dream, but he finished with "really good."

Vran smiled.

Isaac returned the touch. The fabric felt soft and glossy.

"What is this made of?"

"Crushed obsidian, spider silk, and dark matter."

"Seriously?"

The smile deepened, and Isaac knew he'd never get a straight answer.

"Are you still mad at me?" He asked it because he had to, because he couldn't hold it in.

"No, but try to be less dumb, okay?"

"Okay."

Vran reached to take Isaac's hand, and Isaac let him.

They followed the others through the gate and emerged somewhere cooler. Isaac could smell burning leaves and apples. Beneath that was an air too clean to ever be polluted by something as mundane as smoke.

More stars than he'd imagined possible shone overhead.

It wasn't unlike the ocean where he'd rejected Vran's offer, but the ocean was far away. They'd stepped into a grove of carefully cultivated trees, and they weren't alone.

Young elves filled the space.

One wore a dress woven of falling leaves. Gold and purple, they trickled away, skittered and swirled about her, making a dust-devil skirt.

Her two dates favored armor forged of the same style: copper, brass, and bronze leaves. They wore circlets of her leaves.

Another wore a gown of simple white, possibly more spider thread, but undyed. Her hair rose high, woven into the collar of branches spreading from her back. The reddest berries gave it its only color. They smelled like blood and cherries.

Another slender figure was almost as striking in a trailing skirt of blue butterflies. Isaac didn't know if the insects were live or an illusion, but they fluttered about the dancer, weaving and unweaving from gown to suit, sometimes almost revealing their entire body and sometimes forming a wide, iridescent skirt and a pair of massive wings.

"This is . . ." Isaac trailed off.

Beautiful didn't cover it. He settled on overwhelming.

He couldn't even quite find words for the feeling in his chest.

He didn't belong here, he knew that. None of the RCC students did. Their amazing clothes and Hex's spells paled in comparison to immortal grace and enchantment.

No one was bleeding, but the scent of magic lay thick in the air, cold and bracing, like a winter wind.

Vran squeezed Isaac's hand, drawing him back to the moment, to the dream at his side.

"Are you all right?" Vran asked.

"Yeah. It's all just a lot to take in."

"Do you want something to drink?"

"Very much," Isaac said.

Vran led him by the hand. The ground was covered in something too solid for sand but too soft for stone.

There were banquet tables and chairs of woven stalks and branches grown from the earth. The centerpieces weren't cut. They were cultivated, potted flowers of spiny, delicate shapes. Some of them glowed. Some swayed to the ethereal music. Some sang along.

The crowd didn't part for Isaac and Vran, but they gracefully made space, creating a path to the multitiered table capped by an ice sculpture in the form of an impossible filigree castle. A waterfall sprang from its open portcullis, flowing into a spray that divided the table in two. Whole villages and forests stood beneath its walls. Isaac could spy tiny frozen figures working or playing in its shadow.

The Elven Academy side was arrayed with delicate dishes, parfaits of layered flower petals in crystal bowls and pastel-colored drinks that bubbled or glowed.

The RCC side was a mix of fast food still in its paper wrappers, most of it looking cold and unappealing. The cup of soda Isaac tried was long flat. He was used to worse, but could not decide if it was meant as insult or ignorance.

Vran eyed the Academy side and nibbled his lip, trying to decide what he wanted.

"What are you doing here?" a voice asked from behind them.

Isaac would have described it as imperious. That was what the elf was going for, but he came across a bit too adolescent to really pull it off.

He stood with a group of other youths. They'd arrayed themselves against Vran and Isaac in a half circle. He sized up the odds then eyed the forks on the buffet. Those would do if it came down to it.

"I was hungry," Vran said, nodding to the table. "What's good?"

"I meant *here*," the elf snarled. "At the ball. You specifically."

He could have been pretty if he didn't sneer so much. Golden-haired with skin that held a touch of bronze at the edge, he looked like what Isaac had always assumed elves were supposed to look like. He wore a robe and a flowing cape of sky-colored silk woven with bare white branches. The tree limbs flickered in a breeze that Isaac didn't feel.

Vran straightened.

"The king commanded that we attend, that *I* attend." All trace of fun and youth had vanished. This was Ocean Boy, a face Isaac hadn't seen, one cold and dark and quick to drown the unwary. "Would you have me disobey a royal order?"

"As though it matters to the likes of you."

"I can't tell if you're for the king or not." Vran selected a green, fizzy drink from the Academy side and taking a long sip through a reed placed there as a straw. He took a french fry from the RCC side and nibbled it with a look of curiosity.

"You do not belong here, Lost One."

"And yet I am here." Vran took another long sip. His dark eyes narrowed. "You can, as a friend of mine likes to say, die mad about it."

"Is that a challenge?"

The elf flushed a deep, bronze color. Isaac couldn't tell if it was from anger, fear, or some mix of the two.

Isaac stiffened, ready to fight. He inched toward the forks.

Vran smiled and it made Isaac think of the sharks he liked to draw, of some predator lurking in the deep.

"It's just an expression."

Isaac would have sworn that the shadows around them grew taller. They were listening. They wanted to play.

"We're not to duel," one of the other elves said, putting a hand to his friend's shoulder.

Most of the group had shrunk back. Isaac wasn't certain, but he doubted it would be much of a fight.

The golden boy did not back down.

"Did you know, I was the youngest of my court to be named page?" Vran asked absently.

He dipped a french fry in his drink and tried the combination.

"You *were* a page. Your magic is broken now."

"Not exactly." Green eyes opened in the shadows, and the boy's companions took several steps away from the table. "What was broken, *below*, was its cage."

Vran set the empty glass at the end of the table.

"Now do you want to fight or can I dance with my date?" To Isaac he said, "I mean, if you want to dance."

"I do," Isaac said, though he also wanted to watch Vran fight.

The golden elf said nothing. Vran shrugged, took Isaac's hand, and pulled him toward the floor.

Figures twirled and mingled, in pairs or other groupings.

Daffodil and Jack moved in a delicate circle. It wasn't as graceful as the elven students. They could never match that, but they had a happy orbit all their own.

Hex was engaged in animated conversation with an elven girl. Isaac worried she might be having an argument, but her face had that look like it did in Lawless's class, when she was hard at work on a problem. Her dress had waxed to mostly silver and he decided she was in her element.

Isaac had lost sight of Ford, which shouldn't be possible given the troll's garish suit, but the big guy could handle himself.

Isaac met Vran's eyes.

"So am I your date?" he asked.

"If you want to be."

"I do."

"Good."

Vran took Isaac's other hand and he tried to find the rhythm. Vran led, pushing a little, gently pulling, steering them in a slow circle. It was strange, but not bad, that Vran was so much stronger than him.

"What would happen? If you dueled him, I mean."

"I don't know. Nothing good. I'd probably hurt him very badly."

"He kind of had it coming."

"No, Isaac." Vran shook his head. "He's young and proud and more than a little stupid, but nobody deserves to be hurt like that."

Isaac was really bad at dancing but didn't mind because Vran didn't seem to care. He was happy. That was the feeling he hadn't been able to name or place. Yes, they'd almost gotten into a fight, and it felt tenuous, unfamiliar, and impossible, like a too-thin thread to hang anything on, but he was happy.

"Would you hurt me?"

Isaac hadn't meant to ask it. It had just popped out. He didn't like this new habit of his.

"Never," Vran said firmly. Then, sounding sad, he added, "Not until I do."

"What's that supposed to mean?"

Vran shrugged and spun them a little more quickly around the floor. The stars above them became a swirl. Vran drew Isaac closer, closing the space between them. He let go of Isaac's hand and splayed his fingers against his back.

Then they slowed, like Vran's gravity had snared him.

They weren't that different in height, but Isaac bent a little so his chin rested on Vran's shoulder. It felt good, a relief.

He couldn't hear Vran's heartbeat, but he caught that scent, sea salt and burning pepper. Isaac breathed him in, that something that was only Vran.

Peeking, he could see that the strange lines crossed Vran's chest.

"What are you doing?" Vran asked.

Giving up any pretense.

Isaac wanted a kiss. He wanted to kiss this strange, beautiful man and keep kissing him until his own breath ran short.

He decided to answer the question with a question, even though he hated when Lin did it.

"Will you tell me what happened to you? Why they're so scared of you?"

"Is that what they are?" Vran asked into Isaac's hair.

"Yeah." Isaac met Vran's eyes.

"Why do you think it's fear?"

"Because people only ever do something that stupid when they're afraid."

Vran laughed a little.

"Is that something you learned at Murder School?"

"Yes. Make your target afraid and they'll mess up. It will make it easier to hunt them and take them down."

Vran nodded. They took a few more turns. It was nice, hand to hand, hand to shoulder.

"That is it, then," Vran said, dimming. "I make them afraid."

"But why?"

"Because I remind them that the impossible can happen to them."

Isaac kept stealing glances inside Vran's jacket while Vran fixated on the bit of tattoo peeking out of Isaac's shirt.

"Will you tell me what happened?"

Isaac was pushing, but he wanted to know. He wanted to know all about Vran—damn the mission. He just wanted to know.

"Later," Vran said.

Isaac narrowed his eyes.

"*Later* later, or when, like, when we're *dead* later?"

"*Later* later," Vran said with a smile. "Right now I want to dance with you. I doubt we'll get invited back."

"You certainly made an impression." Isaac glanced to where the golden boy sulked at the edge of the field.

Now that his eyes had adjusted, he could make out the trees that lined the clearing. Tall and thick, they were laden with apples. Their leaves tumbled delicately in an autumn rain of ruby and gold. He could not tell if it was enchantment or nature and decided he did not care.

"I try," Vran said.

He pulled Isaac close again. His skin was still cool to the touch, while Isaac felt his must be burning.

The music was strange. He wasn't even certain it had a beat, just a weave of many voices, all entangled in different pitches or tones, but it had no words Isaac could identify. It was beautiful, regal, and perhaps a little sad. That was autumn, he decided.

Every season had an end, but for now he would not care.

He danced with Vran, the boy he wanted to kiss, and let the sounds of the music and the scent of magic wash over them like the wind.

Then Vran stopped. He froze so suddenly that Isaac almost stumbled.

The other dancers came to a halt. Everyone stared toward the empty center of the field.

"What is it?"

"You can't feel it?" Vran asked, his hand still gripped in Isaac's.

"No."

"I forget you don't have your own magic. The king is coming."

In a spiraling, graceful wave, the elves began to kneel.

Vran joined them.

Isaac started to follow, but Vran said, "No, Isaac. He's not your king."

Only the teachers and students from RCC remained standing. Ford stuck out more than a bit in his orange suit, bright enough to give Isaac pause.

Isaac felt exposed.

"What do I do?"

"Whatever you like, but don't piss him off."

"Because he'll kill me?"

"Because I have to spend winter break with him."

Cold and light washed over the crowd like the first freeze in the Graveyard, like the lightest touch of frost.

Isaac blinked and more elves stood in the field.

Dressed in suits of simple gray, each wore a sword and carried a gun. Their backs straight, their expressions hard, they reminded him of statues.

They surveyed the space, gave some signal, and a man appeared in the center of their circle.

All the elves Isaac had seen were beautiful, but there was something about this man whose square shoulders and straight posture spoke of power that set him apart.

Like the queen, he had an air of dangerous power, but like Vran, he also wore a bit of sadness, a bit of that same autumn air.

It made them more human, touchable, Isaac decided. Not that he'd touch a king.

"Is the queen his wife?" Isaac whispered.

"Sister," Vran said.

Isaac could scent it now, the familiar magic. Argent's power was not unlike the young king's.

"Please stand," the king said loudly. "This is a celebration, not court."

The elves rose gracefully.

Isaac offered Vran a hand.

Vran met his eyes through the tangles of his black hair and grinned.

Isaac smiled back.

The king wore a long, narrow sword at his waist.

He didn't wear a crown, but an old-fashioned sort of hat, a fedora, Isaac thought it was called.

"I am honored by your revels," he said. "Honored in this first joining of schools, of difference, as the year turns toward winter. It is more than appropriate that you meet tonight, when the planes are the closest and the veil between them the thinnest. I look forward to further celebrations and to a future of trust."

He gestured, and it began to snow. The flakes mixed with the shifting branches and falling leaves, glittering like ice, but they weren't cold to the touch when Isaac caught one on his palm. It dissolved and the others followed, vanishing before they struck the ground.

An illusion then, as much as Isaac's clothes. He wondered what time it was, how long he had until his elegant suit reverted to jeans and roughened, peeling leather.

He hadn't wanted to come. Now he did not want it to end.

Isaac forced himself to let it go, to push it down into the same place he kept his impending deadline.

And why shouldn't he? How could the Undertaker fear this? It was a party, and it was beautiful.

Vran took his hand and they began to dance again, but Isaac could not completely ignore the room. He could not tell if the king's words about differences and acceptance had made any impact on the young elves who'd confronted them at the snack table. They remained to the side, not dancing, not talking. They stood frozen in contempt.

I cannot tell if you're for the king or not, Vran had said.

Then there were the guards, the lean shadows that had vanished into the trees. He wondered who or what they guarded against.

Suddenly things weren't so warm and beautiful. A shudder moved over Isaac.

Death was everywhere, could be brought anywhere, for the right price.

He was here, wasn't he? If he'd made it past their defenses and suspicions, then who else might they let in?

"Do you want to get out of here?" Vran asked.

Isaac fought the urge to sigh in relief.

"Where to?" Leaning close, Isaac dared to whisper, "My room maybe?"

"First, they can all hear you. Second, mine's closer, but no. I have somewhere else in mind."

"All right then."

He'd follow wherever Vran led, chase him through this place or any other, if that was the game. He hoped not.

He hadn't been too certain of anything lately, but he was quite certain about the kissing.

The feeling had faded with the king's entrance, but it came back strong when Vran smiled at him.

"Then let's go." Vran offered Isaac his hand.

22
BOOKS CAN BE A KIND OF FLIRTING

"Will we get in trouble?" Isaac asked as they left the field.

"Now you care?" Vran teased. He tightened his hold on Isaac's hand. "No. I don't think anyone will miss us."

"How can you be certain?"

"Ford's suit is a great distraction."

Isaac laughed, but the troll didn't lack company. A number of the elves had approached him. They didn't seem hostile, just curious. One or two of them giggled, telling Isaac they were interested in getting closer to the hulking youth.

It was the opposite of how they'd been with Vran, and Isaac had to think that some of them would be relieved to see him gone. If they feared whatever he represented, they could put it out of their minds, the same way Isaac avoided deep water whenever possible.

And yet he'd swum to the bottom of a flood to open a door and drown a fire. Perhaps they'd all be better off if they faced their fears.

Then again, the labyrinth waited. The other demons of his past waited, including and especially the last one, the reason why he had to kill the school, the reason why he had to help Kenji end the Old Man's reign.

Vran led Isaac outside and to a garden gate. The night beyond was black and full of stars. The glow of the ball was bright behind them, as if a bit of the king's light still graced the tops of the trees.

"Where are we going?" Isaac asked, hoping for somewhere private.

"We won't get another chance like this," Vran whispered. "I want to show you something."

More of the glowing flowers lined the path in streams of light, marking the way to the tower that rose ahead. It wasn't made of stone, but something softer, like flower petals carved from mother-of-pearl. Their fronds curved and expanded into buttresses, leaving long gaps, windows glazed in sapphire.

The whole thing glowed faintly, in a way not unlike RCC, but this light was softer, closer to moonlight on Earth. Isaac had to admit that he found it gentler, like a summer night after the sweltering heat had broken.

Vran pulled him along, not pausing as the tower loomed.

"Are we supposed to be here?" Isaac asked.

"Absolutely not, but that's to our advantage. No one would think us this brave."

"Or stupid?"

"Take your pick," Vran said with a shrug.

"So why are we doing it?"

"Isaac Frost." Vran paused to face him, his hand still cool in Isaac's. "I thought you were a badass."

"'An Undertaker only does what he's paid to do,'" Isaac quoted. "'He doesn't show off or take unnecessary risks.'"

"Then it's a good thing you quit."

"What makes you say that?"

"Because you love to show off."

Reaching, Vran traced a fingertip down the open neck of Isaac's shirt and brushed the top of the tattoo.

"Only for you."

Isaac leaned forward.

Vran pecked him quickly on the lips, leaving Isaac wanting far more as they approached the tower door.

More crystal petals were folded across the entrance. They shone like glass, but Isaac didn't doubt they'd be strong enough to withstand his blows.

Vran touched the entrance and it opened, the petals unfolding to the sides, like a tulip in the sun.

"I know you're not the reading sort," Vran said, leading Isaac inside. "But I also know you need some help with your project for Lawless."

Shelves spiraled around them. They drifted in the air. Unsuspended, they twisted and floated in lazy orbits through the tower's open core.

There were books, tablets, and scrolls, more than Isaac could have imagined.

"The Academy Archives are older and way bigger than what we have at RCC," Vran explained. "If there's anything written about Phages, it will be here."

Isaac felt something inside him shift. It wasn't unlike the need to kiss Vran, but it pooled higher and brighter, like a second beat inside his chest.

"It's all in Elvish," Vran said. "But I can read it. Maybe we can find them."

Isaac didn't know what to say. He hadn't even told Vran that he was struggling, that he couldn't find his people.

"Thank you," he said quietly. "Where would we even begin?"

"There's a codex," a voice said. "Not as efficient as a search engine, but it acts as a glossary for everything here."

The king stood in the doorway.

Vran tilted his head in sheepish respect.

"He didn't—he was just trying to help me," Isaac said, ready to move between them, not that he had a chance of protecting Vran from this man.

"Of course." The king strode into the library and approached a tall pedestal. A massive book stood upon it. He opened it, flipped through the pages. Isaac and Vran stood very still.

"It's all right, Vran," the king said over his shoulder.

"I'm not supposed to be here."

"And yet, I say you are, for now. I say it is all right, so it is."

"Just because you say so?" Isaac asked.

Vran squeezed his hand in warning.

The king sighed.

"As much as I'd like to see us evolve past the idea of absolute monarchy, it holds for now. I will that you are allowed in the Archive, and so you are allowed in the Archive."

"You can just change the law like that, anytime you want?" Isaac asked.

"Some of them."

"So then why don't you?"

"Why don't I what?"

If the king was offended by the question, he didn't show it. He cocked his head in curiosity.

"Change the laws. If your power is absolute, then change things. You have to know how messed up some of it is. How unfair."

The king smiled, and it was full of that sadness he wore, that bit of autumn on the edge of winter.

"I wish all changes were so easy, Isaac Frost."

He stiffened to hear his name. Was it a threat? Was the king showing Isaac that he had his number? If so, how much did he know? What did he suspect?

"Traditions are well-worn tracks." The king flipped through the pages of the ivory codex. "The longer they're clung to, and reinforced, the deeper those grooves become. If I change too much, too quickly, the wheels will come off the car. The whole thing will crash."

"Then maybe it should."

"Perhaps, but I play the game to win it, to change it. I cannot simply upend the board. Many, many innocents would be hurt in that chaos. Is that what you want?"

"No. I'm sorry." Though he did not feel sorry at all. "I was just told to ask you, if I ever met you, why you still have kings and queens."

The king chuckled.

"I'll admit that I'm not used to such impertinence, especially of late. I thought the Undertakers were agents of order and Vran was the chaos monkey."

"Chaos monkey?" Isaac asked.

Vran blushed.

"It's what Adam calls me."

"That and *brat*," the king said. "For now, we have what we must have. Maybe someday we'll reach a point where I can will such a change, but it appears even absolute monarchy has its limits."

Isaac remembered the last king and how he'd died. He decided not to mention it. Lin's etiquette lessons must be sinking in.

The king stopped turning pages and pointed to the codex.

"Here. I think this is what you were looking for."

He turned to go.

"Silver?" Vran asked, his voice sounding young. "Why did you come here tonight?"

"To the ball or to the Archive?"

"Both."

"I hoped to quell any tension at the ball, though I suspect I fanned it instead. I appreciate your attendance. I know conformance is not in your nature."

Vran gave a happy little nod of agreement.

"As for the Archive . . . I wanted to see it again. It's been a while, and it is beautiful. I spent much time here, in the seasons when I was your age."

"Thank you," Vran said softly. "For letting us stay."

"You're welcome. Thank you for what you did not do. I will see you at the solstice."

The king tipped his hat.

Isaac and Vran watched him go. They didn't speak for a long moment, and Isaac knew Vran was giving the king enough time to reach a distance where they would not be overheard.

"You're going to tell me, right?" Isaac asked. "Someday?"

"Soon," Vran said. "Very soon, but first, there's this."

He scanned the page the king had left open for them.

"There's a lot here," Vran said, running his fingers over the entries. "At least more than what Jack has."

"Enough to read now?" Isaac asked.

"I don't think so," Vran said. "But I suspect we can borrow what we need via interlibrary loan."

"They're not going to let that happen, are they?"

Vran nodded at the open doorway.

"I think they will. We've got friends in high places."

23
IN THE DEEP END

Isaac didn't know where they crossed to, but the night had cooled and he wished Hex had made him a heavier shirt. It had to be the mortal plane. The air had that taste, infused with chemicals and carbon.

Metal shapes emerged from the darkness as they walked.

"A playground?"

"I like the swings," Vran said, taking one.

Isaac joined him. The chains squeaked as they kicked into the air.

He wanted to get to the kissing, but there was also something nice about wanting and not yet having, about the moment before the strike.

"Would you stay at the school if they didn't make you?" Vran asked.

"Why are you asking?" Isaac countered, mostly out of habit. There was also something nice in their banter, in the way that talking with Vran could feel like sparring.

"I like having you there." Vran kicked himself higher than before. The swing set rattled under their weight.

"You don't even live there." Isaac synced them up so they flew side by side, back and forth.

"No, but I like knowing where to find you."

"You just want me to be a Guardian."

"I do. I'd love for you to be a Guardian with me."

"You make it sound so easy."

He couldn't quite sync their flight. Vran remained a little ahead, then a little behind.

"It is, I think," Vran said. "It's just a choice. Guardians, Undertakers—they're all just people making choices. You can make a choice too, you know. You don't have to be whatever they told you that you had to be."

"You don't understand."

It was the closest he'd come to saying it, to admitting the truth about why he'd come to RCC, about how they'd met and why.

"You could tell me," Vran said quietly, stopping himself with a soft skid of his feet. So perfect, so graceful. Isaac's own pause was louder and uneven.

His heart was pounding for a completely new reason.

He knew what Kenji would do in his place. They were alone, far from the school or the watchful eyes of the others. If found out, Kenji would make Vran disappear and find some way to say they'd been attacked. Then again, he'd never have dragged the mission out like this, let himself get distracted. Kenji would have put an end to it by now.

Isaac could never hurt Vran, never do something like that, and he knew, more than ever, that he probably wasn't capable of hurting the school.

"I'm sorry," Isaac said. "About before, on the beach."

"It's okay. It's just kind of weird that you keep asking when you didn't want to know."

"I do want it," Isaac said. "Just not like that, not all at once."

"Why not?"

"It's scary." Isaac waved a hand. "You. Us. This."

"Okay," Vran said.

They hung there for a while, twisting on the chains. A car horn sounded somewhere close, but no lights encroached.

"What do you want to be, if not a Guardian?" Vran asked.

"I don't know . . ." Isaac trailed off. He'd always thought he'd be with Kenji, helping run things when the Old Man was gone, but that dream was hazy now, less solid or certain. "I mean, what's the point?"

"Of the Guardians?"

"Yeah. Whatever they do, it doesn't fix anything. There will always be bad people."

And there would always be Undertakers, or someone like them, someone looking to profit from those who fell between the cracks and outside the system.

He kept that to himself. The less anyone thought of him as an Undertaker, the better, but he could admit, just to himself, that he didn't want Vran thinking about it. He didn't want Vran thinking ill of him.

"Have you ever seen *Star Wars*?" Vran asked.

"One."

"Which one?"

"I don't know. It was loud. Oh. It was the one with the feral teddy bears. There were a lot of explosions."

"So you hated it?"

"Not at all." Isaac grinned. "I like explosions."

Kenji had taken them to a movie, brought them all to the mortal world to a dark theater where they'd been warm and quiet, awed by the giant screen. There'd even been popcorn. He could still taste the greasy not-quite butter they put atop it. He remembered the oohs and cries of excitement from his brothers, all there, just watching a movie, just being boys for a couple of hours. It had been a cold moment when it had ended and they'd returned to the Graveyard.

"I've seen all of them twice now," Vran said.

"Twice?"

"It's kind of mandatory where I live, but you know how there's Death Stars?"

"Yeah. Sure. The big evil basketballs?"

"I thought it was silly that they kept making more, but they kept getting bigger and more powerful. That's the thing though . . . the bad guys just keep coming back. Evil never stops. Evil people never stop, so the good people can't rest either."

"But nobody wins that way," Isaac said. "Nothing is permanent."

"Maybe not, but if someone gets helped, they'll see it as a win, and I don't think it's a game."

"What, good and evil?"

"Life. Nobody wins at it."

"Because nobody gets out alive," Isaac finished.

It wasn't unlike something the Old Man would have said.

"You talk like you're dying," he continued.

"Aren't I, though? Aren't we all? Some of us just have longer than others."

"I thought you were an elf." Isaac reached out to take Vran's hand, to entwine their fingers. "That you'd live forever."

"So did the old king." Vran squeezed his hand. "I've known for a while how my story ends, and I'm okay with it, I think."

Isaac thought of the handsome man who'd come to the ball and nodded. His father must have expected to live forever. Had he seen it coming? Had he known his son would be the one to take him down?

That thought led down a dangerous road, to the place Isaac didn't like to go. Kenji always spoke of someday. He whispered it when he was certain no one but Isaac could hear, but the Old Man showed no signs of slowing down.

If Kenji wanted the title of Undertaker, if he wanted to protect his brothers, he'd have to seize the Graveyard by force. Isaac's stomach squirmed at the thought, the idea of them fighting to the death. Kenji was the best of them, the quickest, but the Undertaker had been killing for centuries. In all their sparring or training, he'd been untouchable. Isaac could not be certain Kenji would win when the time came.

"What happened to you, Vran?" he asked, focusing on where he was, in the moment and not some hazy future. "You dance around it, but you won't say."

"I went somewhere I wasn't supposed to, far below, where no one living is supposed to go."

"An underworld, and you drank the water."

"Yes. It changed me."

"You said you were a Lost One."

"And so I am."

"You can never go home again?"

"I can, but I'll never fit there."

"Why not?"

"It will never feel right. Nowhere feels right. It's like I'm always a step ahead, or a step behind, the rest of you." Vran put a hand to his chest, rubbed his heart. "I don't know if I can explain it better than that."

"Is that where you got these?" Isaac reached out and laid two fingers to the line on Vran's neck. He traced it for a few inches. Vran's skin was smooth and cool.

"Yes."

"Then why did you go wherever it is you went?" Isaac asked, running a fingertip a little lower.

"To help a friend, because he needed me to. It changed me, changed my magic."

Something inside Isaac coiled, like a spring tightening.

"How?"

"We don't really know yet. Argent is trying to find out, but it scares her, the void, the nothing inside me."

"It's not nothing," Isaac said. "That's not what I see when I look in your eyes."

"No?" Vran's head dipped, though he kept his gaze fixed on Isaac's.

"No," Isaac said. "I see *stars*, Vran. I see a universe. It's like *everything* is inside you."

Vran dropped his head for a moment. The black curls of his hair framed his forehead when he looked up again.

"I think I'd like to kiss you now, Isaac."

"Have you ever kissed anyone, really kissed them? I haven't."

"No one?" Vran's eyes widened.

Isaac shook his head. "What about you?"

Vran smiled. "Not yet, and it would be nice to, and I'd especially like to kiss you."

"I want to kiss you too, but I don't want to taste your blood."

"Okay."

Isaac leaned forward and pressed his mouth to Vran's. It was soft at first, cautious, then one of them opened his mouth. Isaac wasn't certain who, and everything was warm. Void or not, Vran was not cold. Isaac decided he tasted like Vran, like nothing but Vran.

They continued for a while, he wasn't sure how long, but when they finally parted, his clothes had changed back to jeans and leather.

24
YE OLDEN TIMES

Isaac was still riding the warmth left from his make-out session with Vran. A few days of classes had done little to dull its shine. He wanted more, but their paths hadn't crossed since the dance. He waited for Lin's class to come around since they shared that.

He was in the middle of Lit class, trying to care about poetry, when he was summoned to the gym by the intercom.

"All of you, please," the dean announced. "Leave your books."

Isaac and the others made their way through the halls, buzzing with anticipation. Argent waited for them in an outfit that said she was either off to do some high-end shopping or rob a bank in style.

Dean Ryan was dressed in her stiff coat and boots, what Isaac decided was her field uniform. She didn't have her rifle, but her hair was wound into a tight bun that told Isaac she meant business.

"Here," she said, handing him a small canvas package on a belt. "You might need these."

Isaac unzipped it carefully.

It was the right shape, but he did not want to hope.

He let out a sigh of relief to see his knives.

"Don't get too attached. It's just for today."

"Where are we going that he's going to need those?" Hex asked.

"As much as I'd prefer he never need them, or that any of you need to use your abilities as weapons, the world is a dangerous place," the dean said. "Frost can have his toys for now."

"Thank you," he said, hugging the pouch to his chest.

"Do you three need a moment?" Daffodil asked.

"Maybe."

It didn't matter what they thought. He'd missed them. He hadn't realized how much their slight weight had been a part of him until they'd been taken away.

He didn't need them to use his power, but they were his, the only thing that was. Not even his name was truly his, and he kind of hated that Shepherd had made him aware of that. "Am I still on probation?" he asked.

"Oh, very much," Argent said. "But we agreed that you've shown progress."

"Thank you," he said, strapping the knives to his belt.

"And we need all of you for this," the dean said, addressing the class.

"We're going on a mission!" Daffodil squealed. She bounced up and down. "A real mission."

"Everyone?" Jack asked.

"Is this because we didn't, you know, start a war at elf prom?" Ford asked.

"Diplomatic triumphs aside, we need everyone," Argent said. "We need all of your eyes to follow up on Isaac's lead."

"You found her?" he asked, blinking. "You found the goblin?"

"Of course."

"Where is she hiding?" Vran asked.

"On Earth, on the mortal plane," the dean said.

"I think I can whip up enough glamours," Hex said, taking in their numbers. "But they won't hold for long if everyone is coming."

"You won't need them," Argent said. "The goblins are hiding in plain sight, in a crowd no less."

"What about me? Will people be safe with me there?" Daffodil asked, caution muting her enthusiasm. Jack squeezed her hand.

"Yes," Argent said. "I have just the thing."

"You're coming on this mission as acting Guardians," the dean said. "Remember that."

"We aren't children," Hex said.

"No, but you are also still students, which is why I'll be acting in a supervisory capacity." Argent narrowed her eyes. "Let's see if you can perform better than Frost and Vran have."

"Should we be offended?" Isaac asked Vran.

"No," Vran said. "The guy died."

"Good point."

Argent opened the door behind her and gestured for them to cross.

The light shifted from the school's usual greenish glow to bright yellow daylight.

They'd exited a shack and stood in a small alley between two wooden buildings.

Live music sounded nearby, the tune stringy and free of electronics.

"A ren faire! I haven't been to one of these since I was a kid," Jack said, peeking out of the alley's entrance.

Something clanked, interrupting the murmurs of agreement and curiosity.

"How am I supposed to move in this?" Daffodil asked.

Her clothing had transformed into a full suit of armor.

"I can barely see," she said.

"At least you're out and about," Ford said as she tried to shuffle forward.

"I want to help with the mission." Daffodil raised the helm's visor. "I want to be useful."

"I can think of something lighter," Argent said.

She cocked her head to the side, and Daff's armor shifted and stretched.

"That's better," Daff said.

"It's not historically accurate," Jack complained.

"How do you know?" Shy asked from somewhere to Isaac's right. "Maybe there were dinosaurs in the Renaissance."

"There were in the Spirit Realm," Vran said. "We still have megalodons."

His smile put a little flip in Isaac's chest.

"Do you always get this excited about sharks?" he asked.

"*Giant* sharks," Vran corrected.

"Focus, people," the dean said. "Does everyone know what we're looking for?"

"A goblin and her two kids," Isaac said. "Green, big teeth. Don't wrestle with them."

"I brought phones," Jack said. "And earpieces."

"I feel like a spy," Ford said, putting the bud into his human ear.

It was good to see his real form, that he didn't have to cover it up, but Isaac still asked, "Are we sure this is a good idea?"

"They'll just think it's cosplay," Hex said, nodding to a group of people dressed as pirates.

"Exactly," Argent said. "A troupe of elves would draw their attention, but you can blend in."

Cold magic washed over Isaac. His clothes reformed into something else.

"Dude," Ford said. "You look like you fell out of Dungeons and Dragons."

"The goblin has seen Vran and Isaac's faces," Argent explained. "The cowls will help."

Isaac was dressed in green, with a hooded shirt and tight leggings. A bow was slung over his shoulder.

Vran sported a heavy cloak of black velvet.

Argent's own clothes were a delicate-looking armor, filigree but steel. Isaac wondered if it were real, something she'd actually wear back in Alfheimr. She wore a pair of fake ears to cover the points of her real ones.

Vran wore something similar, the shade of the plastic just slightly pinker than his flesh.

"I'm sorry you have to hide," Isaac said, tugging the hood of Vran's cloak forward to disguise his face.

"It's okay. They're just humans," Vran said, shifting inside the heavy garment. "I'm not here to impress them."

"How about me?" Isaac asked, nibbling his lip.

"I'll see if I can do that later," Vran said.

"Partner up," the dean said. "Isaac go with Hex."

"Why?" he asked.

"To spare us all the flirting."

"I can flirt over the phone," Vran said.

"We're on a mission," Argent said. "*Behave.*"

"Yes, Argent."

"Fan out, search in pairs. Call out if you spot anything," the dean said.

"We're heading north," Isaac said, testing the earpiece and their connection.

"Roger," Shy said. "I've always wanted to say that."

"Why does anyone say Roger?" Daffodil asked.

"It's a pilot thing," Jack explained. "They changed it to Romeo at some point but it never caught on."

"I love that you know things," Daffodil said.

"And they were worried about *us* flirting?" Vran complained.

Argent sighed. "Just find the goblins. Is that nose of yours any good here, Frost?"

"There are too many people," he said. "And too much food. I'm mostly getting cotton candy. The air tastes . . . sticky."

"She's not stupid," Argent said. "This was a good place to hide. Lots of cover from people in costumes, and many of the players and vendors are itinerate, going from faire to faire."

"Then how do you know she's here?" Hex asked.

"We have our sources," Argent said as she led them into the chaos.

"Why are there people in Star Trek uniforms?" Ford asked, eyeing a group in jumpsuits. "I thought this was supposed to be the medieval times."

"Don't tell the cappuccino machine that," Hex said as they passed the stall with the longest line.

"Or the T-Rex," Daff groused.

"Focus, people," the dean said.

"I'm beginning to think you need a class on field communications," Argent said.

"I'll decide the curriculum at my school, Your Majesty. You're here as an adviser, but these are *my* students."

"Noted," Argent said in a clipped tone.

Hex and Isaac exchanged a look.

Damn, Hex mouthed.

Isaac agreed. Sassing the Queen of Swords could not be a strategy for a long and healthy life.

"My money's on the dean," Hex whispered, holding her hand over her mic.

"I'd take that bet," Isaac whispered back.

"I'm not getting anything either," Vran said. "Anybody else?"

"If there's magic here, I'm not sensing it," Hex said, looking around. "That's good, right? It means they're probably not using glamours."

"It also means we have to do this the hard way."

Ford shot Isaac a confused glance.

"With our eyes."

Isaac and Hex split from the group.

The dean had been right to put him and Vran with different partners.

It was too easy to get distracted by the sights and costumes. Vran's proximity would have made it much worse.

It was like the mortals longed for the Other Side, the realm just beyond their awareness, and in some cases, they came close to the look of it, though the slightly dreamy feeling and the buzz of background magic was missing here.

"This is . . . a lot," Daffodil said.

"Yeah."

Tasting the air, still trying to get a trace of the goblins, Isaac slipped through a large group of costumed children.

The kids went from booth to booth, examining the wares with excitement or apathy, free and blissfully unaware of all the ways to kill someone. Many of them were dressed as knights or princesses, with paper crowns and plastic armor.

Once, he might have been one of them, sent by the Undertaker to blend into the mortal world, but any happiness would have had to be stolen, taken in the moments between the single, constant lesson.

Isaac realized he'd lost Hex.

Someone jostled him.

"Hey," Vran said.

Isaac let out a breath and muted his mic.

"Hey," Isaac said, unable to hide his smile. "What are you doing here?"

Vran leaned close and whispered, "Same as you, looking for goblins."

Isaac was all too aware of how easy it would be to sneak away, to pick up where they'd left off. He wondered how much trouble they'd get in if they tried.

"Are you all right?" Vran asked, scanning the tents and stalls.

"I'm just not used to crowds," Isaac said. "And I lost Hex."

"Come on," Vran said, offering a hand. "I think she's that way."

Isaac let the elf pull him through the stream of people, darting through them with the same grace he danced with.

Isaac's heart was beating a bit faster when Vran let go of his hand.

Hex stood with her eyes narrowed and her head cocked, as if she was listening to something only she could hear.

"Do you have her?" Isaac asked.

"Maybe," she said. "Wait . . . shut up. Did anyone else feel that?"

"How could you not?" Vran asked. He made a face like he'd tasted something rotten.

"What is it?" Isaac asked.

"Someone just cast a spell," Argent said. "To the north, at the jousting field."

25
STICK, STONES, AND BROKEN BONES

Hex made several gestures, weaving her fingers through the air. She cocked her head to the side, as if to run some quick mental calculations.

"Shit," she said. "I think it's a summoning."

"Head that way," the dean said. "We have to protect these people."

Isaac spied a short green figure striding the opposite way, a giant cone of blue cotton candy in hand. He tapped to unmute.

"I've got eyes on one of the goblets—uh, the kids."

"You and Hex follow," Argent said. "Don't let him see you."

"On it."

"*Boys*," Hex complained. "Why do you always talk like you're in an action movie?"

Isaac ignored her and slipped through the crowd. Vran was gone again, probably off to join the others.

Hex kept up.

"Just watch out for the mom," Isaac told her.

"You're not in charge here, Frost."

"I'm trying to help. She nearly crushed my skull."

"And the babies have long teeth," Vran added over the line.

"He's not even sneaking," Hex said, nodding at the goblin with his bouncing cone of sugar.

"But is he young and dumb or is he leading us into a trap?"

"Uh guys, we've got . . . what do we have?" Ford asked.

"Scarecrows?" Daffodil said.

"They're constructs," the dean said. "Poppets."

"People think they're costumes." Jack sounded panicked. "They're clapping."

"It's a distraction," Argent said.

"So the summoner can go after the goblins," Isaac said.

"How do you know?" Hex asked.

"It's what I would do."

"Are we dealing with an Undertaker?" the dean asked, an edge in her voice.

"No," Isaac said. "We—they—don't have any summoners."

"That you know about," Hex said.

That was a chilling thought. Isaac knew his brethren, knew their names and faces, but the Old Man might have agents hidden away, senior assassins Isaac and the others didn't know about.

"Isaac, you and Hex stop the summoner," Argent said. "Apprehend them. *Alive.* We'll be with you shortly."

"What are we going to do?" Daffodil asked.

"You wanted a field exercise," Argent said. "Constructs are not alive. Use whatever force you want, but protect the crowd at all costs."

"I can smash them?" Ford sounded excited.

"Do as you will," Argent said.

"Are you going to help?" Vran asked hopefully.

"I'm here as an *adviser*," Argent said. Isaac could just imagine the side eye she gave the dean. "I will advise."

He heard the sound of steel ringing.

"Can I get a sword?" Ford asked.

"No," Argent said.

"Be careful," Isaac said. "All of you."

Though he especially meant Vran.

The sounds of fighting came through the line as the goblin headed for one of the buildings. Worse off than the others, the shack either needed a lot of paint or a backhoe.

Isaac wished he was with the others. He was trained to stop a target permanently, not apprehend them.

The goblin didn't even check over his shoulder before he squeezed through a gap in the thick boards.

"They smell terrible," Vran said.

"They're not very stable," Argent said. "Whoever cast this prioritized quantity over quality."

"Well, there are a *lot* of them," Jack observed.

"They're made of mud and straw," Daffodil said. "My power is useless."

"You need a weapon," Argent said.

Daff gasped. "Did you just make my costume's claws real?"

"Yes."

"I've got eyes on the summoner," Hex said. "Great, now I'm doing it."

A figure wearing tattered clothes and even more mud stalked toward the building. She might have been playing at medieval poverty but Isaac didn't think so.

"That's her," Isaac said. "She reeks of whatever spell this is."

"Hex. Frost. Don't let the goblins escape, but don't let her hurt them either," Argent ordered.

"I've got her," Hex said. "Frost, you handle the goblins."

"There's three of them," he complained.

"Suck it up," the dean said. "Life is rarely fair."

He opened his mouth to say something, but before he could speak, Hex made a twisting motion with her hands, muttered something he couldn't quite hear, and the summoner rose off her feet, knocked back by a gust of wind.

The goblin mother poked her head out of the shack and spotted Isaac coming toward her. Her eyes went wide and she ducked back inside.

"Wait!"

She burst through the wood, sending splinters and dust in all directions, a child under each arm, ready to bowl Isaac over as she bolted.

"We're trying to protect you," Isaac said.

"The hells you are."

Isaac nodded to the summoner. She found her feet and hurled something at Hex, a ball of mud and slime.

Hex made a gesture, and the ball split as if sliced in two.

The goblin's eyes darted from side to side, looking for a way past Isaac. He was glad she balked at just stomping him.

"She's here to kill you. We're not. Seems like an easy choice."

The halves of the split ball began to sprout and grow, springing legs and vines.

"Whoa," some guy with a turkey leg said.

"We have an audience," Isaac said.

"We have a *crowd*," Vran said as a cheer went up.

"Your form is improving, Vran," Argent said. "Mr. Ford, you're still favoring your left side."

"That's the strong side," Ford said.

"You need to develop both," the dean interjected.

One of the mud monsters reached Hex, and she put her hands together, the palm of her right behind her left. She made a shoving motion. The thing went rolling, vines and thorns flailing as it struck the summoner and knocked her flat.

Hex gave a satisfied nod.

The other thing shambled toward Isaac and the goblins, its knuckles dragging the ground at the end of its heavy, ropy arms.

"You have to promise us sanctuary!" the goblin said.

"Argent?" Isaac asked.

"Done," she said. "I swear on my favorite car."

"We'll protect you," Isaac said. "The queen says so."

He didn't ask about the car.

The goblin shook her head, set down her kids, and ripped a plank off the decrepit building to wield it like a club.

Isaac drew his knives.

He didn't think they'd help. What he needed was a Weedwacker..

The goblin swept out, bashing the creature with the board.

"I should have stayed in the library," Jack complained. "How many of these things are there?"

"Twenty-four . . . twenty-three . . . twenty-two . . twenty-one!" Ford said, sounding a little too pleased with himself over the sound of tearing wicker and snapping wood.

The vine monster reached Isaac, and he kicked it as hard as he could. Its head snapped back. He was about to smile when its fist reached up, faster than he'd expected, and slammed into his leg, sending him backward.

"Girl," the summoner spat. Her voice was creaky and wet, like sodden wood. "You do not know who you're dealing with."

"Witch, please," said Hex.

The summoner raised her hands and Hex muttered an equation. Force ripped through the air.

It was like the time a bird had bounced off the big window in the chapel. The glass had reverberated. He'd held his breath, waiting for it to shatter, knowing the Old Man would not be happy.

"I have a powerful patron," the summoner bragged.

She fixed her hands into claws, and the nearest trees began to shake.

"Which means you have to trade for your power," Hex said. "Is that what you do? Kill to barter for scraps? I wonder how much you have in the bank?"

"More than you."

The closest trees began to uproot themselves.

Isaac rolled aside as the mud monster tried to crush him with a stomp.

"Earth magic," Hex mused. "You have some chthonic patron, something calling itself a god?"

"He is lord of all the land," the summoner said.

"Huh. So what happens when I break your connection to the earth?"

Hex dropped to her knees and scratched a formula into the dirt.

The ground beneath them fused to glass.

"What?" the summoner said, turning back and forth.

"No earth. No patron. No power."

The mud monsters collapsed. The trees stopped moving.

"How?" the summoner asked. She stomped at the glittering ground, but it didn't shatter.

"Oh, I don't know," Hex said as the goblin strode forward, board raised to do damage. "Silicate and heat. I'm not really sure. After all, I'm just a *girl*."

The summoner ripped something off her neck, a bottle, and tossed it on the ground. A murky puddle oozed from it. She stepped into it and vanished.

"She's gone." Hex eyed the dried-up portal. She let out a long, shaky breath. The glass faded away.

"A glamour?" Isaac asked.

"You think I have enough power to transmute an entire field?"

"I thought you'd cut her connection to the earth."

"No," Hex said, bent at the waist and clearly winded. "But she *believed* I had. That was enough. Patronage to a deity is all about belief. I'm just annoyed she got away."

Worried they'd lost their quarry in the chaos, Isaac turned, but the goblin hadn't run.

"Awesome effects!" someone called over the line.

"Thank you!" Argent said in a cheerful, fake voice. "We're so happy you liked our show! We'll be signing autographs later. Thank you to our effects company, Brighter Daze!"

"Brighter Daze?" Isaac asked.

Argent sighed.

"I am extemporizing," she said into her earpiece.

"That means she's making it up," Jack said.

"I knew what it meant," Isaac said.

"I didn't," Ford confessed.

"Vran, get Isaac, Hex, and the goblins back to the school," Argent said. "I'll cover the rest of us once we escape our new *fans*."

"Are you going to murder us?" Ford asked over the line.

"Keep smiling and waving," Argent said cheerily. "But no, of course not."

"I'm considering it," the dean said.

"They got the job done without any mortal injuries," Argent argued.

"Still, they risked exposing us, and they lost the summoner. B minus."

"B minus?" Daffodil said. "But nobody got hurt and I had to fight wearing a dinosaur costume!"

"I docked a full letter grade for the flirting," the dean said.

26
SKIES FULL OF STARS

"Are they okay?" Isaac asked. "All of them?"

"They're safe," Argent said. "Despite the summoner's efforts."

They'd returned to the school only for Argent to call for Isaac and Vran a while later. Now they stood in the labyrinth, outside a new door. Something crept at the corner of Isaac's vision. He wondered if it was one of the elusive guards.

"She wasn't an Undertaker," Vran said. "Who was she?"

"A freelancer," Isaac said.

Argent scowled.

"Which means whoever hired the assassin that killed the goblin in the Decay has funds enough to afford other assassins."

"It won't go over well," Isaac said. "The Old Man doesn't like it when the client brings in competition."

"I don't like that there are unknowns in this situation."

"Me either."

"Let's get on with it," Argent said. "Bella will only talk to you."

"Why me?"

"I think you impressed her when you tried to save her children. She trusts you, at least more than she trusts the rest of us."

"Then what am I doing here?" Vran asked. "I'm the one who put them in danger."

Argent swung a finger between them.

"Carrot. Stick."

"Will you be listening?" he asked.

"Of course." Argent waved to the door.

Isaac nodded and pushed it open. He paused to take in the room.

Bella sat in a large, soft-looking chair. There were books, a rug with roses, and a vase of some sweet-smelling pale flowers perched next to the teacup on the table to her right.

"Yeah," she said. "I was expecting something else too."

Isaac took one of the chairs across from her. Vran remained standing and pressed himself against the wall.

"Where are your kids?"

"Sleeping. This is the first real rest they've gotten since you showed up."

"I'm sure the sugar crash had something to do with it," Isaac said, remembering the cotton candy and how he'd collapse after an outing when Kenji had overindulged him in sweets.

"This is pretty nice considering what you were doing to people," Vran said.

Bella tensed.

"It wasn't personal. Just business."

It had felt pretty personal to Isaac. It certainly had to be personal for Vran and anyone else whose blood they'd taken.

"How long were you at it?" Isaac asked.

"Decades. Nobody cared until now."

"New king, new Guardians," Vran said.

"Now you're sipping tea at the elves' expense." Isaac leaned forward. "The queen said you had something to tell us about your business."

"Did you kill my husband?"

"No," Isaac said. "And wasn't he your ex?"

"Yes and no." Her face sank. "We were . . . complicated."

"I bet."

Isaac got it. He really did. This job was complicated. How he felt about it was complicated.

"I can't tell you what you want to know," she said. "We're just the farmers. We don't know who's at the top of the chain, who's in charge of it all. I only know that they've been at it for years."

"But you know who you deliver to," Isaac said. "Right? You've got *their* name."

"Yes, and I'll give it to you."

"Let me guess, you want something in exchange?" Vran asked.

He was doing a better job at being intimidating than Isaac liked. He remembered the moment at the ball when Vran had threatened the arrogant boy. More and more, Isaac saw Vran's point about elven nicety and manners being a cover for something darker.

Isaac was the assassin, but he was starting to think his boyfriend was the scary one.

"This. Safety," the goblin said, waving at the room around them. "Give us that for as long as you can promise it."

"That's a long time," Vran said.

"Maybe not as long as you think." Bella leaned forward. "There are a lot of rumblings out there. A lot of whispers."

"What sort of whispers?" Isaac asked.

"Like you said, there's a new king atop the dung heap. Rumors say he isn't as strong as the old one. Sooner or later someone is going to test that." She narrowed her eyes at Vran. "You lot may not sit atop the pile much longer."

Isaac remembered the ball, the number of guards the king had arrived with. He remembered how busy Argent had been when they'd gone into the Decay, and he remembered Silver's warnings about change and the risks of moving too fast with his reforms.

"It doesn't matter though, does it?" Isaac asked. "They've already tried to kill you once. They'll keep coming until we stop them."

"Then let's hope you can protect us," Bella said. "You're Guardians, so guard us."

"We'll do our best to keep you safe," Vran said. "But I'll need to check with the boss."

He stood and left the cell.

The thing was, Isaac knew they would. They would try, do their best, despite the threats they were facing. The Guardians didn't think like killers. They didn't train like them. The Undertakers would cut their losses and run. The Guardians, at least the ones Isaac knew, wouldn't fare well in a war against them. They were too merciful. They cared too much. Maybe that was why the last lot had been so effective. They hadn't cared about anyone but their own power. They'd lost touch with what they were supposed to do—protect people—and they'd been stronger for it.

Maybe the new king was making a difference. He was clearly ruffling feathers, but how long would he last if his authority was in doubt? And how long until he had to become more like his father to keep his crown?

If someone took Silver down, it would mean more than the end of the school. It could mean war and disruption across all the realms.

Damn it, he was starting to think like Daffodil.

"Why me?" Isaac asked the goblin. "You could have told her yourself, made this deal without me here."

"You're an Undertaker." She smiled flatly. "I can see it. You're calculating how to come out on top when it all blows up. You're one of us, the folk just trying to live through it."

Was he? That had been true when he'd set out to prove himself. He wasn't certain anymore.

He had to get it done. He was closer than ever, but it also felt so far away.

Tick tock.

Isaac couldn't ignore the problem, couldn't just blow off the job. The Old Man would send someone else, and soon. Isaac needed to show some results, progress, but he couldn't pretend his hesitation was just about Vran.

He couldn't bear to see Hex or Ford, any of them, laid out on a slab in Shepherd's office.

"You know it's coming," Bella said. "I can see it in your eyes."

He had to stop this. He had to find a way out of the job.

Argent stepped into the room, bringing Isaac back to the moment.

"We agree to your terms," she said.

"How?" the goblin asked. "How will you keep us safe?"

"Vran has an idea. We'll send you somewhere they can never find you. Somewhere far away."

"Could you find me there?" the goblin asked Isaac.

"Me? No, but that doesn't mean someone else couldn't."

One of his brothers, maybe. The Undertakers were as dogged as they were paid to be. Distance was no guarantee. After all, Kenji had beaten them to the goblin in the Decay.

"Your best bet is to tell us what you know," Argent said. "They'll know we took you in. They'll assume that we forced you to talk."

"Would you?" she asked.

"No," Argent said. "We don't work that way."

Maybe they should, Isaac thought. Maybe that's what it would take to survive. Maybe they should play the game to win it. They were capable of it, clearly. The king was at least.

But then they'd be back to where they'd been before, he realized, remembering Lin's class and their field trip. The Guardians were evolving, and that was a good thing, but still, Shepherd might be wrong about defense mechanisms. They might still need them. They might still need some Guardians who could pull the trigger when it came time to survive.

"It's a gamble," Isaac said to Bella. "If you tell us, we might be able to stop this, stop whoever's at the top, before they find you."

"And if you're lucky we'll cause so much trouble for them that they'll be too busy to worry about you," Vran added.

"I am not certain you two are a good influence on each other," Argent said before facing the goblin. "But they have a point."

"All right," Bella said. "Passage to as far as you can send us in exchange for the name."

"There won't be anybody there," Vran said. "Just the three of you. Is that all right?"

"Is there food? Water?"

"Yeah," he said.

"Then that's all I need. Everything else can burn as far as I care."

Vran's shoulders sagged, and Isaac knew he was thinking about their conversation at the end of the world.

He wondered if she would have brought her ex, protected him too. It was complicated, she'd said, but Isaac had seen enough of their memories and tasted enough of their blood to know they still cared about each other, despite whatever had driven them apart.

"Here's what I know," Bella continued. "There's a dealer in the Shoals. We got our payment and drop instructions from her."

"That's not a name," Argent said.

"She's just the Dealer," the goblin said. "She's the only one. You'll find her in the gambling hall."

"Do you know it, Vran?" Argent asked.

He nodded.

"Gather your children," Argent said. "Vran will open the way."

The goblin shuffled off into the other room.

"Is that it for me then?" Isaac asked Argent. "Can I help you or is it back to the school?"

The queen sighed.

"I don't have another option right now, do I, Vran?"

"What does she mean?" Isaac asked.

Vran sighed.

"The Shoals are outside Guardian jurisdiction."

"And neither of you are Guardians, not officially. I can't risk showing my face there. Winter elves are most unwelcome," Argent said.

"What is it?" Isaac asked. "What is this place?"

"Home," Vran said. "It's where I come from."

Argent scowled. Vran nibbled his lip.

"If there's a conspiracy against the crown, it's likely brewing there," she warned. "Our cases may be connected."

"And you can't come with us," Vran said.

"Not without risking another open conflict with your people. That's in no one's best interest right now."

Isaac wanted to ask Vran what she meant about his people, but Bella returned. One of the goblets stood sleepily at his mother's side. The other lay curled into her arms.

"Are you ready, Vran?" Argent asked.

"Yes." He sounded far away.

His eyes had gone dark, but Isaac only saw the stars.

The goblet huddled near his mother. Isaac didn't blame him. Vran's magic still gave Isaac pause, and he'd kissed the guy.

"Open the door, Isaac," Argent said.

He did, and starlight drifted into the room.

He knew it, the white beach, the dark ocean, and the hills of purple flowers. Their sweet scent filled the hall.

"You won't be able to get back," Isaac said.

"As long as we're safe," the goblin replied. "That's all that matters."

She took her boys through.

The walking one gave them a little wave.

How bad did it have to be? How scared was she that she'd risk banishment to someplace so remote? It was beautiful but lonesome.

Isaac closed the door.

"We have to find whoever's behind this," he said.

"Why is this so important to you, Frost?" Argent asked. "Why are you so invested in helping us catch these people?"

Kids, he thought. There were kids in danger. It was the same reason he and Kenji had to stop the Undertaker, but what he said was, "I already told you. Whoever's behind this is taking blood, magical blood. I think they might be like me."

It was also true, but he didn't want any more deaths, any more Samuels in the Graveyard.

"Phages?" Vran asked.

"Who else would want it?"

"But why stockpile it?" Vran asked.

"I don't know," Isaac admitted. "The dead blood, what I tasted in Shepherd's office—it wasn't good. It didn't give me the goblin's abilities."

"But it did give you some of his memories," Argent mused.

"Only for a moment, and only because I had a bit of hers still in my system. I can't imagine they want it for the magic."

"You were right," Vran said. "Your power is kind of gross."

"A dealer in the Shoals . . ." Argent mused. "And someone buying magical blood."

"I don't see how they're connected," Vran said.

"We need to work our way up the chain," she said.

"And we start with this dealer?"

"Apparently. I regret that I cannot come with you. I suspect you'll need more than an adviser this time. I suspect you'll need a sword."

"I've still got one," Vran said. "Should we go now?"

"No," Argent said. "It may be a trap. Let me make certain it's safe for you. I'll send word."

"How can you know?" Isaac asked.

"The same way I found the goblin," Argent said.

"Spies?" Isaac asked.

Argent smiled. She didn't confirm it, but he knew he'd guessed correctly.

27
WHAT WE LEAVE BEHIND

This was it. He could put it off no longer. Everything was building to something, an end.

Knowing that Argent had agents out there, it was very likely she'd uncover the truth about him soon.

At the same time, making his way downward, every sense tuned to his surroundings, he knew he didn't want this anymore.

So why are you still doing it?

Because there was no way out.

Maybe they'd catch him and put an end to this farce. Maybe they'd believe him if he spouted some dumb lie. After all, he belonged here now.

The Graveyard wasn't his home anymore.

The steps to the labyrinth appeared without fanfare. The school trusted him now. It believed that he belonged, and it twisted something inside him.

Kenji had it easy. He didn't have to care. He could just toss a knife and be done. A dove's work was so much worse. Isaac hadn't expected to give a damn, to care about any of them.

So much of him wished he didn't, but time was running out. He had to find the heart. He had to finish this.

He pushed open the door made of keys and stepped into the buzzing yellow lights.

He passed Shepherd's door. The way lay clear, but just like always, he had the sense he wasn't alone, that something more than the school lived here, that he was watched.

The door to Bella's cell had vanished, and the feeling of being watched deepened as he continued, a sort of twist in his guts. Something, the faintest of breaths, brushed the back of his neck.

Isaac almost turned back. He shouldn't be doing this, didn't want to, but couldn't see a choice, couldn't see a way out.

He knew what was coming and braced himself as the lights went out.

"Show me," he said.

He wasn't a child.

He wasn't afraid.

The whispers grew more numerous as he walked. He could not make out everything they said.

Conflicted.

Questioning.

Show him.

Light exploded, and Isaac was back in the Graveyard, in its damp, hazy air.

This was it, another memory.

Isaac felt like he always felt with Samuel, a squishy feeling in his chest, like he'd been given a duty he didn't want to do but had no choice. He'd rather be alone.

The Undertaker led them to the basement door. He took a ring of heavy keys from his belt and unlocked it. It creaked open, revealing a flight of dusty, splintery stairs.

"Go on," he said, gesturing for them to enter.

"I thought we weren't supposed to go down there," Isaac said in case this was a test of their loyalty, of how well they obeyed.

He exchanged a glance with Samuel, who shook, just a little.

The smaller boy was wise to be afraid.

Failure always came with a price.

Isaac waited for the Undertaker to confirm that they should go inside. That too was a risk. Measuring when to hesitate, when to act . . .

he was getting better at it. Honing his instincts, as Kenji called it, but Samuel remained behind.

"Go on," the Undertaker repeated with just enough of a growl that Isaac hurried through the doorway.

It wasn't bright, but enough dingy daylight came from the windows set at ground level for them to see.

Samuel followed, several steps behind him, a shadow with too-noisy breaths.

The Undertaker came down behind them, his heavy steps shaking the narrow wooden stairs. The the Undertaker pulled a string and flooded the room with light.

The bulb buzzed, reminding Isaac of something he couldn't quite remember as he took in the shelves that lined the walls.

They were packed with cardboard boxes. Many were closed but some lay open, stuffed until their contents overflowed onto the floor. Some of it glittered. Most of it did not.

"What is all this stuff?" Samuel asked.

"It's from the dead," Isaac guessed.

"Very good, Dove," the Undertaker said, and the cold, the fear that he might misstep and fail, retreated just a little.

"Why aren't they buried with it?" Samuel asked.

Isaac wanted to know too, but he pressed his lips tightly together so he did not guess too soon.

The Undertaker gave him a little nod, like they had an understanding, just the two of them. Samuel wasn't in on the joke.

Isaac let his eyes drift over the open boxes.

Something glittered in the pile, a bit of silver. He tugged on it, freed a chain. It was almost black with tarnish. Something dangled from the end.

"What is that?" Samuel asked.

"A book," Isaac said. "It's a locket."

It was metal, probably also beaten silver.

He opened it. There were photos inside. A man, a woman, and a child sat fixed in black and white. The pictures were old, he knew that because the people weren't smiling.

"Who were they?" Samuel asked.

"I don't know," Isaac said, forgetting that he'd been trying not to speak until he could satisfy the Undertaker's unspoken requirement.

That was best, to keep quiet until he had the *right* answer.

He wished Samuel asked fewer questions. He wished he knew when to keep quiet. Then it wouldn't feel like he was alone. Even with Samuel as his constant shadow. Even with Kenji, Isaac always felt alone.

"They're nobody," he said. He dropped the locket and chain back atop the pile. "Not anymore."

The Old Man gave another little nod.

"It's the same reason the gravestones are blank," Isaac said.

"That's right," the Undertaker confirmed. "We don't just kill them. We *erase* them."

"But why?" Samuel whined.

"Because it creates fear," the Undertaker said, surprising Isaac. He must be in a good mood to be so forthcoming. "Fear makes the world go round. Fear that you're missing out, that you're too old, that you'll starve. That you'll die."

He waved his arms around at the horde of lost trinkets and jewels.

"Not knowing what happened to them makes others afraid, that the same could happen to them, and fear is good for business."

"But you could sell it all," Samuel said. "There's so much of it."

He had a point. The jewelry, the gold and stones and little silver books full of pictures had to have value to someone, somewhere, but Isaac already knew the answer to this one.

"It would leave a trail," Isaac said. "The ones we bury here have to disappear without a trace."

"That's right, Dove."

He and Samuel followed the big man out of the basement.

The day went on as usual from there. They ran. They sparred.

They played a version of hide and seek where the longer they stayed hidden the more food they got at dinner. Isaac was better at hunting than hiding.

Samuel was bad at both.

Powers were allowed because life wasn't fair and your target might have an advantage you did not. Many of the boys ate little or nothing on the days they played those games.

Samuel was almost always among them, always found too soon to eat much. Isaac tried not to share his meal, but he did. He told himself that Samuel needed to get better, had to get better. Isaac was older. He wouldn't always be there to cover for the boy, to protect him. It wouldn't be long until he was sent on jobs.

They were in their crypt, Isaac in his bunk, his mind turning, when Samuel whispered, "Is that what we do, erase people?"

"Go to sleep, Samuel."

"But, Isaac—is that what happens?"

"To the ones the clients want it to."

He didn't mean to be so short, to sound so mean, but it had been a long day.

"But . . ."

"Go to sleep, Samuel."

He knew that if Samuel got going, they'd be up all night. He always expected Isaac to have the answers, but he didn't. He couldn't. The Old Man didn't tell them everything. He hardly told them anything. He wouldn't, so they'd be strong, be smart. They'd find the answers in the moment, make choices that hopefully kept them alive.

"But Isaac . . . what if that's what happened to us?"

"Shut up and go to sleep."

Isaac let out a seething breath and rolled over.

This was dangerous ground, thinner ice than usual. It was always there, the idea that someone out there had given them up, had given him up.

Did someone have his photo in a little silver book?

Did someone, somewhere, care that he was alone?

"No family but killers," he whispered, reciting the words that hung in the chapel's dining hall. "No memories of the dead."

The past let him go. The weird twilight of the Graveyard's night faded to a more perfect darkness. The cold air of the crypt he shared with Samuel warmed.

Isaac took several seething breaths.

He'd been walking in the dark. He felt sure of it. He'd gone further than before.

The lights remained out, but something had changed beneath his feet.

Isaac knelt and let his fingertips explore the surface of the floor. Shapes were etched into the stone. Dry and a little dusty, he traced one figure, then another. He felt them with his palms, and the shapes were defined enough to feel them through the leather of his fingerless gloves.

Keys. The floor was etched with keys.

Forgotten, the whispers chorused.

Erased.

"It wasn't me," he said. "I didn't kill them."

Samuel, the voices whispered, so quiet Isaac almost couldn't hear them. *What happened, Isaac? What happened to the boy?*

"Stop it," he said. "Just—stop."

At the far end of the passage, around a bend, a single light came on. It illuminated pale skin, pale hair.

Isaac . . . the whispers called. *What happened to the boy?*

The light went out again.

Isaac growled and . . . sat up?

He was in his room, in his bed.

He was still dressed, his gloves on his hands.

His heart raced.

It hadn't been a nightmare, hadn't been an illusion. He'd seen *someone* down there, a boy, but he didn't know if it was Samuel. It couldn't be.

Samuel was dead.

He'd been erased.

28

READING IN ELVISH ISN'T FUNDAMENTAL

"The school changes," Hex said, going through a presentation she'd projected onto a screen.

The stones she'd numbered while Isaac had kept watch shifted as she moved through the images.

"It reacts to our requests, and my observation of its morphogenic field, what most would call its aura, indicates that it both expands and contracts."

"And your thesis?" Lawless asked, her brown eye focused on Hex's detailed map of the stones.

"I believe the school is alive, that it holds at least an animal level of sentience."

The class reacted with a mix of agreement or consideration.

"Does that mean it can feel pain?" Isaac asked. "That it can be hurt?"

He thought about the stones he'd pulled out of place. He thought about the task he was shying away from.

"Perhaps," Hex said. "It's not an animal, so that comparison might not be the best, but it's certainly more complex and advanced than your average plant. It's also growing."

"What does that mean?" Daffodil asked. "How big will it get?"

"The school was created in a fount of magic," Lawless said. "The rebirth of a Watchtower, a rare event. You may be the only students, possibly the only beings, who will ever have the chance to observe this from the inside."

Hex nodded.

"It is slowing, at least since I started measuring it."

"The lava's cooling now that the island's here," Ford said.

Everyone looked at him.

"Sometimes volcanoes go off and make new islands," he said with a shrug. "The school's like that, only magic is the lava."

"An apt analogy, Mr. Ford," Lawless conceded.

"I watched a lot of documentaries when my parents kept me home."

"The rate of change within the school also slowing," Hex said, clicking through several slides. Stones that had been irregular had smoothed. The distance between closed and the green light faded. "Especially in the common areas, those have mostly settled into place."

"Why those?" Daffodil asked.

"It might be because they're the most observed." Hex gestured to a picture of the stones they'd numbered before flipping to another set. These still floated, unconnected and unmoored. "The less observed areas show the most volatility."

"Like particles," Daff said. "They're quantum."

She shrugged.

"Jack was telling me about it."

"Exactly," Hex said. "The school may be reacting to observation, or it may be repetition. The areas that get the most use settle faster, like animals wearing paths into a forest."

"And we're the animals?" Isaac asked.

"Yes," Hex said.

Isaac considered the labyrinth. Maybe his efforts were harder because no one went there. That meant the guards, the demons, didn't count, at least not in the same way. The more attempts he made to reach the heart, the further he got. He was forging a path just by walking where no one else had.

He tuned out Hex as she rattled off a bunch of equations and mathematical proofs he didn't understand until class ended.

"You're wanted at the library, Frost," Lawless said as she dismissed them.

He opened his mouth to ask why but closed it again.

It could only be one thing.

"Thanks," he said and headed that way.

He was halfway there when Vran slid into place beside him, matching his stride.

"Is this it?" he asked.

"I guess," Isaac said, trying to remain cool.

Vran reached out and took his hand.

"How did you know?" Isaac asked.

"You're marching with purpose toward the library," Vran said. "What else could get you to go there without complaining?"

"I think I liked it better when you weren't speaking to me."

"No, you didn't," Vran said.

Isaac grinned. "No, I didn't."

Isaac pushed the door open. Jack wasn't at the desk.

They found him peering into a wide, wooden crate resting in the center of the room. It came up to Isaac's waist, which was a good sign.

Jack reached in and retrieved a thick, leather-bound volume broader than his chest. Laying it carefully on a table, he spied them and asked, "How did you manage this?"

"We ran into the king at elf prom," Isaac said. "He, uh . . . offered to help with my project."

"Well, he seems to like you." Jack waved at the box. "And from what I understand, he doesn't like many people."

Vran peered inside.

"They sent all of this?"

"Apparently," Jack said, laying the book on a table with a heavy thump. "Over a dozen volumes, some of them quite ancient."

"They're all books on Phages?" Isaac hurried to open the book Jack had just laid down.

"No, sadly," Jack said. "There's not one comprehensive treatise, but these contain *references* to Phages. Once compiled, we should know more about you and your people."

"They're all in Elvish," Isaac squinted at the spiraling text on the massive volume's spine. "Aren't they?"

"Yeah, but that's not much of a problem. I'll scan them and translate them before I send them back."

"How long will that take?"

"This many books—this many pages . . . a while." Jack pushed his glasses up. "It could go faster though."

"How?"

"You can help me with the scanning."

"Of course."

"Me too," Vran said before cautiously adding, "if you'll let me."

"If you're careful," Jack said, eyeing the elf with a narrowed gaze.

Vran held up his hands as if in surrender.

"It was one time, Jack."

"It was a fire spell. In. A. Library."

"Almost everything in here is metal," Vran complained. "Including you. Hardly anything burned."

"You singed my favorite bow tie," Jack said. "Besides, now we have—"

He waved at the big book.

"*A Meditation on the Beasts of the Altmarch*," Vran provided.

"That," Jack said. "And I won't have our first loan from the Academy going back so much as smudged. I want this to continue."

"I was just trying to show Hex how it works for me," Vran said.

"What does the sign say, Vran?"

"'*Absolutely no magic in the library*,'" Vran read glumly. "I promise to follow the rules."

"Fine."

Jack sighed and led them toward a table with some equipment that had to be the scanners.

"This is still going to take forever," Isaac said.

"Not necessarily," a voice replied.

Hex came into the library and took a seat. Daffodil and Ford followed her.

"What are you all doing here?" Isaac asked.

"We want to help," Daffodil said.

"Really?"

"You helped me with my project," Hex said. "It's the least I can do, and this doesn't involve slipping on acidic goose shit."

Daffodil squirmed. Isaac didn't know if her reaction was to the mention of the substance, or Hex's language.

"Yeah," Ford agreed. "We can scan books. It should only take a few hours with all of us working on it. Shy's here too, aren't you?"

"Yes," a faint voice replied.

"But how did you . . ." Isaac trailed off.

"I texted Daff," Jack said with a shrug.

"And I texted everyone else," Daff said. "You really need to get a phone, Isaac."

Vran nodded. "Even I have one."

"Thank you," Isaac said. "All of you."

"These look really old," Daff said, taking a seat and looking at the book Jack laid in front of her. "Do we need gloves?"

"No," Jack said. "Just clean, dry hands. It's actually better. You're less likely to tear the pages that way."

Hex unrolled a scroll.

"I think this is papyrus, or whatever passes for it in Alfheimr."

"Winter reed," Vran said, gently brushing a fingertip along the edge. "I like that they used it for a book."

"Why?" Isaac asked.

"I like puns."

Jack rolled his eyes and gave them all a quick demonstration on using the scanners, and they got to work.

Isaac lost track of time, carefully aligning the pages with the wand and watching the images form on the screen.

He stole a glance around the table. He watched the pages of Shy's book turn as if by themselves.

Something in his chest tightened.

He caught Vran staring at him.

"What?" Isaac demanded.

"You look like you're having 'big feelings.'" Vran made air quotes.

"I just—I can't believe you're all helping. Thank you."

"Like I said before, we like you, Frost," Hex said.

"Yeah, dude," Ford agreed. "You're one of us. You belong here."

And he did.

He'd tried denying it, especially knowing what would come of it, but he did. Isaac felt himself warm in a way not unlike how he felt when he kissed Vran.

They finished, and Jack carefully packed the books back into their crate. He stared off into space for a while, his eyes a deep gold, the geometric lines on his green skin pulsing with little sparks of light.

Isaac chewed his lip.

"It's compiling," Jack said. "I should have it all translated in a few days."

"Days?" Ford asked.

"I'm sorry, does me translating an ancient language with multiple subdialects and semantic drift over literal eons in less than a week not impress you?"

"It does me," Daff said, leaning to kiss Jack on the cheek.

"Keep it in your pants, Daff," Hex grumbled.

"I appreciate it, really," Isaac said. "Thank you, Jack. Thank you all."

It didn't feel adequate, but he didn't know what else to say.

"I'll walk you back," Vran said, offering his hand.

Isaac took it.

"Does this mean you two are official?" Ford asked.

"Uh . . ." Isaac couldn't quite meet Vran's eyes.

"If you'd like to be," Vran said, the tips of his ears turning pink. "Then, well, I'd like to be."

"I guess we're official," Isaac said to everyone.

Daffodil made a happy, high-pitched *squee* sound. Hex rolled her eyes. Ford gave Isaac a nod.

Isaac didn't look back, and he and Vran left the library.

They knocked shoulders and cast glances when they weren't touching.

Isaac felt the pressure build in his chest.

It was a new kind of heat.

He pushed the door open to his room, started to say something, and found Vran kissing him. He grinned into it as they backed inside.

"I like kissing you," Vran said as Isaac eyed the bed.

"Me too—I mean kissing *you*."

"But, uh, that's kind of . . . that's as far as I like to go," Vran said.

"Yeah?"

"Yeah. Is that okay?"

Isaac smiled.

"It's more than okay."

So they kissed. They sat on the bed, then lay side by side, and he finally got to trace the black lines over Vran's chest.

Isaac felt full and strange and unbroken in a way he never had before.

When they stopped, they lay there, watching the light dance through the stones, the bit of his wall that remained uneven.

"I'm sorry if I hurt you," he whispered to the school.

He'd try not to do it again, not until he had to.

Vran went to the bathroom for water; at least Isaac assumed from the tap running that he was thirsty.

"Isaac?" he called. "What is this?"

"What is what?"

"The writing on the mirror."

He sprang up and went to see.

Scratched into the glass was a message:

TICK. TOCK. TIME'S UP.

29
EVERYTHING CHANGES

Isaac could lie. He could keep going as he had and pretend that he'd written it himself as a reminder about his project, or something else, but the lies felt heavier and heavier every day. He'd sink into the ground if they weighed him down any further.

"No," he said.

He didn't want to do it anymore. Any of it.

"'No' what?" Vran asked.

"There's something I need to tell you."

"Okay."

Isaac let out a long breath.

"All of you. I need to tell all of you."

"Is this a Dean thing or an Argent thing?"

"Uh . . ." Did he really want to do this? No, but he had to. Time was up. "It's both."

"Okay," Vran said again, heading for the door.

Isaac sighed and followed him.

It would have been nice to have just brushed it aside and kept up with the kissing, but it was too late for that. It might already be too late.

The Undertakers were coming.

"We need to get everyone."

Vran stepped to the nearest door in the hallway, opened it, and called, "Can you meet us in the main hall? It's important."

"Did you just open a door to everywhere all at once?"

"Yeah," Vran said. "So?"

"How?"

"I needed to, so I did," Vran said.

It confirmed something Isaac had been suspecting for a while, that Vran was on better terms with the school than the rest of them. He was never late for class and was always where or when he wanted to be.

Isaac didn't have time to pry as everyone began drifting into view.

"What is it, Vran?" Argent asked, arriving last.

"Isaac has something to say."

It was a lot harder with all of them looking at him, their faces expectant or worse, suspicious.

"I'm not supposed to be here," he said.

"We know," Hex said. "They made you come here."

"No. I mean, I came here on purpose." He couldn't meet Vran's eyes.

"I found you that night because the Undertaker told me to." Isaac raised his hands to make quote marks. "I *rescued* you so you'd bring me in after he spread rumors that I'd run away."

Isaac kept his eyes locked on Vran. He couldn't look at Argent. He did not want to consider what she'd do.

"Why?" Daffodil asked, and that pulled his gaze in her direction.

"To bring down the school from the inside," Isaac said. "To kill its heart."

"But why?" Ford echoed.

"Because someone wants it done. Someone paid the Undertakers to make it happen, so they sent me. They'll try to kill me just for telling you this."

Vran still hadn't said anything. Argent and the dean still hadn't said anything, though for once they weren't in conflict. They wore matching glowers aimed in his direction.

"Why are you telling us now?" Hex asked.

"Because I don't want to do it, and I don't want them to finish the job. Even if you kick me out, or lock me up, or whatever, they'll send someone else. They won't stop until the contract is satisfied. And they're coming."

"What do we do?" Daffodil asked, looking to the dean. "How do we stop them?"

"The Undertakers work for money, or at least for payment," Argent mused.

"Can we buy them off?" Hex asked. "It can't be that simple."

"No. The Undertaker wouldn't risk hurting his reputation that way, but if we take down the client, they wouldn't have a reason to keep coming."

Ford narrowed his eyes.

"And by take them down you mean . . ."

"Arrest them." Isaac held up his hands. "I don't want to kill anybody."

"You mean today," Hex said.

"Not at all, not anymore."

"But you did before? What changed?"

"I did."

Hex clearly wasn't mollified, but the dean hadn't tried to shoot him and Argent hadn't drawn her sword or atomized him, so it was going better than he'd expected. The cup of worms in his gut settled a bit, at long last.

"How do we find out who hired them?" Ford asked.

"We could sneak into their headquarters," Daffodil suggested. "There's got to be files or records, right?"

"The Graveyard?" Isaac considered. "Bad idea. It's warded against anyone but us. Besides, the Old Man doesn't write anything down. He keeps it all in his head. I don't even know who the client is."

"What about that summoner?" Hex considered, looking to Argent. "She wasn't an Undertaker."

"You're assuming that the client who hired her is the same one who wants the school shut down," Argent said.

"It's the best lead we have," the dean said.

"She's right," Vran said. "And even if it doesn't stop the Undertakers, we can still stop the blood thieves."

"I would enjoy a rematch with that summoner," Hex said, pounding her fist into her open hand.

"Why does she piss you off so much?"

"She's using the craft all wrong," Hex said. "She's killing people, and she's bargaining for power from something nasty to do it."

"Then we should bring her in, right?" Isaac asked.

"You're also assuming I'm still willing to let you assist," Argent said.

"Isaac didn't have to tell us," Vran said. "That should count for something."

"Still, he waited this long to do it," Argent said. "He could have told you anytime. You gave him plenty of chances to, Vran. I told you this approach was risky."

"And I told you that I trusted him, that he'd tell us when he was ready."

"Wait, you knew?" Isaac asked.

The queen rolled her eyes.

"I told you when I first met you, that I knew what you were, Frost, and you were hardly subtle during your adventures in the basement."

"And you let me do this, call everyone together to tell them when you already knew?"

"I didn't," Ford said.

Most of the students nodded.

"Some of us had a bet," Hex said. Her expression was stormy.

Daffodil frowned with her entire body.

Vran lifted his hands in a *what could I do* gesture.

"I didn't want to ruin your big reveal."

"Well, I feel stupid," Isaac said.

"Go with that," Argent said. "Let it lead you to better choices."

"And . . ." Isaac started to ask, looking at Vran and not knowing how to finish the question.

Vran kissed him.

"I meant every word," he said, after. "None of that was fake."

Isaac let out a long breath.

"Okay," he said. Swallowing hard, he met Argent's glare. "Let me help, please. You said it yourself, I'm not a Guardian. I can go where you can't."

"But the matter of whether or not we can trust you remains."

"As does the matter of whether or not you belong at this school," the dean said.

"But you already knew what I was doing here. You know I'm telling you the truth."

"You made the right decision," the queen said. "At long last. That doesn't mean I know you will make it again, or that you aren't still keeping secrets."

"Then let me prove it to you," Isaac said.

"How?"

"You want my secrets? Take them. Shepherd and the other demons can show you everything you want to know about me."

"I wouldn't ask that of anyone, Isaac Frost," Argent said. "Not even an Undertaker."

"You're not asking. I'm volunteering."

"Isaac," Vran said, sounding worried. "It's torture."

"Been through it already. They can tell you I'm not a murderer, but that doesn't mean I'm not responsible."

"Are you sure about this?"

"Yes. I'm tired of carrying it. Maybe this will help me let it go."

"What are you talking about?" Daffodil asked.

"I'll show you," he said. "Take me to the labyrinth."

"You don't have to do this," Vran said.

"Yeah, I do. If that's the price to stay here, with you, with all of you, I'm willing to pay it."

"Will it satisfy you?" Vran asked, looking across the assembled professors and students.

Isaac could not read the room, not all of them, but most of them nodded. Some, like Daff or Argent, clearly didn't think it necessary.

"We'll see," the dean said.

That would have to be good enough for now.

"Then let's get it done."

30
NECRO-COUNSELING

Another sob broke from Samuel. They were deep in the woods, farther from the Graveyard and the chapel than Isaac had ever gone.

He didn't know where the property ended, when they'd officially leave the Graveyard, but it had to have an end. There had to be a way out.

Samuel started crying about the time they hit what Isaac thought to be their tenth mile.

This was never going to work.

Samuel was too small, too young, and far too afraid.

He wasn't ready to survive in the outside world, but he wasn't able to survive here either. Almost drowning had been the wake-up call, the near miss, and Isaac had started thinking.

The training would only get harder, riskier.

Isaac knew in his bones that Samuel would not return from his first sojourn.

He could not go alone. He could not stay, so Isaac would go with him.

Samuel gave out another choking sob.

"They'll catch us if you keep crying," Isaac said.

"I know . . . I'm sorry . . . I just . . ."

"We can go back," Isaac said. "It hasn't been very long. They won't suspect anything. We can tell them I was helping you train."

"I don't want to!" Samuel shouted.

Isaac clamped a hand over his mouth.

"We'll go back," he said.

Samuel shook his head and murmured *no*, over and over.

Isaac didn't know what to do. He'd known they had to run, to get away, but only now did he realize the size of what they were trying to do. He could steal enough food for both of them, find shelter and clothes, but Samuel was paralyzed just by trying to walk away.

The outer world would be too much for him, and he could not stay in the Graveyard.

Isaac could feel his own panic rising with the weight of it but stood there, hand clamped over Samuel's mouth, until Samuel stopped crying.

"If I let go, will you keep quiet?"

Samuel nodded. Some of his snot dripped onto Isaac's hand. It felt warm and slippery.

Isaac took his hand away and wiped it on his jeans.

"I'll keep you safe," he said. "I promise."

"Okay," Samuel whispered.

"Let's hurry."

Samuel took his lead and they kept moving. They reached a clearing. It was small, but Isaac hurried them across it. They were at the center when he froze.

"What is it?" Samuel asked, stumbling against his back.

Isaac didn't answer. He couldn't see them, couldn't smell them, but he knew they were there.

"Go on then," the Old Man said from somewhere unseen. "Let's see how far you get."

"You could just let us go," Isaac called. "We're no threat to you."

"It's not about being a threat, Dove. It's about *value*."

"We don't have any, so let us go."

"That's not true, not for both of you."

"You haven't sent me on any jobs," Isaac said, turning back and forth, trying to spot the Old Man in the trees.

They could make a run for it, but he knew they wouldn't get far. He could feel Samuel's back pressed against his.

"Your value to me isn't in what you do, but what you are."

Samuel stiffened.

"Sadly, that's not true for both of you."

"Isaac . . ." Samuel said.

"No," Isaac said. Turning, he wrapped his arms around Samuel.

He could shield him, keep the Undertaker at bay. If he was the only one with value, then surely the Old Man wouldn't risk Isaac's life over it.

"Clever," the Old Man said. "But how long can you stand there? You're not walking out of this, not both of you."

"Isaac," Samuel repeated. "You have to let me go."

"No," Isaac said.

"It's okay. We both know I wasn't going to make it. You still can."

"No. No."

He tightened his hold then grunted as Samuel punched him in the gut. Isaac didn't mean to let go, but he did. His reflexes reacted faster than he could control them.

He waited for the shot, for the bullet or knife, but it never came.

Isaac waited for the Old Man to appear, but no lesson came, no lecture, or blow.

"Come on, Isaac," Samuel said, offering him a hand.

Isaac took it, let Samuel pull him to his feet.

They didn't speak. They'd missed the meal.

They could see what there was to eat in the chapel, but no punishment had been forthcoming. They'd punish themselves and go hungry for the night. Hopefully that would be the end of it.

Isaac knew it wouldn't be. The tests would keep coming, and someday, sometime, Samuel would not make it.

Isaac thought he'd cry, sob himself to sleep like he had so many times before, but tonight he didn't.

"Thank you, Isaac," he said as they climbed into their bunks. "You know, for trying."

Isaac didn't answer. He'd failed, and he did not know what would happen next. He did not know how, or when, but the Old Man would make them pay.

He slept eventually, drifting off because he had nothing else to do, and woke to the sound of his name.

"Isaac. Wake up."

Kenji.

"Isaac. Damn it. Where's Samuel?"

He'd been groggy before. Now he snapped awake, instantly alert.

The bunk beside his was empty, and he knew, just *knew.*

"No," he said. "No."

"Where is he?" Kenji asked.

"The pond."

He didn't bother with his boots. The ground might be cold, but he felt colder. He wasn't certain he'd ever feel warm again.

Kenji ran ahead. Isaac followed, pulled by the inevitable, unable to resist, even as he tried not to see what he had to.

Samuel floated, pale and still, in the water.

Watch me, Isaac. Watch me.

It was all he could hear as Kenji dove in. He knew it wouldn't matter. It was too late.

He'd shut his eyes. He'd slept, and Samuel had slipped away.

It was the only way out.

Isaac wanted to scream, but why? He had survived. Samuel had not. As horrible as it was, there was a part of him washed in red guilt, and under that, relief. It was over. He didn't have to save Samuel, not anymore. He didn't have to worry about anyone else.

It was the only way.

Isaac came back to Shepherd's office, to the now, his face burning and wet with tears.

Returning to the present felt like he'd fallen out of bed and hit the floor, stunned and suddenly cold.

He wiped at his face. It did nothing to alleviate the heat or the pain in his chest.

"Your grief is nothing to be ashamed of," the demon said gently.

"Of course it is," Isaac said. "I let him die. I should have known, should have seen it coming."

"How could you?" Shepherd asked.

"He was just a kid, a child."

"So were you. It wasn't your fault."

"But it was," Isaac said. "I had a choice and I made it."

"You should never have been forced to make such a decision. Neither of you should have."

Isaac let out a long breath, kept letting it out, until his lungs felt fully empty. It didn't help. The ache was too deep, too settled in, like something had broken off inside his body that would cut worse if he tried to yank it out.

"Come," Shepherd said. "Let us speak to the dean and the others."

Isaac rallied and followed Shepherd out of his office and up the stairs.

Most of the school waited in the hall. They'd brought chairs or sat on the floor studying in little groups. Hex had three books open and laid out around her.

Daffodil straightened in her seat like she might spring to her feet and hug him. Vran did, wrapping his slender arms around Isaac and squeezing with that deceptive hidden strength. Isaac started to hug him back and stopped. It felt too much like the memory, like Samuel, even if he was always the weaker one when Vran embraced him.

"Well?" the dean asked Shepherd.

"I can tell you that Isaac believes he was sent here to destroy the school, and I can tell you that I believe he is sincere in his desire to prevent that from happening."

The dean started to say something else, but Shepherd held up a hand.

"I can also say that if you're looking to punish him for his deception, I believe he's done an adequate job of that himself. What he's been through is traumatic, and I resent being used as a lie detector to measure his worth."

"It was his idea," the dean said.

"Even so," Shepherd snapped before turning and heading for the stairs.

"Well?" Vran asked Argent. "I trust him. Are you satisfied?"

31
THE SHOALS

All he could taste, all he could scent, was sea salt and cold brine.

"What does that say?" Isaac asked, nodding up at the massive arch overhanging the dock.

Vran chattered off something in Elvish. It sounded icy and brittle, not at all like the musical tone of the king's people, the soft conversations and musical laughter he'd heard at the ball.

This was something else, something colder and chilling, wet bone and drowned flesh. Isaac suppressed a shudder.

"*The Sea does not forgive. The Sea does not forget,*" Vran translated.

"Oh," Isaac said. "That's . . . well, it's just a little weird to stick it right over the door."

The land beyond them was dark and cragged, a sharp bit of stone rising from the water. Small, no houses dotted it. The only feature, the only sign of habitation, was the dock. Creaking beneath their feet, swaying with the waves, it extended like a single finger into the tide.

"It's meant to be a warning," Vran said.

"To the Guardians?"

"To anyone not aligned with the Cups, the royals who control the sea."

"Wait, are these different royals than the pretty guy in the suit and his scary sister?"

"Yes. The Court of Cups rules over the sea elves, with various vassals and client kingdoms."

Vran took in the shifting tides with their whorls and the drifting isles.

"If they're being territorial . . ." Isaac gave the sign one more glance. "Then you'd think they'd put it in more languages."

"Why?" Vran asked with a tight shrug. "As far as they're concerned, theirs is the only tongue that matters."

Isaac reached to squeeze his hand.

"And these are your people?"

"They were." Vran had lent him some clothes. He'd traded his leather jacket for Vran's long trench coat with the tattered hem. He liked how it looked on him, and more importantly, it smelled like Vran.

Vran wore Isaac's jacket. The shirt he wore underneath was just black mesh, like a net. It wasn't like he needed more. He'd probably be comfortable in swim trunks. Isaac warmed at the image and the gesture, that they'd each worn something of each other's.

He could see them working like this in the future, as partners in the Guardians. Isaac still wasn't sure it was the future he wanted, but it was an option, one he might have to take when the Undertaker came for him.

"Are the Undertakers any better?" Vran asked.

"How did you know I was thinking about them?" Isaac asked.

"It isn't hard. Your face does this thing."

Vran mimed a constipated look that could not be accurate.

"Kind of," Isaac said. "I mean, they kill people but they're not racists or xenophobic, at least not as far as I ever saw."

"Xenophobic?" Vran asked, raising an eyebrow.

"It means—"

"I know what it means," Vran said. "It's just such a fancy word for someone who went to Murder School."

"I guess I'm picking up something in Lit class."

"I guess you are."

Isaac liked this better, the banter. It was familiar ground and far more comfortable than the pit that had opened beneath him since he'd told everyone the truth. It also helped dislodge some of the pain from his session with Shepherd, the freshly unearthed memory.

Now he was here, at the edge of an endless sea, despite himself. He was doing something dangerous because it was the right thing to do.

Vran smiled, and Isaac knew it had nothing to do with vocabulary.

It's like he infected me, Vran had said about Adam, the friend he considered a brother. Isaac understood now. The same thing was happening to him.

Isaac was changing.

He'd thought that the demon would tell them everything, that the last of his secrets would be left exposed to the students and professors. He wasn't sure how to feel that they hadn't. Perhaps it was for the best. Perhaps they'd let him stay if they had sympathy for him, but no—that was Undertaker thinking, that sort of manipulation. He needed a new way of seeing things.

Those old ways of moving through the world were a kind of trap. He could see that now, and he could see a way out.

Vran took Isaac's hand and led him onto the dock.

Theirs wasn't the only island.

Others bobbed, back and forth, up and down, in the waves. Connected by massive chains, they crashed together before separating as far as their iron tethers would allow.

Fog and spray obscured the horizon. Everything tasted of brine, and the sky loomed, too stormy to be pretty. If there was a sun, he could not find it.

"Is it all like this?" he asked, avoiding a hole in the wooden dock.

"Above? Yes."

"I can't believe you came from this . . ." Isaac waved a hand at the bleak churn.

Vran closed his eyes and let out a long breath.

"I fought my way out, to the very bottom, to a crown. It was the only way I saw at the time. I didn't realize I could go anywhere, that not everyone was like my family, that I could belong somewhere."

They weren't so different. He couldn't quite see a future beyond the Undertakers, couldn't quite dream of freedom from what he'd been raised with, but it was there, like a bit of warmth just before the sun rose. He'd chase it. He'd find it, and he'd do it with Vran.

And what about Kenji? What about your brothers?

Isaac had lain crying in the crypt he'd shared with Samuel. He couldn't sleep, could not stop picturing Samuel's limp body, his blue lips—his perfect stillness. The worst thing had been his closed mouth; he'd never ask him another question.

The door to the crypt had opened, letting in a crack of starlight and a shadow. Then it had closed. Isaac had tensed but hadn't moved. He hadn't tried to hide, stayed frozen.

If it were the Undertaker or someone else come to punish him for failing Samuel, then let them come. He deserved whatever pain they brought. He deserved worse.

"Isaac," Kenji had said.

He'd melted into Kenji's arms and sobbed and sobbed.

"I'm sorry," he'd whispered when he was done, and he did not know if he meant for crying, for the snot he'd left on Kenji's shirt, or for letting Samuel down.

"It's all right, Dove."

"How is it all right? How can it be?"

"We're going to stop him," Kenji whispered. "You and me. We're going to make sure there aren't any more Samuels."

"You're going to kill the Undertaker?"

"There isn't another way, but I can't do it alone. I need your help."

"What can I do?"

"For now? Nothing. I need you to train, to get strong enough to help me."

"What then?" Isaac asked.

"Then no more boys who can't survive. No more Samuels. You can't tell anyone, Isaac. It has to be our secret."

"Who else knows?"

"No one. Only you."

"Why?" Isaac felt another round of tears threaten to fall. "Why me?"

"The clearing. You tried to protect him. Because you care." Kenji put his hands on Isaac's shoulders and met his eyes. Issac could barely see in the gleam from the crypt's small windows. "Promise me you'll help. Promise me you'll keep it a secret."

"I promise," Isaac had said.

There would be no more Samuels if he could prevent it.

Isaac squeezed Vran's hand to shake off the past. He needed to be here, in the moment, in the Shoals. It was Vran who needed his help and protection now.

"I'm glad," Isaac said. "I'm glad you survived."

Vran's smile was weak in the sodden light.

"It can't be a coincidence that the contact is here," Vran said. "It's going to get very dangerous if my people are behind this."

"I was thinking the same thing, only that it might be Phages buying up the blood."

"Let's hope it's neither," Vran said. "That neither of our pasts are coming back to haunt us."

"I think it's too late for that, but yeah, let's try to avoid any family reunions."

"That's not what I meant. I know you want to know about them, but I'm worried about you meeting them like this."

"I don't even know if they're still out there," Isaac said.

"Give Jack more time. It's a good sign that it's taking a while. It means there was more information, more for him to translate."

"But what about your people?"

"I think a reunion is unavoidable." Vran nodded at the water.

"Are you safe here?" Isaac wanted to know as much as he wanted to change the subject. He twisted back and forth but didn't see anyone else. He'd never sense them coming, not in all this salt.

"I don't know. My people are here, maybe not the court. They're still hiding from Silver and Argent, but my family are below."

"Any chance they've let you go?"

After all, Isaac's family had given him away, traded him, and never tried to find him. Maybe Vran would be lucky and what haunted Isaac would be a gift to him.

"The sign doesn't lie." Vran nodded back toward the arch. "Sea elves don't forget, and they don't forgive."

"Then I guess I'm lucky you're not like other sea elves," Isaac said, knocking their shoulders together. "What do you want to do?"

"Not what I'm about to, but I think it's the best path."

"What do you mean?"

"Just what you said: a family reunion." Vran pulled Isaac toward the end of the dock and asked, "Trust me?"

"Always."

Isaac said it, but he wasn't sure he meant it. He wasn't sure he ever could, because that wasn't what an Undertaker was, and even if he wasn't an Undertaker anymore, even if that wasn't the road before him, he had to wonder if it wasn't too engraved, too written on his bones, for him to be any other way.

A lifetime of training and nothing to show for it, he thought. The Guardians had no use for a killer.

"On three then," Vran said. "One . . . two . . . three."

Hands still clasped, they leaped together.

Isaac had only a moment to remember Samuel's pale, sodden face. He tried to force himself to remember swimming to the bottom of the flood instead, of the good he could do.

Focus on the moment, he told himself.

It was going to be cold. It was going to ruin his coat, and he couldn't imagine fighting in a heavy, wet garment if it came to that.

Then the air flowed around them, forming a sphere of air that sank with them.

"How are you—"

But Isaac stopped talking when he saw Vran's face.

The lines on his face blackened and spread, branching like cracks. He'd gone paler than usual and sweat beaded his forehead.

Isaac said nothing and willed strength through their clasped hands. He wished he could do more but didn't know how to help, how to try without making it worse.

They sank and sank. The cold pressed in, rubbing at his exposed skin and feeling at the seams and sleeves of his clothes. Isaac resisted the urge to wrap himself around Vran, but he didn't dare risk breaking the elf's concentration.

They had to be getting near the bottom. A light rushed up toward them.

A giant fish rose out of the dark, the glow coming from the appendage dangling from its forehead.

It opened wide, revealing a mouth of spiny teeth. Isaac tensed and squeezed Vran's hand tighter. He couldn't help it. Cracks opened in the bubble of air. Water streamed in.

Then they were down, swallowed whole—and somewhere else, somewhere filled with bottle-green, murky light.

The bubble broke apart, flooding a floor of porous stone already soaked from other such entries.

"Are you okay?" Isaac asked as Vran let him go to bend over.

"Yeah . . . just . . . that's not as easy as it used to be."

"It's the broken cage thing?" Isaac asked.

"Yes. I have plenty of power, but control is an issue."

Isaac nodded, remembering the whispering shadows and the ruined house where they'd met.

He took in the hall while Vran recovered.

Giant stone ribs lined the ceiling, but they weren't inside the pilot fish. This space was far too large for that.

There were nets and bones everywhere, mounted on the rocky walls like trophies. Everything dripped and shone with water.

It was old, marked by years of crusty salt stains.

They'd come in at the top, in an alcove, one cave in a sprawling well of blue-gray stone.

Jellyfish drifted through the air, providing pink and purple light. It wasn't quite enough for Isaac's eyes.

The rock branched and rose like lumpy trees or coral.

An entire town was carved into the stone, little caves and nooks, their openings perfectly round. Water dripped and ran, pooling at the base. It gleamed blue in the eerie half-light.

"Is this the Shoals?"

"Yeah. This is home."

"How do we find the Dealer?"

"I don't know, but I do know who to ask."

The steps worn into the rock were slippery as Vran led him downward.

Twice they used ladders so rickety that Isaac worried they wouldn't hold their weight.

They were near the bottom when Vran paused at a cave mouth.

"This is going to suck, all right?"

"For you or for me?" Isaac asked.

"Probably for both of us."

"Okay."

Isaac wanted to assure him but wasn't certain it would be welcome here.

Vran went rigid, his features schooled to stone. This was Vran's game face, and Isaac did not like it as Vran led him into the cave.

The floor was carpeted with some sort of lichen or seaweed. Bits of white bone littered it. Isaac did not like to imagine what it would feel like on bare feet.

Vran went very stiff, his back straight, as they entered a hall held aloft by twisting columns of coral. At least a dozen sea elves mixed with the watery shadows, blending with the damp of the air.

Isaac leaned close.

"Should we have worn our cloaks and hoods?"

"It wouldn't help. They can smell us."

Isaac could smell them too.

They weren't like Vran. Their scent was saltier, colder, if scent could be cold, but they lacked that other thing, that twist of burnt pepper, the spark that set him apart. It lay beneath an odor of dead fish and rot. The air felt charged, not with magic, but something else. Isaac's senses were alert, ready for an attack. This place was dangerous and for once he didn't feel like snark or bravado would help him.

They froze when a voice called out, muttering a long stream of syllables in the sea elf tongue. Isaac thought he heard Vran's name somewhere in it.

With a sigh, Vran pulled his cat-eared headphones from his coat pocket and passed them to Isaac.

"Put these on."

"Why?"

"Translation and hearing protection."

Isaac slipped them on.

"Hello, Father," Vran said as he stepped forward.

The hall sunk with several steps, ending in a wide pool. At its end, feet touching the still, dark water, sat an elf on a throne carved from coral.

Tridents and fishing spears crossed on the wall behind him.

"You guys really like the aquarium motif," Isaac whispered.

"We do, and they can hear you," Vran said quietly.

Haggard for an elf, his father wore his centuries in fine cracks, much like the ancient porcelain plates in the chapel's kitchen. A hard line ran down the right side of his face. It crossed a milky white eye.

He wasn't wearing a glamour, and something flickered in and out of Isaac's sight, undulating tentacles like an octopus or a kraken. It would have freaked him out if he hadn't seen Vran's scarier side.

"Why have you come home, Page of Cups? Why deign to grace us with your presence?"

"You know I'm not the page anymore," Vran said.

"The Sea remembers," Vran's father said.

"The Sea does not forget," the elves surrounding them whispered.

"What do you want, prodigal page?"

"I came for information." Vran's eyes flicked back and forth over the lurking retainers. "I need to know who the Dealer is, the one who's buying blood from the dry lands."

Vran spoke in an almost imperious tone. Isaac wondered if that was a side effect of switching to Elvish or if it was how he spoke to his father alone. All of his gentleness had gone and Isaac could see him here, sitting in his father's place.

"And what makes you think I know anything?"

The old elf leaned sideways on his not-quite throne.

Vran scoffed.

"You always have your eye on all the fish. You know what I seek."

"I know that you walked away from your title, after everything we did to get you there. You turned your back on the royals. Think of what you could have achieved and what you threw away."

His tone was angry, but Vran's response was calm.

"I threw away a crown that would have brought my doom, or would you prefer I went to oblivion like the others when their plot failed?"

"The Sea will rise again."

Vran shook his head.

"Why did I even ask? I became the page to get out of here. Nothing more. Nothing less."

"You threw away a *crown*," his father repeated. "You could have taken this family lower, brought us to depths unseen!"

He stood and stretched out a hand. The nearest trident flew to it.

"But I kept the sword," Vran said quietly.

A sound like a finger circling the rim of a crystal goblet rang out. The slender blade wasn't metal. It shone, glossy and dark, like black glass, like the water beneath their feet. The hilt and basket were woven of silver and black iron.

The sword in Vran's hand was a pretty thing, and Isaac had no doubt he knew how to use it.

The room went still. The water at their feet rippled slightly, stirred by unseen breezes or coiling shadows.

"I became what you made me. I didn't want that anymore, but I can go back there if you want, Father. I can be that boy, the one you forged. The one who took your eye to prove himself to you."

Father and son stood frozen, staring each other down. Isaac would have suspected that time had stopped, but the water still rippled and he could still hear the rush of waves.

Vran's father lowered his trident.

"I'll take you to her."

32
ROLLING IN THE DEEP

The caves and the decor became posher, more elaborate, as they descended the slippery stairs.

Vran's father led the way. He outright ignored Isaac, which was for the best. Isaac could watch Vran's back better if the old elf wasn't focused on him.

Anyone they passed could be a threat, though most of the elves on the winding ways had some sort of business. They carried baskets woven from green reeds or pots carved from bleached coral.

All of them smelled like brine, but their cargo brought the odor of fish or something with a charcoal tang that he took to be clams.

None of the elves threatened them, so Isaac assumed they were all dangerous.

Their march ended at a low place, a sort of clearing in the forest of stalagmites and soft, undulating plants. A metal tube, a submarine, stretched across the blue gravel ground. It lay slightly tilted, its round windows and a jaunty periscope a bit askew.

"That's it," Vran's father announced. "The gambling hall."

"Is she here?" Vran asked.

"She is."

"I wasn't talking to you."

Isaac took a deep breath.

The scents weren't overwhelming. No one was bleeding, but it was like walking through a spice market. Hints of this and that tickled his nose. There was blood, a lot of it, dozens of types, all of it cold and stale.

"This is the place."

"Then we're done, Father," Vran said. "You can go."

The elder elf walked toward the steps before turning back to say, "Don't darken my door again, boy."

"Not to worry," Vran said. "Like I said, we're done."

Vran's father retreated, and Isaac took in the crowded hall.

Brightly lit boards and tables filled most of the narrow interior. To the sides were rows of slot machines occupied by beings of all sorts, their gaze fixed on the spinning wheels inside the glass-and-metal boxes.

Isaac could not imagine any of it was fun.

The tables were a bit more interesting, if only for the dealers.

He didn't recognize any of them, and he recognized fewer of the races, both staff and customers. There were what he assumed to be dwarves and a number of humanoids with two legs but multiple tentacles and octopus heads. Most of the shapes leaned toward the aquatic. There were plenty of sea elves, and Isaac was glad Vran hadn't put the sword away, having left it hanging from his belt instead.

"Which way?" Vran asked.

"The back, of course." Isaac nodded to the thick red curtains at the rear. "But I don't like the lack of security."

"I was thinking the same thing. Either she's an idiot or she doesn't need any."

"That or it's a trap," Isaac suggested.

"Your mind is a master class in paranoia," Vran said.

"I'll take that as a compliment if it keeps us alive," he said.

The hallway behind the curtain narrowed, and Isaac could not suppress the feeling that they were traveling down the long throat of a snake.

It widened again, into a dry, well-lit space. Isaac might have gone so far as to call it sterile.

The wall, floors, and ceiling were all steel, clear remnants of the submarine. Bulbs not unlike the ones from RCC's labyrinth hung from the ceiling, which did nothing to comfort him. The brine and rust outside had not intruded here.

He ran a fingertip along a metal countertop. No dust came away.

"What do you think these are?" he asked, nodding to the tall, cloth-wrapped shapes lining the walls.

"No idea," Vran said. "Maybe it's moving day."

Movement caught Isaac's eye.

He spun, knife in hand, as the sound of skittering claws on metal retreated.

Black eyes glared at him from a small green lizard that had mounted one of the tables. It flicked its tongue at them.

"Aww," Vran said.

"Yuck."

"Come on, admit it's cute."

"In a dark and scaly sort of way," Isaac agreed.

More lizards and snakes crept and coiled as they went deeper, approaching the heavy door at the very back of the room.

It swung open before they could reach it, and a woman walked through it. She had a musky scent, one similar to the nest Isaac had cleared out of the crypt. She wore a lab coat and heavy, sensible boots. Her hair, a wriggling nest of serpents, flicked their tongues at Vran and Isaac. They studied the interlopers with bright beady eyes, and Isaac wondered if the Gorgon's were the same beneath her thick welding goggles.

"You . . . It can't be," she said. The snakes focused fully on Isaac. "It can't be you, can it?"

"Do I know you?"

She laughed.

"You wouldn't remember me." She took several steps toward them. "You were just a baby when they stole you."

"Stole me?"

"Yes. From right here." She sounded awed. "I can't believe it. Come. Come."

She waved for them to follow her.

"Okay," Isaac said. "That wasn't what I expected."

"At least she hasn't tried to kill us."

"Not yet."

They followed her through the swinging door.

More steel, but the light was so much brighter here. The impossible mix of blood nearly overwhelmed Isaac's senses.

Cabinet after cabinet held vials and bottles, all carefully labeled.

"I've come close a few times." She waved at the collection. "But never matched you."

"Could you please start at the beginning?" Isaac asked. "I feel like I've missed several episodes of a TV show."

"The Phages," she said excitedly. "It's you. You're the key to bringing them back—to saving them."

"What happened to them? Where are they?"

"They're here." Vran tuned back toward the door. "They're the statues."

"Yes," the Dealer said. "They were dying, so I froze them in stone."

"Dying? How?" Isaac asked. "What was killing them?"

"A plague, one tailored just to them."

"But not to me?"

"No, not you," she purred. "I made you to resist it, and you have, but someone stole you before I could test the results."

"Why are you doing this?" Vran asked, looking over the room. "Why are you down here in the Eversea?"

"No one is looking for me here, or for them."

"Are they . . . my parents . . . are they here?" Isaac stumbled over the question.

"Absolutely," she said. "They risked so much, remaining out of suspension to have you, to let me test a cure."

Isaac and Vran followed her to a corner of the lab.

"I put them back as soon as I could, before the virus could take hold."

"But they are infected?"

"Yes."

She pulled the cloth from a pair of figures.

He strained, trying to remember anything, a scent especially, but all he got was snake musk and dry stone.

They didn't look all that special, if he had to be honest. He wasn't entirely certain they even resembled him. Maybe he had his father's nose. Maybe. He couldn't tell their eye or hair color.

"You were my last, and best, attempt," the Dealer explained. "I could not try again without risking more of their lives. The virus works too fast."

"Is that why you needed the blood?" Isaac pointed to the shelves and racks.

"Exactly. The combination for a cure is somewhere out there. If I couldn't breed another Phage with resistance, then I'd synthesize one." She faced the nearest counter, but the gaze of her snakes remained fixed on Isaac. "I've been testing and experimenting for decades! But now you're here. I just need a sample, some of your blood, and I can cure them."

"Why are you doing this?" Isaac asked. "Why are you helping them?"

"They paid me to." She shrugged. "But they knew I wouldn't be able to resist. A virus engineered to kill a race immune to disease? That was a puzzle I had to solve."

"Engineered?"

"Someone made this. Someone wanted them off the board."

"Who would do that?" Isaac asked. "Why would they do that?"

"Because they were the most dangerous assassins in the realms, because they worked for the Sea, and without them in the way, the winter elves could seize the northern tower."

"Is this true?" Isaac asked Vran.

"I don't know." Vran shrugged. "I really don't."

He could be lying. He could be trying to keep Isaac from finding out the truth, but no—Isaac decided to trust Vran.

"It started small," the Dealer said. "The effects weren't immediate. Their line of work was dangerous after all. They never noticed until it had spread through the entire population."

"And all this time, you've been working on curing it?" Vran asked.

"I went underground for a while, when the tower changed hands, made some money in the wars, then when I finally got back to work, I made you. Then you were stolen. I thought you were dead. No one could find you."

And they wouldn't, not in the Graveyard, not hidden among the

Undertaker's boys. But he'd been stolen, not killed, not erased. Why? Others had died.

"You killed your suppliers," Isaac said. "The goblins. You sent assassins after them."

He hoped she heard the plural and would believe Bella and her children dead.

"I had to. They got sloppy. I can't afford royal intervention. It doesn't matter now." She headed for a table and prepped a syringe. "All I need is some of your blood and I can bring them back."

He tried again to find the resemblance between himself and the statues and thought he found it in the eyes. They'd posed, frozen together, almost embracing. He decided that he favored his mother, with her sharp features. She was not pretty, not in any way he would call it, but she had a determined and maybe hopeful expression.

"They're all killers?" Isaac asked quietly.

"Each and every one."

The Dealer sounded impressed.

Isaac didn't know how to ask what he needed to, but Vran sensed the question.

"I think it's a bad idea without knowing more, but it's your choice, Isaac. I'll support it, whatever you do."

"They are your people," the Dealer said. "You can save them. It's what I made you to do."

"I'm not sure it's the right thing."

"You can't compel him." Vran put a hand to his sword.

Isaac studied his parents. It was a genocide, the virus that had brought the Phages to this, and yet . . . they'd been killers. It was a sort of prison sentence. What would happen if he set them loose? Would they seek revenge? Would they start killing again?

Someone had wanted them off the board. He had his suspicions as to who.

"I can't," he said. "Not yet. I have to think about this."

"A Phage with morals. How droll," the Dealer said. "But I wasn't really asking for your consent."

The doors to the hall opened, and a crowd of sea elves filled the entrance.

"I told you this was too easy," Isaac said.

"I guess your paranoia is justified *sometimes*."

Vran drew his sword and shifted to stand back-to-back with Isaac.

"This okay?" he asked.

Isaac grinned.

"The best."

"I don't need him alive," the Dealer said.

"I guess that sets the rules of engagement then," Vran said.

"Finally," Isaac said. "I've been wanting a real fight since I got to the school."

"Kiss me," Vran said, and Isaac understood.

He did, quickly, and took in the drop of blood without tasting it. There wasn't time.

His ears immediately heard more. His sight was no longer dimmed. He could almost see the details of the faces under the canvases, the frozen features of his people, despite the cloth. Many of them were as cold as the elves rushing their position.

These weren't Argent. They weren't Vran, but they were still powerful and damn quick. They were armed with everything from clubs to blades of jagged bone.

"On your left," Isaac said as the first elf lunged to his right.

Vran flowed out of the way. Isaac matched his sidestep.

He wasn't trying to look like a good guy here. These weren't Bella, and he wasn't pretending to get in anyone's good graces.

Isaac slashed out and was rewarded with a cry and the bloom of blood in the air.

Vran jabbed outward, catching an elf before he even got close enough to use his club.

The shadows began to crawl. They began to whisper. Isaac could make them out better now, in-between dodging and stabbing. Vran's coat left him room to move. It was loose enough that he could dance. He kicked just for a change and received an angry grunt in response.

Alone, he'd have worried about the longer weapons, but he wasn't alone.

Vran spun and sliced, disarming his people with precision. More blood bloomed, and the shadows swam like eels or threads of glossy ink.

Isaac no longer needed to hold back. With Vran's blood in his veins, they were in sync, moving almost as one. This was so much better than the prom.

The shadows snapped out, dragging an attacker into them, distracting the rest.

Vran ran an opponent through. The elf made a gurgling sound that ended in a grunt. Bluish light haloed him as Vran kicked his body off the long blade. Isaac was seeing the magic, he realized, the life. He watched it dim.

"It's not too late to run," Vran called, loudly and calmly. "You can still leave here alive."

Some of the elves did just that, but the rest kept coming, even as the shadows dragged more of them into the darkness.

Isaac got distracted and paid for it with a slash along his side.

Vran spun, running his attacker through. Isaac let the motion carry him so they'd reverse. He swept out with his leg, taking down a red-eyed elf before he had time to run Isaac through with a fishing spear. Thrown off balance, the elf dropped the spear, and Isaac brought his knives down together into the elf's belly.

He searched for the next moment, the next opponent, and saw the shadows had it in hand. They snaked through the attackers, rending and coiling, squeezing and dimming the light of beings who should never had died.

The last of the elves shouted in fear or pain. Then the darkness had them, and it was over. Isaac and Vran stood among the wounded and the dead.

"You didn't have to do this," Isaac said to the Dealer.

She reached for her glasses, ready to petrify them.

"I can fight without my eyes," Isaac warned her, grateful that Kenji had drilled him in the darkness.

"We're going now," Vran said. "Isaac will let you know if he changes his mind."

"Okay," she said, holding up her hands in surrender.

"You hired the assassins to take down your suppliers?" Vran asked.

"Yes."

"What about the school, are you the one who ordered that hit?" Isaac asked.

"What? What school?"

"I don't think she's lying," Vran said.

"Me either."

The only question left was what to do with her.

The Guardians had no jurisdiction here. She'd killed people, hired killers. Isaac could take her off the board. He could end her. It might mean leaving the Phages petrified forever. It might not.

He saw Vran watching him, knew he was waiting to see what Isaac would do.

"Let's go," he said.

Vran opened a door and they stepped through to RCC.

"Are you all right?" Vran asked.

"Yeah." Isaac lifted his arm to examine the scratch. "It's just a little blood."

"I didn't mean that."

"I know. Do you think it's true, what she said about the Phages, that they were all killers?"

"I don't know," Vran said. "Hopefully Jack can tell us more soon."

Isaac nodded.

"Let's go tell Argent what we found."

33
THE ENEMY OF MY ENEMY

The Queen of Swords sat behind her modern desk and listened intently to their report. Isaac made certain she had every detail. When his voice faltered, Vran stepped in. For a few moments longer, they were two sides of the same coin.

When they'd finished, Argent leaned back in her seat.

"I fought a Phage once," she said.

"Did you kill them?" Isaac asked.

"It didn't come to that."

"Why did you fight?" Vran asked.

"She was working on behalf of the Sea. I needed something she'd stolen to incriminate our court. It was invigorating."

Isaac was curious if the Phage had managed to taste the queen's blood. He doubted it, not unless she'd been far more able to withstand magic's burn than him. Just the bit of Vran he had in his system had left him shaking.

"She was telling the truth then?" he asked. "They were all killers?"

"As far as I know. I only met the one, but what you've learned aligns to my suspicions, that the Sea employed them. The exclusivity does not surprise me."

"Was it you? Did your court create the virus?"

"Isaac!" Vran protested.

"No," she said. "Though I can see why you ask. The Sea court was deposed, and control of their Watchtower was claimed by my father."

"Did *he* kill them?"

"I do not know. Once, Isaac Frost, I would have taken great offense to that question, to the implication that my sire could support such an act, but he surprised me in the end, showing himself capable of contemplating the extinction of humanity. It is more than strange that he met his end by aligning with the Sea."

"I don't know what to believe."

"Then your education is getting somewhere," Argent said. "Doubt is your friend. Keep questioning, especially those in power and their motivations."

Did that include her brother? Did she trust him?

"You almost sound like the Undertaker."

"It is important to question. Sometimes I think true learning begins when we realize our elders do not know everything and do not always have the best of intentions."

Isaac thought of the various professors and their quirks.

"Then why have them teach us?"

"Because they still know more than you two. You're dismissed. Get back to the school."

"Is it safe?" Vran asked. "We still don't know who's out to destroy it."

"We sealed anyone but staff or students from coming or going."

"How?" Isaac asked.

"My brother set the wards," Argent said. "I'd almost feel sorry for your former master if he chose to test them."

Vran let out a relieved sigh.

"Thank you," Isaac said as they stood.

"For what?" she asked.

"For calling him my former master."

"Go learn something, Isaac Frost."

They stepped through before it registered with Isaac that she hadn't taken back his knives.

"Library first?" Vran asked. "Or do you want to get cleaned up?"

He nodded to Isaac's arm. The cut had closed, proving that Phages healed almost as well as goblins, but a darker splash stained the sleeve of the coat.

"Library," Isaac said. "I'm ready if Jack is."

Jack didn't smile when they entered, but he gave Isaac a little nod and led them to a computer.

"This is everything." He nodded to the screen. "It's not very pretty. Are you sure you want to know?"

"I think I already do."

Isaac pulled out the chair.

Vran didn't say anything. He took the seat next to Isaac as he began to scroll.

It was all there, in lengthy prose clearly written by people who had more time than they knew what to do with.

The Phages had been assassins for hire, mercenaries and freelancers, until the Sea, until Vran's royals, had brought them under exclusive contract.

Had the elven king brought about their doom? None of the writers Jack had translated suggested such a thing. Then again, the sources had come from the current king, from Argent's brother. Was that a secret they'd let out? Had Silver's kindness been a way to keep it safe?

Vran had said it himself.

Sometimes Isaac's paranoia was justified, and Argent had admitted that her father had surprised her in terrible ways.

With a long breath, he closed the browser. It was all true, everything the Dealer had told them.

"Isaac . . ." Vran said.

"It is what it is."

"What are you going to do?"

"Write my paper for Lawless, but otherwise . . . I don't know." His voice sounded small, not unlike Samuel's.

He'd always thought that somewhere, out there, he had parents, that he was loved. It had been a fantasy, he'd always known that on some level, but it had warmed him, kept his heart beating when the cold came into the crypt. It had been a dream, a good one.

Now he knew his only purpose had been to save a race of killers, people no better than the Undertakers, than the family he'd been stolen into.

He didn't even know if he had a name. From what he'd seen of the Dealer, he probably had a number.

He hadn't been traded, that much was for certain.

The Undertaker had either taken him as a job or as a means of keeping his competition from rising again. That or someone had paid him to do it, which was somehow worse, to think that he'd been so unwanted, just a prize, locked in the Graveyard like an urn in a vault.

That was why he'd been held back so long. He wasn't a trainee. He'd been a hostage.

"Let's get out of here." Vran stood and pulled Isaac to his feet. "You need a shower and some rest."

Isaac let Vran tow him along. He managed a muttered thank-you in Jack's direction.

They reached Isaac's room. Isaac did as Vran suggested and showered. He left most of his clothes off and found Vran waiting, stretched out in his bed, the soft emerald glow of the stones acting like a nightlight.

Isaac settled against Vran's chest, against his cool skin, and let himself drift away.

The memory, the golden dream of someplace warm, didn't rise, didn't become a clearer picture. He knew why now. There was nothing there to find, just a laboratory, cold steel and stone faces.

"Whatever you decide," Vran whispered. "Decide for you."

Isaac woke when the world shook, snapping his eyes open. The green light pulsed like a wild heartbeat.

A stone fell out of the ceiling.

Vran rolled Isaac off the bed as the rock crushed it.

"What the hell?" Isaac asked, gaping up at the hole. The pulsing continued, like a green alarm.

"Get dressed," Vran said. "Something is very, very wrong."

Isaac raced back into his clothes. He tugged on Vran's coat.

They ran for the main hall and found the rest of the school

gathering there. The building shook again. More stones fell, along with a rain of dust. The light pulsed again, quickly, over and over, racing now. Several open doors showed nothing beyond, a void of stars or utter darkness. One let in a gust of snow, another dry desert air.

"Earthquake?" Ford asked.

"We're not on earth," Hex said.

"You know what he meant," Isaac snapped.

Another rumble shook the building. A great crack grew in the wall, the stones tumbling down to let a long slice of emerald sky in.

"What is it?" Daffodil asked.

"It's the heart . . ." Isaac realized. "We've got to get to the basement."

"None of the doors are working," Jack said.

"Vran?" Isaac asked.

The elf nodded.

He knelt and spoke gently.

"You have to let us in," he said. "We're trying to help."

A circle of green light surrounded him.

"Everybody in," Isaac said.

The students gathered. Isaac could see the professors and the dean running toward them as the floor gave way.

They crashed into the labyrinth, landing in a pile of rock and dust.

"Anybody hurt?" Ford asked with a groan.

"I think my arm's broken," Daffodil said.

"Let me see," Jack said.

"You two stay here," Isaac said. "The rest of you follow me."

For once, Hex did not remind him that he wasn't in charge.

He checked his knives as they sprinted.

More tremors shook the school. Dust rained from above. It glittered, green to black.

"You've got to be kidding me," Isaac said as the lights went out ahead. "We're trying to help!"

"It has to be you," Vran said. "Run ahead."

"What?"

"You've cleared most of the trials. We'll catch up when we can."

Vran was right.

He pulled Isaac to him and kissed him hard on the lips.

"For luck," he said.

Isaac nodded and ran, his boots slapping on the stone floor.

The darkness swallowed him but he raced on, the carvings of keys passing beneath him.

He hoped, this once, they'd let him go without visions and torments. The whispers, usually so chatty, had fallen silent. That couldn't be a good sign.

A door waited at the end of the hall.

Isaac stepped through it and found himself beneath an endless, empty sky.

He'd gone somewhere flat, a sea of yellow grass stretching in all directions. The wind rippled through it, making waves and flutters, breaking against the battered house that sat like an island at the center.

Any better days it might have had were long behind it.

Weathered wood, wind-stripped of paint, barely held up a roof full of holes.

Two eyes, bright blue, peeked from a window.

Isaac walked to the door. It opened before he reached it.

He'd been wrong.

The boy he'd caught a glimpse of was not Samuel.

Pink from the dusty wind, with hair almost the color of raw cotton, he stared at the body on the floor. It was the same person. Isaac knew that somehow, despite the corpse being withered with age. Both wore faded blue pajamas. Blood stained the dead man's stomach. He'd been stabbed in the gut.

"You came here for it, didn't you?" the boy asked. "The heart?"

He was fuzzy at the edges, like he was unraveling.

"Yes, but it wasn't me," Isaac said. "Who did this? Who killed you?"

"I never saw him."

The boy took in the worn-out wallpaper and cracked wooden floor.

"I'm sorry," Isaac said.

"It's okay. I think I'm ready now. I'm not scared anymore."

"I don't understand," Isaac said.

"I wasn't talking to you." The boy pointed to the house's open back door. "He went that way."

Then he was gone.

Isaac stepped outside and into a room filled with thick cords. They curtained the walls and ceiling. He did not know if they were veins or vines, but they all ran to one place, a mass of bright green light, an emerald star. It pulsed black and the school shook again.

A laugh came from somewhere. Isaac drew his knives.

"You mad, Dove? You shouldn't be. You knew it was coming."

"*Shy*," Isaac growled. "You've been here this whole time?"

"Yep."

"How long have you been trailing me?"

"I wasn't trailing you, brother. I was way ahead of you. It just took me longer to get through the trials. Too many feathers you see, not that you can see them. It was clever of them to hide the heart in a cell, but I found it."

"The Old Man sent a ringer."

"Nah, I was here for another job, for the boy, but since you weren't getting it done . . . well, two birds, one knife."

The heart pulsed again. Darkness ran through the veins, and the room blackened at the edges. The heart had begun to still.

Isaac didn't need to ask why. The job was the job, or jobs. Someone had wanted the boy dead. Someone had wanted the school destroyed.

"Who's the client? Who wanted this?"

"Don't know, and it doesn't matter. The job is done."

"You'll pay for this," Isaac said, scenting the air. "For all of it."

Shy laughed.

"Because you're a Guardian now? You should know it doesn't work that way. There's only one way out, Frost, the way Samuel took."

Something rushed by him and pain flared in his side.

"You can't scent me."

Another rush, another cut, this time through the coat and across his back. Damn, he was fast.

"Can't catch me."

"What do they call you, really?" Isaac asked, hoping to buy a moment free of the teasing cuts. He wouldn't last long in this fight.

"The Ghost. Fitting, isn't it?"

He laughed.

"Oh yeah," Isaac said.

"Why do you think so?"

"Because you're a dead man."

"So bold. So confident. What are you going to do? You can't see me, can't hear me coming."

"No, but an elf can."

Borrowing the last of Vran's blood in his system, Isaac spun and threw.

Shy made a choking sound. It wasn't a fatal blow, only a glance. He didn't become visible, but his blood did. It flowed from the side of his neck, dyeing his sweatshirt red as it poured out.

Isaac ran and sliced. He followed it with another hit, then another. He brought his black knife back and forth. Shy became more visible as the wounds appeared, as his strength gushed away. He gurgled.

"Tag," Isaac said, driving the blade into Shy's chest, up into the heart the way he'd been taught. "Brother."

They fell together, Shy onto his back, in a spreading pool of red, Isaac to his knees, weak from his own wounds.

The last of Vran's hearing told him the others were almost to him.

"Isaac?" Daffodil gasped. "What happened?"

"Shy," he said, pointing to the translucent corpse and trying to find his breath, "was an Undertaker."

He was only a little older than them. Isaac used the tip of his knife to lift Shy's sleeve. His arm was covered in feathers. He knew the other would be the same.

"Is that the heart?" Hex asked, nodding to the dying star.

Its light had almost completely darkened.

"If it goes . . ." Lawless stared, transfixed.

"What happens?" the dean asked.

"The tower will implode," Lawless said.

"It's happened before," Lin said.

"Not with us inside it!" Hex said.

"The last tower's death happened in a time loop," Lawless said. "Even then the damage was significant. This one hasn't fully taken root. It could destabilize whole planes."

"It won't," Vran said. "Not if we give it another heart."

"A transplant? How? It would take something transplanar, something really compl—" Hex trailed off.

Vran's smile was sad.

"Exactly."

"What?" Isaac asked, catching up. Finding his feet he grabbed Vran's sleeve and knew his grip was too weak for another fight. "You can't."

"I have to," Vran said. "I'm sorry."

"Vran?" He choked out.

"I said I wouldn't hurt you until I did."

"But how . . . how could you know?"

"Because, Isaac, my love, my story isn't a straight line."

Leaning in, Vran kissed him.

Breaking off, he whispered, "I'll explain later."

Then Vran let him go.

Isaac tried to grab him, but he didn't have the strength.

"There's got to be another way."

"There isn't."

The heart pulsed a final time. The school shuddered as the light died.

"It's now or never," Vran said. "Goodbye."

He turned, ran, and leaped into the crack. It sealed behind him in a blink.

The tears were hot on Isaac's face.

"What just happened?" Ford asked.

A sound like a generator, an electrical buzz, filled the space.

Green light burst from the heart. It ran through the mortar, infusing the stones with something strange and familiar.

"What did he do?" Daffodil asked between sobs.

"What he had to," the dean said.

34
TAKE ME TO CHURCH

Argent was waiting when they reached the main hall.

"The ward is unsealed?" the dean asked.

"It took some time, but yes." The queen took in the bruised and dusty students. "What happened here?"

"No one had to come in." The dean's voice cracked. "We already had an Undertaker among us."

Argent glared at Isaac.

"Another one." The dean stepped between the two of them. "Shy. Isaac killed him."

"Where is Vran?" Argent asked.

Isaac couldn't tell her. He couldn't explain. Then someone was hugging him from the left and the right. Ford and Daff. Her arm was wrapped in a cast of copper wires.

They held him up.

They had to. He'd collapse otherwise.

"He's gone," Hex said. "Shy struck the heart down and Vran entered it to stabilize it, to save the school."

"I see," Argent said in a voice several degrees below freezing.

"The tower is transplanar," Hex said to Isaac. "If he's merged with it, he'll live a thousand lives, maybe more."

"But not this one," Isaac said, his voice quiet. "Not anymore. And not with me."

He'd learned that much from Lawless's class.

Argent gave a nod.

"How bad are your injuries, Frost?"

"I'm fine," he lied.

"Do you remember where the Graveyard is?" Argent asked.

"Not exactly. I can only go there in dreams."

"How?"

"A drop of my blood. It knows the way."

"Hex?" Argent asked. "Do you know what to do?"

"Yes." She pulled a piece of chalk from her pocket and began to draw a circle ringed in proofs and equations.

Isaac shuffled forward when she gestured, and with more gentleness than he thought her capable of, she wiped a little blood from the cut on his side and smeared it on her circle.

"What is this?" Jack asked.

"Forensic magic," Hex said. "It's a flavor of sympathetic, a tracking spell, only we need it to work across the planes."

"You can do that?" Daff asked.

Hex didn't answer as the chalk dust rose, swirling like a dust cloud. It resolved into a spiraling shape with tendrils like blood vessels. Letters and numbers drifted around it, fading until a spark lit on one of the branches, illuminating a single point.

"There," Hex said with satisfaction. "It's there."

"Come with me, Frost," Argent said.

"What are you going to do?" Isaac asked, voice trembling as cold crept from her, chilling the hallway. Ice crawled up the walls.

"For once, what I want to."

"We're coming too," Hex announced, looking over the students. The group nodded in agreement, even Jack.

"All of us," the dean said, cocking her rifle.

Argent drew her sword, a sliver of polished mirror, and sliced at Hex's conjuration.

It wasn't a door that opened. This wasn't gentle magic, a quiet snowfall. It wasn't the bright light of crossing when Isaac had met the queen. This was an angry tide of ice and deadly cold. This was a glacier, an avalanche.

Gray sky shone through and then they were elsewhere.

The chapel stood ahead, its crumbling spires rising over the crypts and blank tombstones that gathered like ducklings in its shadow.

"Your Majesty!" the Undertaker called. He stepped from behind the chapel, dressed in his heavy greatcoat and top hat, a dirty shovel resting over his shoulder. "You are out of your jurisdiction."

"I'm not here as the Queen of Swords, and I'm not here as a Guardian."

The Undertaker shook his head.

"Did you come for tea then?"

Isaac was aware of his brothers. They circled the scene, sizing up the RCC students.

"No." Argent's expression was grim and fixed, like a statue. "I came to end you."

"Because I'm evil?"

"Because you took one of *mine.* A life for a life, isn't that what you teach the boys you steal away?"

"I see," he said.

The ground swelled. Bones and hands began to push clear of the graves.

"Gross," Ford said.

"Did you think I wouldn't have contingencies in place?" the Undertaker asked as the zombies and skeletons writhed free.

"Did you think I would give a damn?"

Argent swung her sword, and shards of ice rained from the sky, pinning dead flesh to the ground and breaking old, brittle bones.

"What do we do?" Jack asked.

"Whatever you can," Argent said.

"Fight as a team," Isaac said. "They don't know how to counter that."

A crack preceded a choking sound.

One of Isaac's brothers lay on the ground, writhing in pain, Daffodil's bare hand open from the slap she'd just delivered with her good hand.

"Works for me," she said.

Ford twisted to let a trio of throwing knives bounce off his wooden skin.

"Oh, it's on, asshole!" he roared before charging the brother in a quarterback's run and plowing the junior assassin over.

Ford circled back toward the group.

"Hex!" Isaac called as a trio of the skeletons surrounded her. "Watch your six."

She twisted her hands in a clawing motion, muttered some numbers, and a gust of wind broke loose, ripping the brittle bones apart. They flew like daggers in the direction of the oncoming brothers, and blood of many types filled Isaac's nose.

He heard the coming strike before it connected and spun to let the knife go wide.

"Nice coat," the brother, Ezekiel, said.

"Thanks," Isaac said, remembering how happy he'd been to wear it.

He kicked out, but Zeke locked Isaac's leg in his arms and twisted.

Isaac rolled with the motion so they both hit the dirt.

"You need new moves," Zeke said as they stood.

"How's this one?" Jack asked, grabbing Zeke in a sleeper hold from behind.

The Undertaker stabbed and stabbed, but his knife did little more than make a chinking sound against Jack's metal skin.

"Pity," Jack said, dropping the unconscious assassin and taking in the holes in his clothing. "I really liked this sweater."

Argent and the Old Man were dueling, sword to shovel. Light erupted with every strike of the queen's sword. It cracked the sky and earth, letting in slashes of emerald light, breaking whatever planar wall separated the Graveyard from the Spirit Realm.

The RCC students were in a slowly shrinking circle. The professors were holding their own, but between the Undertakers and the undead, they were vastly outnumbered.

Isaac ran for the chapel.

"Where are you going?" Ford asked.

"You'll see!"

Isaac slammed into something hard, a wall of muscle. He rebounded, falling onto his back.

"Going somewhere, Dove?" Kenji asked.

Isaac nodded to the chapel.

"Not exactly, but I need to open those doors."

"What's the play here?"

"We can take him out," Isaac said. "That's what you want, isn't it?"

"Then what?"

Isaac found his feet.

"We'll leave. He'll be gone. Then the Graveyard's yours. All you have to do is stand aside."

"Not ours? You're supposed to do this with me, Dove. You're supposed to be at my side."

"I don't belong here anymore." Isaac sheathed his knives. "You have to let me go."

"And if I say no?"

"I can't beat you, Kenji. Look at me." Isaac gestured at his bloody state. "I'm barely standing. Just let me go. The Old Man crossed a line. He went too far this time. She won't let him go."

Kenji followed Isaac's nod to where bones and dirt whipped around the Undertaker in a whirlwind shield. Argent carved away at it as delicately and efficiently as she might a cake on a turntable.

The students and professors weren't faring as well. A number of Isaac's brothers lay unconscious or wounded, but the circle was shrinking. The students and professors were losing ground.

"You can't go back there," Kenji said. "It won't be around much longer."

"Yeah, it will. I killed him, Kenji. I killed Ghost. V—we stopped him."

Kenji's golden eyes went wide.

"How?"

"You trained me too well," Isaac said. "I stopped your plan, and it was you, wasn't it? You were the client. You set this up so the Guardians would take the Old Man out for you. You forced him to go too far and get the royals' attention. It was a good plan, but you missed the whole point. There weren't supposed to be any more Samuels."

Isaac nodded to the students.

The students and professors were back-to-back now, fighting for their lives. The Undertakers might not know teamwork, but they also didn't know mercy.

"They're Samuels, all of them. RCC is their home. It's mine now too."

"Is that really what you want?" Something like hurt wrinkled Kenji's golden eyes. "You've really gone that soft?"

Isaac laughed.

"What's so funny?"

"You. Because the only softness I'd known before now came from you. Let me go, brother. *Please.*"

"I won't be the only one to come after them."

"Then it's a good thing they'll have me to protect them."

Narrowing his eyes, Kenji stepped aside.

Isaac pressed a hand to the chapel doors.

"Can you hear me?" he asked. "Are you there?"

He wasn't certain, but maybe there was a pulse in the wood, the gentlest rattle to tell him he'd been heard.

"I hope you know what we need. We don't have much time."

Ford clutched a wound on his human side. Jack's clothes were in pieces and his glasses were broken. A trio of brothers had realized they couldn't cut his skin and were trying to pummel him with rocks and broken tree branches. Professor Lawless had a pair of pirate cutlasses in her hands. She swung wildly and screamed bloody murder.

Another little pulse, a rattle that hopefully wasn't Isaac's imagination, went through the door.

Isaac threw it open and dove out of the way.

Cries of surprise and confusion filled the air as a rush of scales and feathers poured onto the field.

The Undertakers scattered before the charging triceratops.

Isaac winced as a dire goose landed on a nearby fighter, honking and pecking at the broad-bodied man.

Something massive squeezed through the door, a head. The T-Rex charged as Isaac hurried back toward the other students.

The Undertakers broke as it bore down on them. They ran for the hills. Kenji had climbed atop the chapel.

Isaac followed his eyes to the main event.

Bones littered the ground like discolored hail, mixing with the melting ice that Argent had conjured.

Breathing hard, the Undertaker brought his shovel around. Argent sliced through the handle, severing the shaft. He tried to chop out with the head, aiming for her gut. She brought her blade down, a look of cold satisfaction on her face.

The Undertaker howled in pain as his arm landed with a thud in the dirt, the shovel head beside it.

That was it then. He wasn't untouchable after all.

The Old Man faced the brothers. They'd made their way to the chapel. Gathered around Kenji's perch, they waited for him to do something, to say something. Some limped, some dragged or carried their fellows. Killers or not, something twisted in Isaac's gut to see them in pain.

The dinosaurs stood in a row, oddly united, ready to charge should the Undertakers rally toward the Old Man. The geese had flown away.

"Kenji!" the Undertaker called.

Whatever leaked from his severed arm wasn't blood. The limb itself lay twitching, writhing, and flopping, trying to find its way home.

She walked over to it, staring at it in disgust.

"Give me that," the Old Man said.

"Okay."

Daff lifted it with her bare hand. The arm twitched once more, blackened, and dissolved into ash.

"Oops."

She dropped the empty coat sleeve.

"Boys!" the Old Man howled in rage. "Come here. Now!"

"They won't," Isaac said.

"Help me!"

"They won't," Isaac repeated. "Because they do not love you. They only fear you."

He turned to Kenji, who nodded.

"And they'll be happy to know you're someone else's problem now."

"You're not a Guardian, Frost," Argent said. Her sword gleamed. Ice bled from the blade like white smoke. "What do you want to do with him?"

A word, and she'd do it. He knew she wanted to.

And how he wanted it too.

For Samuel. For all the boys he'd stolen or killed.

A word, maybe a nod, and he could end the Undertaker, here and now. He could even do it himself. The Old Man was out of tricks, defenseless. Isaac could drive a knife into his heart as easily as he had Shy's, but that had been battle, survival. This would be murder.

"Take him in," Isaac said.

"You have no jurisdiction here," the Old Man panted.

"I'm not a Guardian," Isaac said. "Technically, most of us aren't."

"Is that what you want?" the dean asked.

It was a test of course.

"No, it's not, but it's what Vran would do."

"You'll never hold me," the Undertaker said. "You'll never—"

A crack split the air. The Old Man's mouth opened in shock as red bloomed across his chest.

The dean smiled over the sights of her smoking rifle.

"I'm not a Guardian either," she said. "And he was mine too. Enjoy the silver bullet, asshole."

"That's not going to kill him," Isaac said as the Undertaker made a choking groan and fell writhing upon the ground.

"Oh, I know. I'm no murderer, Frost, but I suspect it hurts like hell."

"You know, Katherine," Argent said calmly. "We might have our differences, but I do love your style."

The dean nodded.

"Well?" Isaac asked, looking to Kenji.

"He's all yours."

35
LATER LATER

The others had already gone through, herding the dinosaurs. The dean shoved a cowed and weakened Undertaker along. Isaac thought back to the beaten farmhouse with the dead boy and the flowery room Bella had stayed in. He had to wonder what sort of cell the Undertaker would enjoy.

Above it all, the sky stood cracked. Slashes of green light fell across the Graveyard. It would be Kenji's, but it wouldn't be hidden anymore.

"You broke the sky," Isaac said to Argent.

"It had it coming."

He exchanged a final nod with Kenji and followed Argent through the door.

The light when Isaac passed through was dimmer than he expected. He wasn't at the school. He wasn't in Liberty House.

A little sun fell from the skylights, but the vast, cavernous space was mostly dark.

Isaac's eyes adjusted and he smiled.

He reached out a hand and Vran took it. Isaac tried not to notice that the grip was faint and Vran's always cool skin felt a little colder.

"Thank you," Vran said. "I didn't want to go alone."

"You knew, didn't you?" Isaac asked. "You always knew it would come to this."

"Yes. I've known since I went below, but I'm still scared."

"Why didn't you tell me?"

"Because I didn't, and because if I had, you might never have danced with me or let me kiss you."

The mall no longer teemed with shoppers. The storefronts were all caged and dark. The food court sat empty, though an odor of grease and cheap food lingered. Isaac doubted demolition could wipe it away. The Greek place had the air of a haunted temple. The out-of-place fountain stood dry and sad in the gloom.

"Is this how it is now?" Isaac asked, taking in the scene.

Vran shook his head.

"This was about twenty years ago. They tore it down soon after."

"Could we go back?" Isaac asked, almost wincing at the hope in his voice. "To, you know, *before*?"

He suspected the answer. He dreaded it, but he'd give anything to stand there again and for a single moment, not care about anything but the feel of Vran's lips on his.

"It doesn't work that way," Vran said. "I'm sorry. I can go back, but you can only go forward."

Isaac clenched his fists, but there was no one left to strike. They'd won the battle, but who cared? He'd lost what really mattered.

"I hate this."

"I know," Vran said.

"But you don't? Hate it, I mean?"

"This is how it was always going to go," Vran said. "How I was going to die and what I was going to become."

He faded a little, growing hazy at the edges, blurring into the darkness of the abandoned storefronts. It was dimming too. Time was washing away their little island of the past. The school was an anchor, dragging Isaac toward the present, to a future without the boy he'd known and loved too briefly.

The whispering shadows filled the corners, swirling around them, and Isaac recognized them now. They were all Vran, versions of him, all different heights and ages, different races and shapes. One wore an apron and carried a kitchen knife. One, dressed like a soldier, had a bandage on his head, over one eye, and held a drum. One had veins of blue in his black hair and skin the color of beach sand.

"You told me we had choices, that we could choose who we got to be."

"Not always." Vran shook his head. "Not this time."

"This really sucks," Isaac said because he didn't know what else to say.

"It does." The shadow Vrans nodded or whispered agreement. "But just for a moment, I got what I wanted."

"And what did you want?"

"You, and to be a Guardian with you."

It wasn't enough, wasn't nearly enough. Isaac felt something in his chest crack. He couldn't breathe. It was Samuel all over again and it was worse. Samuel was guilt and failure. Vran was the future he wanted, something he could never have, something stolen. Erased.

Vran smiled and leaned in for a kiss.

Their lips met. The sensation was brief. Then Isaac was back at the school. No door, no trick. He was just there, alone in Vran's room.

It was as it had been before, the seashells and rocks, the bits of coral and battered books.

Vran never lived here, not really, and yet the space felt emptier.

Isaac sat on the bed.

"Goodbye," he whispered.

He sat there for a long while, staring at nothing, at the wall, at the green light that no longer pulsed like it might die.

"Can you even hear me?" he asked, fighting back tears.

"We don't know," a voice said. "Even Argent doesn't know."

A sandy-haired man stood in the doorway.

He didn't look imposing. The air around him didn't taste like immortality, but Isaac stiffened at his angry expression.

He wore jeans, beaten work boots, and a button-up flannel over a T-shirt.

He had a bit of magic to him, something strange and uncertain, like distant, tiny storm clouds, like death and life rolling together. That worried Isaac more than the sword he wore on his back.

"What happened to Vran?"

"I—don't you know?" Isaac asked, his voice cracking.

"I want to hear it from you, Isaac Frost."

He didn't draw his blade.

Isaac nodded and found his voice.

"Then you'd better have a seat. This will take a while."

Isaac didn't cry through the telling, which surprised him.

The man, Adam, didn't say anything until he'd finished, until he felt drained, like telling the story had made the loss, all of the losses, real.

He'd found his parents but hadn't. He'd lost his brothers, and it shouldn't hurt—but it did. He even mourned the Old Man, how stupid was that?

I guess I've earned some feathers, he thought. He'd get three tattoos, three feathers. One for Vran, one for Samuel, and one for Shy.

They wouldn't be erased. Isaac wouldn't let them be.

He choked, swallowing a sob.

He stiffened, then broke when Adam wrapped his arms around him.

He cried for a while, which was the least killer-like thing he could do, but that didn't matter anymore, did it? He wasn't an Undertaker. He wasn't going to be.

Vran might have known his own future, but Isaac's road was dark. It was thrilling and terrifying, like the climb of the car to the top of a roller coaster, or it would be, when the ache in his chest let up.

With a shuddering breath, Isaac untangled himself from Vran's brother.

"Don't let it be for nothing," Adam said through gritted teeth. "Don't let him have died for nothing."

"I won't."

With a nod, Adam left.

Isaac sat there a while longer.

At some point he stretched out on Vran's bed, tried to catch some hint of him in the pillows. He found nothing. He sniffed the coat's collar and there, just a bit of burnt pepper and salt. Curled into it, into himself like something was kicking him, over and over, he drifted.

"There you are!" a voice said, waking him. His buddy.

Daffodil seemed subdued. Her copper cast shone. She had a few bandages on her face, likely Doctor Cavanaugh's work. His buddy.

"The dean wants to see you," she said.

Isaac didn't feel like showering, like putting on any kind of a show, so he didn't. He put on the coat. He might never take it off. He brushed his teeth though, and tried not to look at his sunken features in the mirror.

"Are you there?" he asked.

Of course Vran didn't answer.

"Let's go. You kicked ass today," Isaac said to Daff.

"It was yesterday," she said, stopping out front of the dean's office. "But, yeah, I did."

She stopped outside the dean's office.

Isaac went in alone.

The dean sat behind her desk.

"We don't know what to do with you, Frost."

"Are you kicking me out?"

He couldn't bear it, couldn't bear the idea. He had nowhere else to go, and yet he wouldn't blame them. He wasn't like them. He wasn't a Guardian.

"There was a vote." The dean hung her head. "And I was overruled."

"*You* voted for me to stay?"

"You need this school, Frost, and despite why you came here, I think you've been a good addition. I think this institution needs you too."

"I'm sorry," he said. "For all of it."

"Shepherd was right. You've paid for your deception," she said. "A hundred times over, but you also killed a man."

Isaac wanted to point out that it had been self-defense, but he could have stopped. He'd had Shy on the ropes. He could have chosen that moment to subdue him, and he hadn't.

He'd done what he'd been trained to do. He'd listened to his instincts.

He was, despite all his protests, a killer.

What else was there to say?

Isaac nodded and stood.

Outside, the students and professors had gathered in the hall.

Their expressions were a mix of angry and sad. Even showered and bandaged, everyone had a battered and tired appearance.

Isaac knew how they felt. All he wanted was to crawl back into bed and sleep and sleep. Maybe he'd dream of black hair and eyes full of stars and the secrets of the universe.

Maybe he'd dream of ocean waves and the taste of cool skin. Maybe he'd sleep forever.

"This isn't right," Daffodil said. "It isn't fair."

Isaac shrugged and stiffened when she threw her arms around him, keeping her uncovered face away from him.

"Thanks, Daff," he said, returning her hug and being careful of her arm.

"I'm sorry, Frost," Hex said, her tone not icy, but fixed.

He knew she'd voted against him. She wouldn't condone Shy's death, no matter what he was responsible for.

"I understand."

He'd loved Vran too. He felt the same anger, but had nowhere to put it.

"Where will you go?" Ford asked, raising his human hand to give Isaac a sad little fist bump.

"I don't know. Maybe I'll go hunt down that summoner and bring her in."

Yeah. A little justice. That sounded nice.

Maybe he could work his talents into some kind of bounty hunter type of thing. The Undertakers and the Guardians couldn't be the only game in town. Someone had to need a non-assassin.

The dean opened a door. Green grass and trees marked the other side, but in the distance, Isaac could see buildings. The climate felt kinder than anywhere the Old Man had ever sent him.

Isaac gave them a little wave and stepped through and found himself walking out of the dean's office and back into the hall.

"What the—?" Ford asked.

"They voted," Isaac said to the ceiling.

"We did," the dean agreed.

Isaac walked through the door again. He came out on the other side of the hall.

"Vran . . ." Isaac pled.

The open doors slammed shut. All the exits vanished, melting into the stone as if they'd never been, enclosing everyone in the main hall.

"I think the school has vetoed your decision," Ford said, arms crossed over his chest.

"Isaac stays," Daffodil said, crossing her arms too. "Or . . . or I'm out too."

"Daff," Jack said, sounding shocked. "You can't mean that."

"Yeah," Ford agreed. "Me too."

Hex gave a little sigh.

"There's always Howard," she conceded. "I'm changing my vote. If Frost goes, so do I."

"He belongs here," Jack said. "It can't be Rogue Community College without a rogue."

Daffodil made a disgusted face.

"No dad jokes until you're a dad," she chided.

The dean glared at the other professors.

"Well?"

"I guess this settles the question of the building's intelligence." Lawless threw up her arms. "Whatever. I have papers to grade."

She marched away.

"Cavanaugh? Lin?" the dean asked.

The doctor nodded. Lin too, albeit a bit reluctantly.

"I'm staying?" Isaac asked.

"You're staying," the dean said. "The school has forgiven you, even if everyone else has not."

"I have one condition," Isaac said to the ceiling.

"What?" the dean groaned.

"I wasn't talking to you. I want Vran's room."

She narrowed her eyes at him.

"Why?"

Because waking up there was the first time I felt safe, Isaac thought.

Because I loved him, because being around him brought out a part of me that I don't think I will ever get to see again.

He didn't know how to say any of that, so what he said was, "To remember him."

The dean nodded. Maybe she understood. Maybe she was just tired and had her own paperwork to do.

"Request approved. Get back to class. All of you."

Daffodil gave Isaac one more hug and walked away.

CLASS DISMISSED

THE ENEMY OF MY ENEMY IS MY INTERN

Isaac went to his old room, intending to pack up his things, but he opened the door and found himself stepping into Argent's office instead.

She wasn't behind the desk. The queen stood to the side. The silver king sat in her place. He wore his pinstripe suit and gangster hat.

Isaac froze.

He'd known he'd face the music, face everyone who'd loved Vran and cared for him. He'd known that he was on borrowed time, but he always had been. Still, he'd expected Adam to be the one to run him through. Instead the guy had held him while he'd cried.

"Come in, Frost." Argent said. "Have a seat."

"I'd prefer to stand, you know, if you're going to kill me."

"Kill you?" Silver leaned forward. "No, Frost. That's not why you're here."

Isaac sat.

"So why am I here?"

"Because you have skills others don't, something unique even at RCC."

"I won't kill for you. That's not what he would have wanted."

"We agree," Argent said.

"But a trained assassin can see what another may not." Silver's head tipped so his hat nearly covered his eyes.

Isaac almost laughed. He'd been thinking similar thoughts. Maybe Vran hadn't been the only one with insight into his future.

"What do you want me to do?"

"I want you to become what Vran wanted you to. I want you to be a Guardian."

"And I don't want that." Isaac met Argent's gaze. "That hasn't changed."

"Hear me out." She leaned to place her hands flat on the desk.

Isaac gave a little nod and settled back into the uncomfortable chair.

"You already realized that we have agents who move between the lines."

"Like the ones who found the goblins for you, or did recon in the Shoals."

"Exactly."

"You want me to be one of them. You want me to be a spy?"

"Precisely," Silver said.

Isaac thought of Samuel. Maybe he would have survived if Isaac hadn't gotten tired of his endless questions. Maybe this could be a sort of penance. Maybe Isaac could do some good with what the Old Man had taught him.

"What about the Undertaker?"

"He's safely locked away," Argent said. "Shepherd will work with him to learn what he can, but we already know there are other threats. We need to find them and stop them before any other students are harmed."

"You can start with whoever hired Shy," Isaac said. "The school wasn't his initial target. He came to kill that boy in the labyrinth."

"We know." Silver's voice was cold.

"And you know who hired him?"

"We do, but it's a problem we cannot address at this time."

"Why not?"

"It is not your concern, at least not now. There are plenty of other plots to keep you busy, Isaac Frost."

He pretended to think it over.

The school needed Isaac. It needed a protector. It needed a Guardian.

It wouldn't be what Vran had wanted for him, not exactly, but Isaac liked it. It was a way to do good and stay himself.

"All right," he said. "Where do I sign up?"

ACKNOWLEDGMENTS

This book is for everyone who loves to learn and read but didn't have the usual path. It's especially for the queer kid hiding in the library because that was the safest place we knew.

I especially want to thank the teachers, educators, librarians, and professors who saw something in a high school dropout from Guthrie and challenged me (usually by handing me a book and telling me to read it). Too many of them are no longer with us:

Doctor Kim Klimek

Doctor Martin Miller

Doctor Paul Farkas

Doctor Susan French Ferguson

Ellen Slatkin

Jamey Trotter

Judy Porter

Julie Blume

Mrs. Coke

Mrs. Clark, I'm sorry I was so awful in math class.

As always, I couldn't do any of this without the incredible team at Blackstone. You all make my words shine and come alive.

My agent, Lesley Sabga is a rock star and tireless advocate for my work.

Michael David Axtell kills it on the audiobook every time.

Sarah Riedlinger always makes the cover something special and this one blows me away.